To Auntie Moira
With love

Murder
at the
Meridian Club Ball

Maura Kennedy Fair

Maura Kennedy Fair

A CIP catalogue entry of this publication is available from the British Library.

ISBN: 978-1-80440-399-0
Silver Quill Publishing

www.silverquillpublishing.com

To my boys

Donald and Frederick

ACKNOWLEDGEMENTS

A novel is a collective effort. This one would never have seen daylight were it not for a marvellous group of people, all of whom richly deserve thanks:

I am extremely grateful to Silver Quill Publishing and Wendy Leighton-Porter who agreed to publish the book.

A special thank you to Iona Carroll for a detailed and thoughtful proofread, and for all her help and encouragement with the book which is always greatly valued.

I would also like to convey my gratitude and thanks to Oliver Eade for giving his time and energy in the formatting of the book and much appreciated encouragement.

To Janet for providing medical advice and cake.

To Marion Goddard for a meticulous proofread and providing inspiration for the book covers.

And of course, to Donald with whom I enjoy tripping the light fantastic and reeling with my perfect partner. My husband.

ABOUT THE AUTHOR

Edinburgh born and bred, Maura Kennedy Fair is the author of Murder at the Meridian Club Ball which is her debut novel. An avid book reader since childhood, she is inspired by, amongst others, Daphne Du Maurier, Agatha Christie and Stephen King.

A keen Scottish Country dancer and an equestrian enthusiast, she now lives in the Scottish Borders with her family and her animals.

Chapter One
The Meridian Club, December 2013

'Amy. *Amy*? Are you OK?'

Serena's favourite evening of the year. The Meridian Club Christmas Ball. The dancing had been in full flow. Groups of couples dazzling in full evening attire, the men in mostly tartan trousers with velvet smoking jackets or Highland dress, the ladies in shimmering silks and sequins in a rainbow of colours stood around sipping champagne. It was now midnight, time for a break from dancing. The champagne bar had just opened and there was a queue already forming.

Suddenly the Ball attendees heard an unexpected sound. The siren jarring with the tune of 'The Road to Dundee' being played in the background. The Club Secretary strode into the middle of the ballroom. He clapped his hands. The music stopped immediately.

'Ladies and gentlemen. That is the fire alarm – let us hope it is a false alarm. If we can all make our way out the fire exit onto George Street,' the Club Secretary announced, resplendent in his Cameron tartan evening suit. Everyone grabbed their coats and moved in an orderly fashion out into the freezing cold street.

After twenty minutes or so the fire brigade gave the 'All Clear'. The Ball guests and staff rapidly filed back into the club. Serena and Robin were amongst the first inside. They headed up the first flight of stairs. Serena wanted to discuss with Robin what had happened before the fire alarm sounded. The stairway area was dimly lit. At the bottom of the stairs leading up to the third floor there appeared to be a great pile of white material. They rushed over. It was Amy. She was lying in an untidy heap. Was Amy *that* drunk? Serena patted her shoulder. Amy did not stir.

'We need a doctor. *Now*!' Serena said to an ashen-faced Robin.

Robin nodded and raced down the stairs.

Serena couldn't believe what had happened. She collapsed on the step above Amy, her head in her hands. A train track of tears travelled down her face. She brushed them away. Amy was dead. She had not liked Amy. Amy who attached herself to Serena like bindweed *and* they had just argued. But how had it come to this?

Chapter Two
Corbie Primary School, 1990

Primary School was fun. The first month whizzed by. She loved learning and trying to be the best at everything. Serena was five years old, tall for her age with a delicate heart-shaped face and the innocent questioning green eyes of a kitten. Neat as a pin she was. Dressed in her black felt blazer, grey pleated skirt and white shirt with the obligatory school tie.

'Come on, Mummy. *Come on*!' Serena stamped her foot. 'We're going to be late.'

Phyllis smiled as her small daughter dragged her along the street towards the school. 'Serena, we've got plenty of time. You won't be late.'

'But I *want* to be there before the bell goes. I want to play with Anne and Helen!'

She made friends easily and even got on well with her austere teacher Miss Fenton. Looking forward to the school day ahead. Until the illness.

Serena had caught a bad cold and then developed an un-shiftable cough. She was off sick from school for three weeks. Eventually, the doctor prescribed cough medicine which tasted like an expensive adult liqueur or so her mother said to encourage her to drink it. Slowly getting better, she was able to return to school with a couple of days remaining of the medicine to take.

She was thrilled to be back. Reading was her favourite subject. They had completed reading 'Chicken Licken' and were now on 'The three Billy goats gruff'. Her teacher stood for no nonsense and was unpleasant to the children in the class, but Serena always tried to please her. Three of her friends had already got the belt for coming into the school at playtime to avoid the driving rain. Miss Fenton, a spinster, was extremely strict and appeared to be from a previous generation where 'spare the rod, spoil the child' was the mantra. In her late fifties, each day at school she wore a brown tweed suit and most unusually, for the time, flesh-coloured tights with seams at the back.

Break time came and went. The class was then permitted by their teacher to have a drink, the children picked up the small warm bottles of milk from the crate that stood next to the blackboard. Sitting at her desk, Serena finished her milk and put up her hand. She was conscious of a nauseous sensation deep down in her tummy.

'Yes, Serena?'

'Miss Fenton, please may I go to the toilet?' She begged.

'No, you may not, Serena. You should have gone at breaktime,' Miss Fenton replied, her bulbous eyes peering over her large, pink-rimmed glasses which she usually perched on top of her dull brown frizzy hair.

'Miss Fenton. *Please*?'

'No, Serena.'

'But my mother said she had written to you about the medicine?' Serena persisted.

'No, I have told you already! You may not go to

the toilet and that is my final answer,' Miss Fenton said, turning away to write on the blackboard.

'What *is* wrong with you?' blonde, pony-tailed Janice who sat next to her asked.

'Nothing,' said Serena but her face contradicted what she had just replied.

Serena squirmed in her chair and attempted to concentrate on what was written on the blackboard. She held her breath and clutched her tummy with both hands. Nothing seemed to help. Serena could hold on no longer. Suddenly there was a strong pungent smell, as Serena's pants became saturated. The children sitting beside her, looked at her holding their noses and commenced making 'pooh' noises.

'Baby, baby – baby needs a nappy!' the class began to chant.

Serena lowered her eyes and hid her reddening face in her hands. Miss Fenton grabbed her by the hand and dragged her out of the classroom. Cleaned up in the girls' toilets by the sympathetic school nurse, Serena burst into tears.

'There now dear, you're fine. Please don't cry.' The school nurse wiped Serena's face with a tissue.

'My mother told Miss Fenton the medicine could act as a lax...?' Serena said dolefully.

'I know, dear. Your teacher was told about the laxative effects of the medicine – I saw the letter. Now you run along back to your class. You'll be fine now.'

But she wasn't. Nor would things ever be the same again completely. Her friends looked at her with pity. Miss Fenton, who she always wanted to please, when on the rare occasions she spoke to her, her tone cutting, as sharp as a carving knife. The only time she now talked to Serena was to find fault. All praise was withheld. Her classmates noticed how the teacher spoke to her. Even her best friends Janice and Jane picked on her. Nobody wanted to play with her and called her 'Stinky Sue'. The child who once happily skipped along to school just trudged along and during playtime now stood alone in a corner pretending she was a little bird who wished she could fly away.

Time passed. Thankfully, Miss Fenton was no longer her teacher. She was a monster who wrecked young children's lives and destroyed their confidence and self-belief. Years later, Serena heard of other children taught by Miss Fenton who had started bedwetting and one who even chewed the arm off their school blazer. Serena was thrilled to have a different teacher. But the damage was done, and she was not the confident and carefree child she was before.

The new teacher, who had now taught Serena for two years, was straight out of teaching college. Serena got on well with Mrs Forsyth and school began to be fun again. She focused on working on her class project. There was a prize for the best four efforts.

Before the end of the summer term, Mrs Forsyth announced the winners. She stood beside the blackboard and slowly peeled open a sealed envelope for maximum effect. The whole class was silent. Serena crossed her fingers on both hands and focused on the envelope. Mrs Forsyth winked at her.

'The best pirates of the Caribbean projects were done by Andrew, Gary, Jane and Serena!' Their teacher announced. 'They will be going to the local swimming pool on Wednesday afternoon!'

The winners cheered.

Everyone had a super time, enjoying splashing around and hurtling down the slides. The afternoon was memorable for two reasons. Zooming down the slide for the third time Mrs Forsyth's blue bikini bottom *almost* came off. To the great amusement of Gary, Andrew, Jane and Serena. Red-faced, she managed to pull it up just in time. Then, embarking on the journey home in Mrs Forsyth's yellow Metro, the driver's car door wouldn't shut properly so it was held secure by one of the boy's ties looped onto the inside door handle. Safely back, they had had a wonderful time and wished they could go again.

Chapter Three
Park Lane Stables

'Go on, get up on Venture. He won't bite,' Ruth, the riding instructress said.

Serena stared at the nondescript bay pony. Venture. Venture scowled back.

'Come on now, up you get.'

On a windy Wednesday afternoon, Serena and her mother stood in the middle of the indoor school at Park Lane Stables. Serena hauled herself up on the pony's back. Reminding herself she was only doing this to please her mum and beat her so-called best friend Janice at it. After walking many times on a lead rein around the indoor school, Venture took exception to the rattling roof and promptly bucked Serena off.

'Are you ok?' Ruth asked.

Serena gritted her teeth and with one hand brushed the dusty peat of the school surface from the seat of her jodhpurs. 'I'm fine.'

Venture bucked multiple times again flinging Serena off. Again, she climbed back on. *I will not be beaten by this stupid pony*, Serena vowed. And she wasn't. Over time she progressed to riding the more difficult ponies including 'Mo' who frequently put his head down without warning to eat grass. Most people slid down his giraffe neck and over his head but never Serena. She realised she enjoyed horse-riding and felt a different, confident person when on a pony's back.

Years passed and Serena now helped at the

stables on a Sunday. The helpers included two gawky older girls – Brenda and Jill. At the ages of seventeen and eighteen respectively, they were in charge or so they thought and left all the dogsbody work to Serena and a younger girl named Kelly. Serena didn't mind as she had now come to love being around horses and ponies. It also meant she managed to avoid attending Bible Class on a Sunday morning at the local church.

The riding stables changed hands, and the new owner purchased several horses and ponies from Ireland. There was one that caught Serena's eye. Cola Cube. A flashy, chestnut pony with a flaxen mane and tail, he stood around fourteen hands tall. She loved riding Cola. He was young and uneducated. Her mum, who had always wanted a horse, liked him too. There were secret conferences between her mum and her grandma. One afternoon at home a vet phoned up about vetting a pony, Serena took the call and told the vet there must be a mistake. A few weeks later Serena after finishing a riding lesson on Cola and when going to pay for the lesson was told:

'You don't pay as much now as you're a livery here,' Ruth the instructress said.

'What do you mean?' Serena said. She was confused.

'Cola is *your* pony now,' Ruth revealed.

'What!?' Serena said and fainted clean away.

The good times had begun.

Serena and Cola got on like a house on fire. True, he was young and barely schooled. When faced with jumping a wide fence the first time he landed on top of it. The jumping improved. Rosettes followed. Serena took immense pleasure in 'blu tacking' the rosettes to her bedroom wall. A fast learner, Cola was a steady pony who loved nothing better than galloping on the sand out to the sea at the local beach.

Serena encountered some new friends amongst the other girls who kept ponies in livery at the stables. But she was looked down upon by the rest of them. Having worked in the stables as a helper she wasn't considered a real livery and considered inferior to the other liveries. Serena was neither fish nor fowl. Brenda and Jill, her previous fellow Sunday helpers, caused no end of trouble saying she was getting above her station in life. She ignored them and concentrated on schooling Cola so he could perform even better at pony competitions.

*****

One day Serena was leading Cola to the indoor school, a blonde girl with forgettable features came up to her.

'You can't ride in the school as Delia is using it,' she drawled and stood in front of the open sliding doors.

'Yes, I can. There's loads of room in there,' Serena said. 'What's your name?'

The girl with the plain face and her hair styled in a single blonde plait, which reached down to her waist, introduced herself as Amy, Delia's best friend. Delia owned an expensive grey showjumping pony and was a plump, dark-haired girl.

'How come *you* got such a nice pony?' Amy said,

wrinkling her snub nose.

'I was lucky. Very lucky,' Serena stroked Cola's nose as she tightened his noseband.

'You're too big for him. You, you're like a beanpole on him and shouldn't be riding him,' Amy tossed *her* long-plaited mane to one side.

It was true. Serena at fifteen years old was almost five foot ten and as slim as a reed. At times, her feet hit the jump poles of a jump after Cola jumped them clear, knocking them down. Amy, by contrast, was tiny. She resembled a bouncy rubber ball with short stumpy legs but still managed to look neat riding the ponies at the stable.

'You'll look stupid on him in the working hunter competition on Wednesday,' Amy remarked.

'We'll see. I'll show you,' Serena said.

*****

The day of the horse show dawned clear and bright. Serena left her home early, catching the number eight bus to the stables. She concentrated on beautifying Cola for the working hunter class she had entered. At least, she had washed his mane and tail the day before so just had to plait them that day. Tying Cola up beside his hay net she divided his mane into ten neat bunches. The bunches were braided into neat plaits to Serena's satisfaction. Cola protested at her removing his hay net so she could plait his forelock. His forelock took no time at all, as did the plaiting of his tail.

Amy passed by just as she was tacking him up and giving her stirrups a final polish.

'You know that thing won't win anything today,' Amy said.

'Well, *you* don't know for certain. The judge might like him,' Serena replied.

'In your dreams,' Amy jeered. She then sauntered off to get the pony called Rolo she'd leased from the stable ready for the show. A rotund, dark bay.

'We'll show them,' Serena whispered to Cola. Which they did.

The show was taking place in a large field behind the livery yard stables. There were three fenced-off arenas. One contained the rustic jumps for the working hunter classes, an empty ring for the showing classes and the other filled with a variety of obstacles for the handy pony classes. Beyond the arenas was a row of horseboxes and trailers with lines of gleaming ponies tied up outside them.

Serena walked the course of jumps for the working hunter competition. Memorizing the order of the jumps as she went. Nothing too difficult or spooky for Cola. The only issue Serena could see was the large spread fence, the penultimate jump before the narrow rustic stile which was the last fence.

Serena warmed Cola up in the outdoor school and jumped him over four practice jumps. He sailed over. 'What a difference a year makes,' reflected Serena, thinking of their horrific efforts the previous year. Time to go. Once in the ring the bell rang, and they cantered towards the first rustic pole and rails. Clear. Cola sped round. He continued to clear all the fences and increased his speed to the last which was a narrow stile fence. He cat-jumped it at the last minute. They landed over the jump and Serena waited to hear the familiar thud of knocked down poles. None. Serena gave Cola's neck large pats, and they left the ring to the sounds of the spectators' applause. In the end, there were only three clears, Serena, the stable owner's sister Emily and Delia. While each of them individually walked, trotted and cantered their ponies, the judge conferred in the centre of the ring with his helper. The judge approached Serena and Cola and pinned the red rosette on Cola's bridle. First! She couldn't believe it. Could things get any better? There had been two earlier working hunter classes for the smaller ponies. Serena and the two other class winners went into the ring for the working hunter championship. After a few moments of deliberation, the judge pinned the large red, white and blue championship rosette on Cola's bridle. Serena was over the moon. Cola galloped a victory lap followed by the two other ponies around the ring. He knew Serena was thrilled with him and expected the customary supply of After Eight chocolate mints. Serena couldn't wait to get home to tell her mum about her and Cola's triumph.

After winning her working hunter class and the working hunter championship, the final class Serena had entered was the handy pony. Serena walked the handy pony course. It consisted of several obstacles, designed to test a pony's obedience. How long it took to complete the course was timed. Whoever completed the fastest round with the least penalties won.

It was soon time for her round. Amy's pony had faultlessly dealt with the course. Nothing had phased him. Serena went into the ring, the last competitor after Amy. Cola easily negotiated the gate, traffic cones and the small jump. The last obstacle was a blue plastic sheet with yellow rubber ducks glued on both sides.

'Oh help! Cola's not going to like those ducks!' Serena grimaced.

But it was Cola's Day and they navigated the ducks without any trouble. Serena patted his neck many times. She then gave him even more After Eight chocolate mints when back in the collecting ring.

Amy walked past on Rolo. 'You'll never win this class; you just weren't fast enough. I'm sure I've won it,' she said.

'Well, the results will be out soon. You clever boy,' Serena said to Cola who was licking his lips.

Five minutes later they were. Serena had beaten Amy by two seconds. Amy was almost incandescent with rage. Her face turned scarlet and her mouth puckered up like a dog's bottom. How could that drippy girl Serena have beaten her? On that stupid pony with that silly name. Cola Cube.

They lined up to collect their rosettes in the ring. Cola at the top of the line of ponies, Rolo second. Serena thanked the judge when he pinned the red first rosette to Cola's bridle.

'Smashing pony,' he said to Serena.

'Thank you. I love him,' Serena patted Cola's

neck.

'I can see that!' The judge smiled.

The judge approached Amy and Rolo with their blue second place rosette. Amy barely thanked the judge then turned and glared at Serena who grinned back.

Once the judge moved onto the next pony, Amy reached over and pinched Serena's knee. Hard.

'Beginner's luck,' she sneered.

Serena prised Amy's sharp fingers from her knee and moved Cola out of Amy's reach.

When the four remaining placed ponies had their rosettes on their bridles it was time for a victory lap. Cola galloped round the ring followed by the other ponies. The spectators clapped.

What a brilliant day, Serena thought. She was dying to get home and tell her mum all about the show and to let her see the rosettes. Especially the championship one. But firstly, she had to sort Cola out for the night. After removing his plaits and giving him a thorough brush, it was then time for his tea. Hugging him one final time, and after telling him, he was 'the best pony in the world', she gave Cola his evening feed with extra carrots.

Serena rushed home. She thundered up the stairs to the top-floor flat where they lived. Quickly inside, she thrust the two red rosettes and the championship rosette into Phyllis's hand.

'Mum, I've had a marvellous day,' she said. 'The best ever.' Serena couldn't stop smiling. 'You should have seen these horrid yellow rubber ducks in the handy pony class. Cola was great! He just placed one hoof on the blue sheet, then another and walked over it in seconds. It was as if he did this every day.'

'Darling, that's marvellous, I'm so thrilled for you and Cola.' Phyllis hugged Serena. 'How did that horrid girl Amy get on?' she asked.

'She was second in the handy pony class. Nothing else. I'm worried she'll do something nasty to me or Cola because of how well we did today.'

'You need to try and ignore her and think about Cola and the friends you do have there,' Phyllis advised.

'I wish we could leave Park Lane stables and move Cola somewhere else.'

'In spite of all the horse shows they run and the beach to ride on?'

'Yes, in spite of those nice things,' Serena said.

'Well, I'll try and find out if there's somewhere else we can move Cola to,' Phyllis agreed.

Cola's two red rosettes and the championship one was displayed next to a large photo of Cola and Serena jumping a huge gate at a pony club One Day Event. The rosettes stayed there for many years, as did the memory of a golden day in Serena's mind.

Coming down to earth the next day Serena turned up at the stables to groom and ride Cola. His mane looked different. Significantly different. It was now short and straggly and all different lengths. Someone had hacked it to bits. Amy sauntered past.

'You shouldn't have won the championship anyway. YOU got what you deserved.' Pointing a podgy finger at Cola's mane.

Serena glanced down at the stable floor. Strands of Cola's beautiful golden mane could be seen, intermingled with his straw bed. She bent down to retrieve them. Cola ambled over and stuck his head over the stable door. Amy grabbed hold of his muzzle and twisted it. Cola squealed and reversed towards the back of his stable. Serena stood in front of him. 'How dare you! Just get out of my sight and leave my pony alone.' Her eyes blazed emerald fire in Amy's direction. Serena stroked Cola's nose. 'Go away! Now!'

'A jumped-up stable helper like you on your cheap pony. Beating Delia and the owner's sister, too. She was in a right state, crying into her pony's mane last night, she was. I still don't get why that judge placed you first? Must have been blind,' Amy shook her head, her blonde plait bouncing up and down. 'I told Delia you must have known the judge. After all, why else could YOU have been placed first?' She waddled down the passageway between the stable stalls.

'Well, I did win, and Cola didn't deserve to have his mane cut,' Serena shouted after her. 'One day I'll get back at you.'

'Never in a million years,' Amy smirked. 'What could *you* possibly do to me? You're hopeless. You're no good at anything!'

Serena ignored her, put Cola's saddle and bridle on and led him out of his stable. Minutes later she was on his back and soon afterwards on the beach galloping out to the sea.

Matters did not improve. Serena's hoof picks were frequently stolen. She started keeping one in her jacket pocket. Her stirrup light for riding out in the dark had been deliberately smashed. Serena suspected Amy of doing this but had no proof. Amy still stirred up trouble for her at the stables and spread lies about her. Serena ignored her. She was just jealous that Serena had a pony and she didn't.

Chapter Four
West Lothian

Jubilee was a mystery lady. She appeared in *The Scottish Farmer* up for sale just before Christmas. At the right time. The advert read:

'Bay mare, 15.3hh, six years old, kind nature, good jumper, bombproof in traffic, easy to do, near Glasgow, eight hundred pounds ono.'

Now too old and too tall to ride Cola in pony competitions, Serena's parents decided they should buy a horse for Serena. This was one hobby they very much wanted to encourage, given the positive effect horses had on Serena.

Accompanied by her parents, Serena set off to see Jubilee on a very wet and windy day at a farm in what seemed like the middle of nowhere. Inside the muddy farmyard horses massed around in a herd. It could have been a scene from a western movie apart from the lack of warm and sunny weather. Her bandy-legged owner, walking crab-like across the cobbled yard, pointed to a bright bay mare with a small white star on her forehead. She had the fine legs and flat feet of a thoroughbred. 'That's Starry,' he said. *What a stupid name,* Serena thought.

'Do you want to try her?' he asked.

There was an old railway line to try her out on with a single jump halfway down. The rain stoated down on the cobbled yard. The horse was quiet and well behaved for her owner, jumping the high single pole jump with ease. Serena then got on 'Starry' and put her through her paces and jumped the jump. No bother. To see if she was sensible in traffic Serena had the old Glasgow main road to ride her up, which was parallel to the motorway. She didn't bat an eyelid at the traffic which zoomed past her.

Serena knew Starry was coming home with them. When riding her on the road the noseband of the bridle had come loose and was repeatedly hitting her on the nose. No reaction. An honest horse. After just passing the veterinary inspection 'Starry', now renamed Jubilee, came into Serena's life just before Christmas. She was an enigma, there was no record of her breeding or when and where she had been born noted on her passport. However, Serena loved her immediately.

Jubilee certainly lived up to her new name. Serena's father was mad on railways and had installed in Serena a love of iron horses. Leafing through a book of LMS engine classes looking for inspiration for Starry's new name, she came across the 'Jubilee' class. The Jubilee class of steam engines were of uncertain temperament and were apt to run away. Jubilee certainly loved to run away. The merest shortening of the reins and she was off into canter asking, and on occasions demanding, to go faster and faster. Serena and her mother, amongst other more knowledgeable 'horsey' people they knew, concluded that Jubilee was previously a racehorse and had taken part in hurdle races. Certainly, she was extremely fast. A pony club instructress could not bear to look at the speed she displayed when taking on the show jumps at a practice session for the pony club showjumping team. Unsurprisingly, Serena and Jubilee weren't selected for the team.

Cola was currently out on loan with a pleasant family at the livery yard they had moved to after leaving Park Lane stables. Serena was now able to devote all her attention to Jubilee. But what to do with her? Eventing? One of Serena's favourite television programs was the Badminton horse trials which took place every spring. Six-time Badminton winner Lucinda Greene was Serena's all-time heroine. She wanted to be her. A beautiful and stylish rider, Serena had seen her once in the flesh at Thirlestane Castle horse trials but chickened out of asking her to autograph the event programme. Serena now embarked on getting Jubilee fit, entering cross-country events and showjumping competitions. The dressage left much to be desired, but Serena was confident it would improve, over time.

Chapter Five
Charterhall horse trials

Charterhall One Day Event. Jubilee was entered in the novice class. Jubilee now had a show name – Jubilee Fizz. From an early age, Serena was not averse to the odd glass of champagne. Being possessed of a fizzy forward going nature the show name suited Jubilee perfectly. The dressage was still less advanced, than the jumping but there was no point in putting off competing in One Day Events if she wished to emulate her heroine, Lucinda Green.

The One Day Event was held on a picturesque estate in the Scottish Borders. Serena, her mum, dad and of course Jubilee arrived early. Her dad had obligingly driven the trailer to the horse trial. Her mum was the designated 'event groom'. A hive of activity greeted Serena on arrival at the former airfield. Horseboxes and trailers were parked on the old runway, competitors rushing about, preparing their horses for the first phase of the event. The horses' coats shone in the May sun. Hooves were being painted with oil and leather riding boots given a final polish.

Serena tacked up Jubilee. She looked magnificent, her jet-black mane was neatly pleated and her bright bay coat shone like a quality cognac. Once mounted, Serena warmed Jubilee up for the initial phase of the competition, the dressage by putting Jubilee through her paces. The canter was all right, but the trot was terrible. Serena ended up walking Jubilee about on a loose rein hoping to encourage her to calm down. All too soon it was time for her dressage test. They entered the dressage arena. Five minutes later it was all over.

'How did it go?' Serena's mum asked when Serena left the arena. 'I was too late to see the test.'

'Well, you didn't miss much! The trot work felt OK to start with but after we cantered the first circle Jubilee decided that the remainder of the test should be performed in canter. I finally managed to persuade her to trot but she did this sort of goose-stepping trot, her head stuck out like a camel's. You know what she's like.' Serena scowled. 'We ended up cantering down the centre line to halt at 'X'. I thought she wasn't going to stop and I had to haul on the reins. She stood – eventually – a nice square halt which of course she spoiled by tossing her head up and down. It was as if she was saying thank God that's over, now let's get on with the fun bits.'

'I'm really sorry to hear that Serena – after all the hard work you've done to improve her dressage.'

'It's not easy – she just wants to go fast. *All* the time,' Serena said as she patted a now happy Jubilee and loosened her girth before the next phase of the One Day Event. 'It was so ghastly that I wished the ground would swallow me up. I don't think she'll ever improve at dressage. Look – I'd better get ready for the showjumping phase.'

Serena gave Jubilee a cursory pat as she made her way back to where her trailer was located. A tall girl, around Serena's age, the spitting image of one of

Serena's favourite actresses, Vivien Leigh, smiled sympathetically as they stumbled past.

An hour later the dressage scores were up. Their test score was fifty-three penalties. Out of thirty competitors in their section they were fifth last. *At least I'll enjoy the show-jumping and cross-country,* Serena consoled herself.

They fared better in the showjumping phase. An unlucky pole down at the last jump, a brightly coloured parallel, left them with five penalties to add to their score.

There was an hour between the showjumping and the final cross-country phase. Serena and her parents sat on deckchairs beside the trailer and ate their packed lunch. Jubilee was tied up to the trailer beside them and enjoyed looking at the other horses around her. To her, it was one big "pony party".

At ten to two, Serena in her purple and green cross-country colours, rode Jubilee down to the starter's box situated, in plenty of time, ready to start their round.

'Good luck, Serena. Look after yourself and Jubilee,' her mum said.

'I will do.'

'Just pretend you're Lucinda Green.'

'I'll try!'

Jubilee's legs had been 'coated in white grease' in case she should hit one of the solid wooden fences and hopefully slide over as opposed to falling. The 'lucky green' bandages Cola had worn to protect the lower part of his legs, when competing, were still visible despite the grease on Jubilee's four legs. At only eighteen Serena had felt nervous about taking part in this competition but remembered Lucinda had been younger than her when she competed in her first novice horse trial. Serena and Jubilee jogged over to the starting box. Inside the starting box Jubilee stamped her hooves and half-reared as they waited. For the umpteenth time, *why am I doing this*? buzzed through Serena's mind. And suddenly they were off.

'5,4,3,2,1...go! Good luck,' the starter shouted.

Jubilee bolted out of the starting box and galloped towards the first jump. It was an imposing steeplechase jump, a smaller version of what was present at Cheltenham racecourse. She soared over it and Serena felt her confidence come trickling back. Swiftly over the next fences in the ancient parkland, ahead was the start of the more challenging jumps, a bank with a large drop on the landing side, followed closely by a narrow post and rails fence leading into a shadowy woodland. Jubilee handled these superbly, galloped between the pine trees and was soon out, over a large log pile, back into the broad sunlight. Thundering on, the cadence of the hooves went faster and faster. Jump, gallop, jump. Serena's legs felt like jellied eels clinging to Jubilee's sides.

Two spectators, enjoying a picnic at the side of the course, looked on as Jubilee, who was ignoring Serena's requests to go slower, hurtled past.

The man with a tweed cap pulled down, almost obscuring his eyes, said, 'Wow! Did you see that bay mare going past? The girl riding it must have lost control – she keeps pulling on the reins – she looks like she could be in trouble.'

'Yeah, the horse obviously has no brakes!' his companion, a woman, dressed in a waxed jacket and jeans agreed. 'Most definitely not. I'm just glad I'm not the person riding it!'

'Well, I hope the rider manages to gain control before the next obstacle – it's the trickiest fence on the course.'

They watched in horror as Jubilee clipped the highest point of the jump with her front hooves.

'Aw, no – she's going to fall; she shouldn't have taken off so far away from the fence. I hope they'll both be OK. I can't bear to look.' The man unscrewed his hip flask and took a large gulp of brandy.

'Look, John. Look! I can't believe it – how did the mare manage to scramble back up on her hooves? That's amazing. And she's off like lightning. Again! She's like a Ferrari!' the woman exclaimed.

'Sally – how on earth did the rider not fall off? I really thought the competition was over for them. That girl must have super glue on the saddle. And what a brilliant courageous horse! Look at her go!' The man said rubbing his eyes. 'She's eating up the ground between her and the grey horse in front.'

Ahead of Serena and Jubilee was a slow horse and rider. Jubilee the ex-racehorse, her ears pricked, flickering backwards and forwards. No way was she going to let *that* horse reach the next jump before her!

The woman put down her sandwich. 'Goodness, she's overtaken the horse. And the way she sailed over the next jump. The bay mare *must* have been some racehorse in her day.'

'Definitely,' the man agreed and said, 'and I wish she was mine.'

The couple stood silently, watching Jubilee gallop off, into the distance.

'Jubilee Fizz is fizzing down the hill,' the commentator announced.

You're right there! flashed through Serena's mind.

There was an ever-increasing distance between the two horses although the grey horse had now gained a new lease of life and followed Jubilee enthusiastically over the next few jumps.

The rest of the course sped by. Jubilee jumped and jumped and leapt over the remaining jumps. The penultimate jump loomed – a large hedge preceded by an enormous ditch brimming with water. Jubilee galloped towards the jump; Serena's legs became jelly-like again and sharp pains of adrenalin shot through her chest. She avoided looking down into the yawning chasm of the ditch and instead concentrated on the distant telegraph poles. Jubilee on the other hand, had no such qualms. Both black-tipped ears pointed straight ahead, in perfect symmetry, locked on to the fence.

'Come on, Jubilee. Come on, we're nearly there. Only one more jump to go!' Serena whispered to the mare.

Serena touched her heels to Jubilee's side, and they flew over the jump. How could she have *ever* doubted Jubilee's courage? The last fence was upon them in no time at all, or so it seemed to Serena, they were then galloping over the finishing line. Jubilee knew the cross-country round had come to an end and pulled herself up to a steady walk.

'You, clever, clever girlie,' Serena said to Jubilee and stroked the warm sweaty neck heaving in front of her.

Serena's mum ran towards her.

'How did you get on? I couldn't bear to watch?' she said.

'Clear. Jubilee went clear! I can't believe it.' Serena's legs shook when she dismounted from the puffing mare.

By the time Jubilee was washed down by Serena and put in her trailer with a well-deserved hay net, the results were out. Serena was near the bottom of the results. The dressage score was naturally the reason why. The girl who had smiled understandingly at Serena after Jubilee's appalling dressage test had won their novice section. Once the prizes were handed out Serena went over to speak to her.

'Congratulations – you were amazing,' Serena said.

'Thank you. Of course, I can see that my horse is easier to ride than yours,' said the young Vivien Leigh lookalike who then introduced herself. 'I'm Ginny Favell by the way,' extending a grubby hand.

'And I'm Serena Kennedy. Yes, but you were brilliant in all three phases. You made it look so easy,' Serena said. 'I just wish Jubilee and I could be like that too.'

'Well, your horse Jubilee Fizz is an extremely talented mare. A super jumper, amazing scope – she made nothing of the cross-country course,' Ginny said. 'She just needs her flatwork sorted out for the dressage,' Ginny suggested. Removing her spotless show jacket, she loosened the snowy white stock around her neck.

'Just!? Easier said than done,' Serena explained. 'We now believe Jubilee was a racehorse and all she wants to do is go faster and faster! You know that film with Tom Cruise where he talks about wanting to go fast. That's what goes through Jubilee's head *every* time she's ridden!'

'Right, I see... I think!' Ginny laughed. 'Anyway, I'm a freelance instructor, so if you ever need help with her let me know.' She handed a business card to Serena.

'Thank you very much,' Serena said. 'I'll be in touch.'

Numerous people had tried and failed to sort Jubilee out, Serena mused on the drive home. Ginny might be *the* one.

Soon after Serena began having regular lessons from Ginny. Over time Jubilee improved. There was always an unpredictability about her dressage tests, but she managed to achieve minor placings at horse trials. Serena and Ginny became firm friends. In the years that followed with other horses she owned, Serena benefited from Ginny's eagle eyes and attention to detail. Nothing escaped her notice.

Everything she suggested to try for the horses worked. Serena had previously remarked that Ginny was a goddess on a horse whereas she herself was a mere mortal.

Chapter Six
The Bank, Edinburgh

Time passed. Serena worked hard at school, realising a well-paid job was necessary so she could afford to keep a horse in a livery yard when she grew up. Computers were the way forward. Serena graduated from university with a degree in computer science.

Serena was lucky enough to be offered the job of a developer in the IT department of a prestigious bank. There were around eighty people in this department if you counted contractors and the staff who worked for the third-party software suppliers, also developers, system analysts, technical support team, system testers and four project managers. This was a far larger and grander setup than where Serena was employed previously. She was extremely impressed and naturally a tad nervous. On her first day, Serena was taken into a large, light, airy, oblong room with a long corridor on both sides of which were rows of numerous banks of desks. The room resounded with the noise of laptop keyboards being pounded away on. The office gave the impression of being a terribly busy place.

The department admin assistant introduced her to her sharp-suited project manager, Daisy. The stark black suit was softened by the expertly tied amethyst purple scarf and the gem-set floral brooch on her jacket lapel. Compared to Daisy, Serena in her 'safe' navy suit felt incredibly frump-like. Well, it was her first day and she wanted to play it safe, she told herself. Daisy looked like she wouldn't stand for any nonsense and indeed she didn't. Always polite and to the point, the only time Serena ever saw her angry was late one afternoon. This was shortly after Serena started. That day the bank's figures didn't balance. Daisy was racing around the department demanding to know how this had happened. The air was blue with her invectives. Screeching like a fishwife at the developers, she wouldn't have been out of place at Newhaven harbour a century or so ago.

'What will happen if these figures don't balance by the end of today?' Serena asked Daisy.

'The Bank of England could close us down,' Daisy clarified before rushing off to speak to the project manager of the third-party software supplier.

Thankfully, this crisis was averted but it made Serena appreciate how easily problems could develop and the wider implications for the bank and not just for the IT department.

A youngish man was trotting along the office corridor, whistling. Daisy introduced Serena to him. 'Serena, this is Graham Rae, something of a technical whizz kid or so HE likes to think!'

Serena shook hands with Graham. Noticing Graham's stocky build, he reminded her of a Suffolk Punch horse, an endangered breed. Then considering the pint-size legs, more like a Welsh cob she decided. Looking down she could clearly view the beginning of a bald patch on the centre of his head. This made him look slightly like a monk, albeit a cheerful monk.

'Lovely to meet you, Graham. I now know who to

speak to if I need any help with environments or databases.' Serena smiled.

'Yes, well you know where I am if you ever need me!' Graham beamed, a smile brightening up his plump face.

Another person Serena met on her first day and became close friends with was Mary. She sat diagonally opposite Serena at the line of desks near the far end of the office fourth floor.

'Hi, I'm Mary Colquhoun. I'm pleased to meet you.'

She was a woman slightly older than Serena. Mary's glossy copper hair styled in a bun, glinted in the light from the fluorescent tube lights high above the banks of desks. 'I hope you will enjoy working here. I certainly do,' she said whilst typing away furiously. She smiled earnestly at Serena taking in the tall young woman who was fidgeting with the strap of her handbag.

'Hi, I'm Serena, I'm looking forward to working here. It seems a terribly busy place,' she added.

'It certainly is. Never a dull moment here!' Mary said, 'You won't be bored!' She frantically flicked through a document in front of her.

'Good!' Serena said settling down at her new desk. She put an old photo of Jubilee and one of her cat Shadow near where her laptop would sit.

Mary glanced over and noticed the photos. 'Are these your pets?'

'Yes. The cat is called Shadow. Cats are my favourite animals followed by horses,' Serena said taking off her navy blazer. It was especially warm in the office.

'Cool. Mine too,' Mary said and that was the start of their friendship.

'What about the horse? What's its name?' Mary eyed up the photo of Serena riding bareback on a shiny bay horse.

'She was my old horse called Jubilee, or Jubilee Fizz to give her show name,' Serena awkwardly said. Her face reddening, her eyes dropped to her desk and she smoothed the long flame coloured hair behind her ears.

Mary sensed there was something wrong here. 'There's a department meeting at eleven, then it'll be lunchtime. Would you like to go to the canteen for lunch?' she asked.

'That would be good. Thanks,' Serena said. She was also glad to get off the subject of Jubilee.

Chapter Seven
Jubilee

It would be many weeks before Serena could bring herself to tell Mary about Jubilee. For years after when she thought about Jubilee she wanted to burst into tears.

Jubilee had been retired from eventing, after producing a filly foal the image of herself. Although now in her twenties, Serena occasionally rode her. Despite her years, Jubilee continued to be a lively and fun horse to ride.

One sunny summer's day Serena was riding Ruby, Jubilee's daughter, in the field by the cottage where Serena and her parents now lived. Jubilee was allowed to stay in the same field when Ruby was being ridden since they were both sensible horses. Or so Serena thought. Serena rode Ruby up to the top of the hill in a brisk trot. Jubilee followed them. Serena and Ruby then proceeded to walk back down the hill and were almost at the foot of the hill when Jubilee sprang. She had obviously decided she was going to beat Ruby to the gate.

Memories of her old racehorse days had come flooding back to Jubilee. The field gate represented the finishing line. Jubilee hurtled down the hill galloping, accelerating at breakneck speed. Serena asked Ruby to stand as they both watched Jubilee speeding towards them. Suddenly Jubilee's forelegs appeared to be going faster than the ground, which was rising to meet them. In slow motion or so it looked to Serena. The next moment Jubilee came to a jerky halt. She was unable to move. Serena flung herself off Ruby and charged towards Jubilee.

'What have you done to yourself?' she said to Jubilee as she stroked her shuddering body.

It was hopeless. The mare could barely walk. She was crippled. The tendons had snapped in both her forelegs.

'You stupid old woman,' Serena sadly said to Jubilee. 'At twenty-five years old you should have known better than to show off to your daughter.'

Putting Ruby in her stable. Serena rushed back to attend to Jubilee who remained as still as an equestrian effigy. Jubilee's progress to the stable was painfully slow as she slowly hobbled, shuffling one hoof after the other.

'Please Jubilee. You *must* walk. I must get you into your stable.' Serena lovingly patted Jubilee's heaving neck in encouragement. Many minutes passed before Jubilee eventually managed to stagger into her loose box. Serena immediately phoned the vet and only at that moment away from Jubilee's stable did she allow herself the luxury of bursting into tears.

The vet arrived in no time. Jim was a kind and sympathetic young man who knew how much Jubilee meant to Serena. He had foaled Jubilee's baby, Ruby. He too loved Jubilee's kind and sensible nature.

'Oh no, Serena, I'm so sorry.' Jim glanced at Serena. 'I know you know there's nothing we can do for Jubilee,' Jim said standing outside the stable, caressing Jubilee's nose. His eyes averted from Serena's. 'I just wish there was something more I could do – I know how precious she is to you.'

Serena nodded. *And to Ruby,* she thought. A single tear travelled down the side of her face. She raised her eyes and looked up at the bright blue sky.

Jim prepared the lethal injection. Ruby's stable doors were both shut so she couldn't see what was happening. She whinnied frantically. 'What are you doing to my Mummy?' she was saying.

Serena led Jubilee round to the side of the stables. Jim sedated Jubilee and several minutes later he administered the lethal injection. *I must be brave for Jubilee,* Serena thought, raising her chin up and gazing overhead at the azure sky. Serena began feeding Jubilee her favourite biscuits. At this point, Jim said to move away. Jubilee fell to the ground. She was dead before she hit the ground. Her once kindly regarding eyes would flicker no more at Serena and her warm body stiffened; a statue made of stone. Serena crouched down beside the dead mare and stroked her face. The dark eyes remaining open, frozen in time, the unseeing eyes of the dead.

'Why can't I close her eyes?' Serena turned her own tear-heavy eyes towards Jim. She noticed a solitary drop of blood on his left hand. Jim rubbed his hand against the pocket of his jeans.

'They don't close. Not when they're dead.' He hugged Serena.

'Jim – thank you for looking after Jubilee, so well. All those years. Would you like a cup of tea before you go?'

'No thanks, Serena – I better be going,' he replied, his eyes not quite meeting Serena's. 'I'll arrange for her body to be picked up tomorrow. I'm so sorry.' He got into his car and drove off without a backwards glance.

Serena ran into the cottage and burst into tears. 'You stupid old fool, why did you have to show off to your daughter? Why did you have to leave me so soon?' she said to herself.

Ruby was equally desolate. She constantly walked back and forwards along the paddock fence. Wearing down a path and neighing hysterically. The light had faded from her shining brown eyes. A friend was found for her, but she was never the same horse again and died, a couple of years later, after succumbing to grass sickness.

Serena acknowledged the huge debt she owed Jubilee, for she had made her horsey dreams come true. She had also given Serena the gift of belief in herself if not confidence. Other horses came and went, but there would never be another one like the mystery lady. Jubilee.

Chapter Eight
The Bank, Edinburgh

Work kept Serena busy and as Mary had previously remarked there was never a dull moment. The months flew past and in no time, Serena had worked at the bank for three years. She had recently been tasked with developing website screens for the new mortgage product. There was a demanding deadline to meet, resulting in Serena working extra hours at the weekend. She now lived in Edinburgh. Her current horse named Rose was stabled in a livery yard on the outskirts of Edinburgh. Serena didn't have far to travel to see Rose and the yard owner kindly rode the mare twice a week.

The project's implementation date drew closer. The infrastructure of the website being developed was found to have issues. This meant liaising with the technical teams. The problems continued. Serena had to raise several defects one of which was assigned to 'cheery Graham' in the technical support team. They had always got on well and frequently had a laugh during lunch with Mary and others. The defect was assigned on 13th February and the next day Serena could see there was so far no progress, so she sent Graham an email. The email's subject was 'Thinking of you on Valentine's Day'. Graham clicked the email to view the contents. The email read:

'Thinking of you on Valentine's Day.

Defect 391!'

'You're a right joker,' Graham said to Serena as he

dawdled past her desk after the daily project meeting. Graham had mentioned Serena's email when the unresolved bugs were discussed at the morning meeting.

'What do you think? Do I have a chance?' glancing upwards as he asked Robin who was with him. Robin shrugged his shoulders.

'Well, she's obviously keen on you. Her eyes light up whenever she sees you or when your name is mentioned!' Graham said. *I must be mad telling Robin that*, he thought.

'Really?' Robin said. 'I'm sure she's fond of you too.' Pushing back the long floppy fringe obscuring his eyes. His deep brown eyes sparkled. He too, was not immune to Serena's charm. Close to her desk, Robin sauntered by with an easy elegance, his tall figure dwarfing Graham who trotted along to keep up.

Serena beamed at Robin and a smirking Graham. Little and large she commented to herself! Like a greyhound accompanied by a Jack Russell terrier. *What an attractive man Robin is*, she thought. Although possibly too much of the honeyed tongue, she wondered.

Robin stopped at her desk and admired the photo of Shadow. 'I like cats, too,' he said.

Serena smiled. 'That's Shadow. She really is the most lovable of cats and literally my shadow. She follows me around all the time when I'm at home.'

Mary overheard Robin. 'Really?' she said, tilting her head to one side.

'Yes, really,' he said. 'When I was a boy, my dad

was posted by his job to the Hong Kong office. We all went with him. One day I was walking home from school alongside a busy road, close to where we lived. I spotted a tiny, bedraggled kitten squeaking in pain dangling one paw, in the middle of the road. Someone had flung her out of their car and left her to die. Dodging the tooting cars, I grabbed the trembling little body and took her home. Unfortunately, one leg had to be amputated, but she managed fine on her three remaining ones. When we returned to Scotland, the kitten, now grown up and christened Midnight, went too. She was such a friendly cat and lived to the ripe old age of nineteen.'

'How can people be so cruel?' Serena said. 'It's so sweet that you rescued her and she became your family pet. Do you have cats now?'

'No, I'm going to wait until I have a bigger house. One day.' Robin smiled at Serena.

'Come on, Robin. Stop coffee housing – we've got a meeting to go to,' Graham interjected.

'Sure,' Robin said and winked at Serena. She blushed.

Robert (or Robin to his friends) Dudley had joined the IT department shortly before Serena. She didn't see much of him. He was a solutions architect and sat with the other more serious 'techies' at the opposite end of the office. Serena, a Tudor history aficionado had promptly christened him the Earl of Leicester after Elizabeth I's favourite. Taking after his namesake, Robert Dudley or so Serena thought, he was one of the handsomest men she had ever seen. To

Serena, the thick mahogany hair was cut in a style reminiscent of a public schoolboy appearing in the film 'Another Country'. He was several years older than Serena she reckoned, around thirty. And he likes cats! Perfect. She thought.

Serena kept her head down and concentrated on completing her remaining development work. The finished website screens and related JavaScript she handed over to the system testers. She had always prided herself on her work and attention to detail was one of her strong points. Conversely, she lacked confidence in herself and her work. She was still the little girl at heart, who had been picked on by her primary school teacher and subsequently bullied by her classmates all those years ago. Nor had matters been helped by her experiences with Amy and her cronies at that livery yard. Seeking approval, always striving to please.

Her website work passed the system testing stage of the project with no show-stopping defects and was handed over to the business users. They would use the new system when it went live.

User acceptance testing commenced almost immediately or so it felt to Serena. She did a walkthrough of the new screens she had developed of which the business users approved. The screens met their requirements and performed as they wanted them to.

A couple of weeks later, Daisy, the development project manager, came over to Serena's desk. Lagging behind her was a girl about her own age who looked vaguely familiar.

'Serena, have you got a minute?' Daisy asked, 'Now I know you're terribly busy preparing for the implementation, but can I introduce Amy MacDonald, the new business testing lead? She'll be working alongside Steve and the other UAT testers.'

Serena was stunned. She gulped; her throat felt constricted. Here was Amy from Park Lane stables, all those successfully forgotten years before. Serena's nemesis. Serena was pleased to see that Amy's looks hadn't improved and she was still the same buxom girl, who at the age of fifteen barely reached Serena's shoulders. A hint of a sneer emerged on Amy's face when she recognised Serena.

'Hi Amy, it's nice to meet you again,' Serena said through gritted teeth. 'I'm sure you'll enjoy working here.' She struggled to produce a tight-lipped smile.

'I didn't realise you two knew each other.' Daisy glanced at Serena and then Amy.

'It was a long time ago. When we were younger,' Serena said.

Amy looked at Serena, her Wedgewood blue eyes displaying all the warmth of an icy winter's day. 'I'm sure we'll get along fine. Working together. Simply fine,' she said, glaring at Serena through narrowed eyes.

'Now, Amy, any issues regarding the website software, please raise them with Serena,' Daisy said.

'I'm sure I'll find plenty,' Amy said. 'It won't be hard to do so.'

Daisy's eyes flickered up and down as she studied

Amy. Maybe Amy MacDonald wasn't the nice, pleasant person she'd been led to believe. Not her problem though. On the other hand, Serena was a talented developer who she didn't want to lose to another company. 'Well, I'm SURE you'll find very few problems.'

'If you have any questions, Amy, you know where I sit.' Serena smiled.

Amy said nothing and averted her gaze away from Serena's eyes.

'Well, we mustn't keep you back from settling in and starting work.' Daisy bustled Amy away, persimmon chiffon scarf flowing behind her.

Great. Just what I need, Serena thought. The Amy she knew of old had spread rumours and lies about Serena at the stable where Cola was kept. All untrue. Although she was relieved to see that Amy's looks hadn't improved with age. Previously the long lustrous golden tresses were her sole claim to beauty. The bobbed hairstyle really did nothing to enhance her looks. Just like having a yellow bowl stuck on her head. She resolved to tell Mary all about Amy at lunchtime.

Lunchtime finally arrived. Serena and Mary were ensconced in their usual corner table at the back of the canteen.

'And you think Amy cut Cola's mane after you won the working hunter championship?' Mary quizzically asked. Serena had blurted out what Amy had been like at the livery yard.

Serena picked unenthusiastically at her baked

potato filled with grated cheese. 'Amongst other things. Well, I'm not totally sure. I couldn't prove she did. But she caused a lot of trouble and turned most of the other girls at the stable against me. I know that for definite.' Serena shrugged her shoulders.

'Surely that was a long time ago. I'm guessing more than ten years?' Mary sipped her lukewarm cappuccino.

Serena nodded in agreement. 'Yes, a long time ago. It seems like a different life. One that no longer exists. In my dim and distant past.' She stabbed the potato with her fork. 'Or so I thought.'

Mary glanced at Serena. She could see how upset Serena was. 'I won't believe anything she says about you. I know what you're like. A crazy horse woman!' Mary chuckled.

'Thanks! Glad to hear it. But I could do without her working here.' Serena made a face.

'Try not to let her get to you. Forget her,' Mary sympathetically said.

'Easier said than done. But I'll try.' Serena frowned. 'I didn't trust her then and I still don't.'

'Just focus on getting the implementation out the way and look forward to going to *Bellinis* for celebratory cocktails when the project is live. Think of all those yummy cocktails.' Mary licked her lips.

However, Mary was not convinced and sensed there was more to this story than Serena was letting on. They had been best friends for a couple of years, but Mary had never seen Serena so rattled before.

In the weeks that followed Serena focused on her

contribution to the project implementation plan. The plan had been put in place to ensure the new mortgage product transitioned smoothly into the 'live' environment, live being the environment where the new product could be accessed by the public and the business users.

The morning after the midnight implementation dawned. Back in for seven am the IT staff, including Serena who had worked on the project, 'walked the floors' where the business users sat. This was to check for any complications which had arisen due to the new software going 'live'. Everything had gone without a hitch. Nothing was forgotten due to the pre-implementation planning. Those involved in the implementation were able to leave early that day.

Serena strolled past Amy's desk on the third floor. The desk was cluttered with screen shots of the bank website and Excel spreadsheets. There were photos of Amy's prize-winning white poodle tacked onto the partition behind her laptop. Amy had her back to Serena focusing on her laptop screen. Sensing Serena's presence, she turned round.

'Going well, so far,' Amy said sarcastically, 'In spite of *you* working on it.'

'Glad to hear it,' Serena smiled.

'Beginner's luck,' smirked Amy.

Serena ignored Amy's comment, shrugged her shoulders and strode towards the next bank of desks to inquire if there were any issues.

Chapter Nine
Edinburgh

Light was starting to stream through the gaps in the bedroom curtains. Clothes speedily discarded from the previous evening were intertwined on the bedroom carpet. A half-empty bottle of red wine and glasses containing dregs rested on the dressing-table. It was still quite early. A Saturday morning and not yet time to get out of bed.

'Bedsitter' by Soft Cell could be heard blaring from the radio alarm on the bedside table. The man groaned. He *hated* that song. 'Oh God,' he said. He didn't want to revisit *his* recollections of what happened the night before. Quite the opposite. He wanted to forget they had ever happened. Obliterate them from his mind. Forever. Pushing the switch on the radio alarm, the room became silent. Again.

The woman in the bed woke up. She stretched contentedly like a cat. Replete. Or maybe not quite. A smile played on her lips as she noticed the rumpled duvet, on the edge of the bed. She had captured him. He belonged to her. At last. Rolling over in the bed towards him, Amy caressed his face.

'I can go and make some coffee. If you'd like a cuppa?'

There was no response from the sleeping man.

Leaning over closer she covered his face in kisses. The man stirred and shook his head. 'Look, get off,' he said.

She stopped and flinched at his words. 'But I

thought you liked me. Liked me very much. Now,' she pouted, tracing a finger on his bare chest circling slowly downwards. No reaction.

Amy decided to try another tack. After last night's amazing encounter, she was not yet sated and was ready for more. It had exceeded her wildest fantasies and she was on fire. She straddled the man, revelling in her nakedness and voluptuous figure.

The man protested. 'Please get off me. I'm not interested.'

'But you were last night. Very much,' she said.

He ignored that remark and pushed Amy off. Jumping out of bed he started to scrabble about for his clothes. He dressed hastily.

She stood up and draped her warm body around him. The man gently untangled himself. 'I need to go,' he said.

'But it's still early and I could do a full English...?' She persisted. Feeling like a spider trying to unsuccessfully entrap a fly in her web.

'No! No, I really need to go.' He zipped up his jacket.

Amy reached up for a kiss. A long lingering kiss, she envisaged. She shut her eyes. The man pecked her on the cheek instead.

'Call me?' she said. A plea.

'Yes, I'll call you. Soon,' he said and with that she had to be content. For the moment.

Thoughts raced through the man's mind. None of them pleasant. What *was* he thinking of? How *could* he have let this happen? He knew the reasons why.

Uncharacteristically drunk, feeling lonely and sorry for himself he had succumbed at last to Amy's questionable charms. That still didn't make up for what had taken place. Last night. Slowly unlocking the flat's front door, he closed it quietly behind him, flicking the floppy fringe from his forehead.

Chapter Ten
Bellinis, Edinburgh

The laughter was loud and raucous in *Bellinis*. The much favoured and legendary cocktails were flowing. *Bellinis* was handily placed just around the corner from the office and convenient for celebrating a successful post implementation review. The pub was slightly dingy inside with brass fittings and dark wood panelling. But it felt spacious enough, with tables clustered round a small dance floor close to the bar situated in the centre of the room.

The IT project managers had put a tidy sum of money behind the bar and the IT department showed every sign of taking full advantage.

Serena was sitting next to Mary at a long table nearest to the bar. Serena felt glamorous in her purple halter-neck top which showed off her well-toned shoulders. Leaving straight after work to go to *Bellinis* she had no time to change into anything else to go with her black suit skirt. Mary on the other hand couldn't be bothered and had settled for a liberal spray of Miss Dior.

'Go to the bar and get me another Beachcomber Baby.' Mary, waving her empty cocktail glass, pointed to the bar, 'Before it gets busy again!'

'OK,' Serena smiled. 'But since when have you lost the use of your legs?'

An hour or so ago!' Mary grinned.

The Beachcomber Baby cocktail was Serena's favourite drink at *Bellinis*. It was a supped-up Pina

Colada with a large measure of créme de banana thrown in. Serena came back from the bar and placed the drinks on the table and plonked herself back down beside Mary.

'That'll do me nicely, for starters.' Graham, who had joined them, attempted to grab Serena's drink.

'No chance!' Serena laughed, 'Go and get your own!'

'I've been waiting for a girl like you' was blaring from the disco speakers. Serena scowled; she detested that song.

'See whose flavour of the month then,' Graham scoffed as Robin strutted past with Amy clinging to his arm and every word.

Serena turned and looked away. This was the last thing she wanted to see.

Robin stopped beside Serena. 'Hi, guys! Having a great evening? Serena?'

'Yes, it is. I'm enjoying the cocktails.' Serena forced herself to swivel round to face Robin and a Cheshire cat grinning Amy. Raising her glass, she clinked Mary's.

'How are you, Amy?' Mary asked.

'I'm having a marvellous time.' Amy winked at Robin. Her short slinky black satin dress was creased across her middle, highlighting every lump and bump over her stomach. Fluttering her long black caterpillar-like false eyelashes she gazed up, with sheep-like eyes into Robin's.

She really should go on the TV programme 'What not to wear', Serena thought. They would soon sort her out. Not that Serena would want them to do that!

In the background, the karaoke machine was starting up.

'I just love karaoke,' Amy announced, 'Robbie, we could do a number? *Please*?'

'In her dreams!' Graham chortled under his breath to Serena.

Serena pulled a face. The night was rapidly going downhill. She knocked back her cocktail. Seconds later Amy had dragged Robin over to the karaoke machine.

'Come on, Robbie. Let's do a duet,' Amy suggested.

'OK, Amy, you win,' Robin agreed. Anything for a quiet life and an excuse to go off to the bar by himself afterwards.

The opening chords of the Heaven 17 song 'Temptation' started. Amy and Robin held the microphone together, to sing their duet. Robin struggling to keep a straight face as Amy attempted to hit the top notes but failed miserably. Amy sounded like Shadow miaowing for her tea, Serena concluded.

Amy shrieked, again and again.

Graham put his hands over his ears.

Eventually the song ended. Amy and Robin bowed to the cheers from the now very merry IT department.

After another round of Beachcomber Babies, Graham persuaded Serena up to sing 'Don't You Want Me' by the Human League at the karaoke machine.

It was unexpectantly amusing to do. Mary gave her a round of applause when she returned to her seat. Serena noticed Robin and Amy sitting closely together at an otherwise unoccupied table.

'Can't get you out of my head' by Kylie Minogue was now being belted out by Daisy, the project manager.

Mary observed Serena staring at Robin and Amy. Serena was engrossed, her gaze never wavering. Mary glanced over, 'So he's the one, is he?'

Serena snorted; 'Hardly, given the company he keeps.'

'I don't think so. He's just putting up with her,' Mary said. 'Anyway, he really likes you.'

'What makes you think that?' Serena raised her left eyebrow.

'Well, he has asked me about you in the past. Are you single, what are your hobbies? Stuff like that.'

'Really? I don't speak to him very much.' Serena shrugged her shoulders and contemplated her now empty glass.

'Well, he does, just doesn't show it,' Mary explained. 'I've known him longer than you. He's smitten with you.'

Serena grimaced. 'What an old-fashioned expression.'

'Wait and see,' Mary smiled. 'I can be the matron of honour at your wedding!'

Serena laughed and lobbed a cocktail napkin at Mary. 'Yeah, right! More like at Amy's at this rate!'

Serena felt better after that. She tried to ignore

what was happening nearby. Amy sat closer and closer to Robin. *Any closer and she'll be sitting on his lap,* Serena sourly thought.

A group of well-oiled girls from a hen party attempted to dance 'The Slosh' and fell over. Loud cheers of encouragement could be heard from members of the IT department.

Surely it must be time to go home, Serena deliberated. She tapped her nails on the drinks table, I can't take much more of this. The karaoke had concluded, and Amy had yanked Robin up onto the small dance floor. Amy looked like the proverbial cat that had got the cream.

Serena glanced at her watch. Almost time to leave. Thank heavens. She didn't think she could bear watching Amy endeavouring to wrap herself around Robin like a boa constrictor. It was nearly Christmas, she had lots of presents to wrap and a lengthy list of presents still to buy. A busy Princes Street beckoned tomorrow.

The DJ announced the last song to be played, 'Fairy-tale of New York' by the Pogue's.

My favourite Christmas song, Serena thought. She was looking straight ahead at the dance floor when a pair of slim black jean clad legs approached.

'May I have this dance?' Robin smiled and gestured with his right hand. Serena, surprised, stood up and took it. They drifted onto the dance floor. Serena couldn't bear to look at Amy. Mary did though. She was taken aback at the malevolence she saw in Amy's eyes, gouging into Serena's back. She made a mental note to keep an eye on Amy on the off chance she did anything nasty to Serena.

The first chords of 'Fairytale of New York' were played. Robin took both Serena's hands in a waltz hold and they started to dance. Robin twirled Serena round the dance floor. They made an eye-catching couple. Both were tall, slim, and stylish in appearance. Robin twirled Serena under his arm, her flame hair streaming out behind her, the colour clashing gloriously with her bright purple top. Amy was furious, her lips clamped together, her face a deep crimson. Mary didn't like the expression of hate on Amy's face. She turned to Graham who was still sitting beside her.

'Graham. *Graham*! I know you've been dying to ask me to do dance all night. Mary tapped Graham on his shoulder.

Graham groaned, 'If I have to,' and following Mary's gaze, looked in Amy's direction. Then at the happily waltzing figures on the dance floor. He was getting an idea of where the land lay. Drunkenly stumbling to his feet, he grabbed Mary by the hand and they took to the floor.

Serena wished the dance would continue forever. Robin spun her faster and faster around the dance floor. The electricity sizzled between them. Regrettably, all too soon, the music stopped. Robin escorted Serena back to her seat.

'Remind me to ask you to dance again,' he laughed. 'Guys – I must go. See you all on Monday,' he winked at Serena , then nodded to Mary and

Graham who were back seated together at the table. Wandering off to retrieve his jacket, Robin left the bar. Serena sat down; her legs had turned to jelly.

'Wow! You were like something out of Strictly!' Mary gushed.

'Hardly,' Serena brushed the compliment off. 'But I did enjoy myself.'

'Yes, we could see that. Sparks were flying.' Graham and Mary both laughed.

'But seriously though, watch yourself with Amy – she's not a happy bunny and I'd hate to see you hurt,' Mary advised.

Amy had left just before Robin and Serena stopped dancing.

'Yes. I'll be careful and will keep away from her. I didn't like her previously and I didn't trust her then. Nothing has changed.'

'Anyway, it is time for this Cinderella to leave the ball. A busy day's Christmas shopping lies ahead tomorrow,' Serena stood up from her seat and stretched.

'I'll share a taxi with you,' Mary jumped up too.

Chapter Eleven
The Scottish Borders

One Saturday, several weeks later Serena visited her mother. Christmas had come and gone; it was now a bleak March. She enjoyed the forty or so mile trip. Trundling along at a steady sixty miles an hour down the familiar A697. The soft rolling countryside of the Scottish Borders flying by. The fields were starting to have lambs in them, some running races in little gangs, others sitting closely by their mothers. Past Greenlaw, Serena turned off the A697 and drove down a single lane road. Her mother lived in a stone built Victorian cottage. Daffodils danced on the garden lawn. The field with the now empty stables stood behind the house. Jubilee flashed through Serena's mind, and she shivered. *Do you and your daughter Ruby have ghostly gallops together here at night?* She wondered.

Her mother greeted her with a fierce hug.

'Darling, it's been ages since I've seen you! Are you doing OK?' A sprightly seventy-year-old, Phyllis wore a lime and turquoise striped jumper and baggy blue tracksuit bottoms. She examined Serena closely; she was too slim for Phyllis's liking.

'I hope they're not working you too hard in that place?' Phyllis questioned, 'You do look a bit peaky.'

'No, I'm fine, thanks, Mum. I've just been very busy, that's why I've not been down since Christmas. I'm a bit tired nothing else, but I feel all the better for seeing you!' Serena said.

‘I had a reason for asking you down today. I want you to meet someone.’

Serena was intrigued. ‘Who?’

‘Come into the sitting room and plonk yourself down on the sofa,’ Phyllis said. ‘I’ll explain.’

Serena did as she was told and was soon tucking into fruit scones dripping with butter and home-made raspberry jam. She glanced around at the familiar pictures on the sand-coloured walls. Phyllis had painted several of the Northumbrian castles and seascapes herself.

Phyllis heaped some logs on the glowing fire and sat down on the armchair opposite. A large Calico coloured cat jumped up and settled on her knee. The amber eyes glowered up at Serena. The cat dug her front claws into Phyllis’s knee.

‘Oh, stop being jealous of Serena, Marmalade,’ Phyllis remarked as Marmalade glared at Serena.

Serena smiled thinking of her own darling grey cat Shadow who enjoyed visitors coming round.

‘So, how’s work? Met anyone special. Yet?’ Phyllis enquired. She always hoped Serena would meet somebody nice. One day.

‘No, not really,’ Serena said. Although in the months since the post implementation night out she had seen more of Robin. He now regularly joined Mary, Graham and herself for lunch in the canteen. There were a couple of boyfriends in her past but nothing serious. In her mind she envisaged Robin and herself as Aragorn and Arwen from one of her favourite films. The Lord of the Rings. And that was where it was going to remain, she had told herself firmly. In her imagination. Focus on work and horses. An unwanted additional factor was Amy. She was obviously still sniffing round Robin without much success it seemed. Or so Serena hoped.

'Anyway, Serena, I have a big surprise for you. A pleasant surprise – well, I hope it is. What I wanted to say to you is that you have a half-sister.' Phyllis smiled.

Serena almost fell off the sofa. 'What? *What* half-sister? Mum – what *are you* talking about? Who's her father, then? It's obviously not Daddy. Is it?'

Phyllis stroked Marmalade's head. The cat purred in ecstasy.

'Well?' Serena said.

Phyllis thought for several minutes before she started to speak.

'No of course not, Serena. Ten years or so before I met your father, I had an illicit love-affair with my university art lecturer. I thought he loved me, but he didn't. He was married. And intended to remain so. That old, old, story. Alicia was the result of our liaison. Your grandmother made me give her up. She said it would bring disgrace to our family. Nowadays that sounds terribly old fashioned.' Phyllis explained.

Serena stared at her mum. *Her* mum, had done *this*? She was gobsmacked.

'Nonetheless when Alicia was in her late twenties, she tried to find me. She had been living in Devon which was where her adopted parents lived. A village called Kingston.'

‘Close to where we stayed on holiday. Once,’ Serena recollected. She couldn’t take it in. This was totally unexpected from her outwardly respectable mother. ‘How old is she now?’

‘She was thirty-eight in January, so eleven years older than you.’

‘Ok. So, you’ve known about her being around for nearly ten years. Why didn’t you tell me before?’ Serena demanded.

‘I was worried you’d be upset.’

‘I AM upset. I wish you had told me though,’ Serena countered. ‘Did Daddy know?’ Serena’s father, a country solicitor, had died a couple of years ago, when an undiagnosed aortic aneurysm had ruptured. Serena didn’t make it to see him in time before he unexpectantly passed away.

‘No, Serena, your dad didn’t know.’ Phyllis shook her head. ‘It’s too late now.’

That must be one of the saddest expressions in the English language, along with ‘if only’, Serena thought.

‘Well, when will she be here?’

Around three. I hope you like her darling.’

Serena and her mother sat in silence. Serena didn’t know what to say. Thoughts raced through her mind. She was astounded. This was a thunderbolt out of the blue, totally unforeseen and not something she would have ever expected to hear from her outwardly ultra respectable mother. What if her new half-sister was horrible? Spoilt? A right pain in the neck? Didn’t like animals? Couldn’t, wouldn’t like Serena? Time dragged. The clock hands crawled round on the mantelpiece clock. Serena stared into the smouldering wood in the fireplace. The embers causing shadows to flicker on the wall.

Sure enough, promptly at three pm, there was a loud knock on the front door.

Phyllis rose to answer it.

'Come in dear. Yes, it's lovely to see you too.' Phyllis held open the sitting-room door. Yes, yes she's here. Come through and meet her.'

An unfamiliar woman entered the sitting room.

'Serena – this is Alicia,' Phyllis said. 'She now lives in Kelso.'

'Hi, 'I'm Alicia. I've been so looking forward to meeting you.' The skinny, delicate, erstwhile secret half-sister made her way swiftly over to Serena. Alicia Fairfax had tastefully streaked, short, auburn hair and impeccably applied makeup. She was wearing a bottle green velvet shirt which emphasised the colour of her eyes. She thrust a scrawny and bruised right hand in Serena's direction.

Serena scrutinised Alicia. Naturally, there were similarities in looks. Each sported green eyes, Alicia's a deeper mossy hue. They were both above average height and graceful. Whereas Serena was slim, Alicia was undeniably thin and what could be described as rather gaunt in the face.

'It's nice to meet you,' Serena said. 'What brought you up here? Now?'

'I've wanted to meet you for ages. It's been far too long,' Alicia said with her Devon accent. 'Being a painter like our mother, I was determined to relocate to Scotland to find inspiration for my new interest – landscapes and to continue to paint animals, which I love doing. I ended up buying a place in Kelso overlooking the river Tweed. It has an impressive view. And, of course, I wanted to meet you.' She played with the rings on her hands.

The 'our' mother bit jarred. Serena stared at her so-called, long-lost half-sister. Why couldn't her mother have told her previously?

'I know, I should have told you before,' Phyllis sensed what was running through Serena's mind.

Alicia smiled at Serena. 'I've heard so much about you and have been dying to meet you,' she added.

Serena was speechless. She didn't know what to say.

Phyllis, looking at them both, left the sitting room to make some more tea. Serena and Alicia sat side by side on the sofa. The ticking of the old grandfather clock filled the quietness. Serena gazed at the paintings on the wall. Alicia picked at her nails.

'So, how long have you been in Scotland?' Serena finally asked.

'A year or so, but I wanted to get settled before I met you. Our mum told me about a pretty house in Kelso which came up for sale a month or so ago and, since I had nothing to sell, I was able to buy it almost immediately.'

'I love it up here,' she added. 'It would be super if you could visit me. You know Kelso well. When I've got things sorted out in the house. If you'd like to, that is?’

‘Yes, it would be good to get to know you better. We’ve got tons of catching up to do.’ Serena agreed.

Phyllis came back into the room with a refilled teapot.

‘It’s so nice to see you girls chatting,’ she said.

‘Well, it’s rather a shock to find out I’ve got an older half-sister,’ Serena scowled at Phyllis and stood up. ‘You could have told me before.’

It was time to leave.

‘A rather *nice* shock. I should hope,’ countered Phyllis. ‘I always thought you were lacking in friends and Alicia will be a faithful friend to you.’

What about Mary and Ginny? Serena pursed her lips. They were her best friends. Better quality than quantity.

Before Serena left, she arranged with Alicia to come down and visit her soon. She had entered her horse Rose in a couple of horse shows which she was looking forward to. She didn’t know quite what to make of Alicia.

Chapter Twelve
Kelso, the Scottish Borders

Summer arrived before Serena managed to spare the time to visit Alicia properly. They had met briefly in Edinburgh when Alicia had driven up to replenish her oil paints and other painting materials. Alicia wasn't overly enthusiastic about 'the big city' as she called Edinburgh and anyway, she didn't like leaving her grey whippet Tosca too long. Tosca and Pimms, the black cat, got up to all sorts of mischief when Alicia left them to their own devices.

Alicia suggested Serena came down for dinner and stayed over. Midsummer's Eve had been a perfect summer's day. After a two-hour hack with her horse Rose, Serena then headed down to the Borders. The drive as pleasurable as ever. The lush, green fields sped past. Horses, sheep and cows grazed in many of these, seeking shade from the beating sun, under random trees and for a lucky few sheep beneath a discarded children's trampoline. The countryside was at its prettiest. Wildflowers grew profusely on the grass verges and peeped through the stone dykes. Once over the crossroads at the village of Gordon, she felt like she was on the home straight. She had no trouble locating where Alicia lived as she was familiar with Kelso. It had previously been her local town. Alicia's house was situated in a row of handsome house overlooking the Tweed on the way up to the entrance to Floors Castle. The sky was still a vivid blue when Serena arrived at Alicia's home. Serena knocked at the door. Alicia, wearing a pumpkin-orange dress, opened it.

'It's so lovely to see you,' she said to Serena enveloping her in a bear hug.

'Yes, it's nice to be here,' Serena agreed. Returning the hug less enthusiastically. She wasn't really a hugging person. 'Your dress is fab by the way.'

'Thanks – I didn't know if the colour suited me or not.' Alicia said leading the way, through the kitchen. 'What a glorious day it's been. Come out to the garden?'

Serena left her overnight bag on the stone floor and placed a bottle of white Burgundy wine she had bought on the oak table. Looking round the kitchen, she noticed the seascapes of Devon painted by Alicia. Serena shivered; Devon beaches did not hold happy memories for her.

Alicia read the wine label. 'Thanks for the wine, it's my favourite,' she said. 'I'll put the bottle in the fridge and we can drink it later.'

Alicia opened the French window which looked straight out into the garden. An idyllic garden. A veritable suntrap. The garden was surrounded by a high stone wall on three sides. On the wall opposite the house, there was a tall gate which when opened, led down to the banks of the River Tweed. The garden was heavenly scented. Perfumed by Chinese lilies in Greek urns and from the jasmine growing against the walls. Banks of hostas, lady's mantle interspersed with lavender and nepeta bordered the rectangular, manicured lawn.

'This is amazing, you must have inherited my mum's green fingers. I certainly haven't.' Appreciatively sniffing the fragrant air, Serena glanced around the delightful garden. Alicia evidently had green fingers.

'I'm so glad you like it. I enjoy pottering around out here.' Alicia snipped some pink roses from a large rose bush. 'Anyway, come outside and meet the animals!'

Tosca, the grey whippet lolloped towards Serena and placed her velvet muzzle on Serena's hands. She stared up at Serena with her hazel eyes. Tosca then rolled over on the grass, her tummy in the air. Shaking herself, she then stood up and padded over to sit alongside Alicia's deckchair.

'She's gorgeous,' Serena said watching Tosca elegantly arrange her paws as she settled down on the grass.

Pimms was lying in the nepeta and couldn't be bothered coming over to meet the newcomer. She rolled over again and again, revealing a snowy white furry tummy.

'Don't be so antisocial,' Alicia yelled fondly at Pimms. Pimms looked up at Alicia as if to shrug her shoulders at her and proceeded to wash her paws.

'Fab! You've got a swing seat!' Serena said, 'I always wanted one.' The swing seat faced onto the lawn, Serena kicked off her Hobbs red espadrilles and sat down on it rocking the seat steadily back and forwards.

'Is it too early for Pimms... the drink I mean?'

Alicia laughed.

'Never too early,' Serena grinned as Alicia disappeared into the kitchen and returned brandishing a large jug garnished with mint and cucumbers.

The afternoon drifted by. Alicia showed Serena to her room upstairs. It featured a coomb ceiling and one small window which overlooked the river Tweed.

'Make yourself at home. Come down when you're ready.'

Serena unpacked her nightie and toiletries. She breathed in the scent from the crystal vase of cream and cherry red-edged roses. The bed, with its cream satin throw, looked extremely comfortable and inviting. She lay down on the bed. It had been a manic week at work and Amy catting around Robin hadn't helped. Unable to keep her eyes open, she nodded off to sleep. It only felt five minutes had passed when Alicia came into the room and woke her up.

'Wakey, wakey, Serena! It's time for dinner.' Alicia patted Serena on her arm.

'Have I been asleep long?' Serena rubbed her eyes.

'An hour or so, anyway everything is ready to eat. Come down, I'll have a glass of wine waiting for you!'

Outside at the picnic table, they sat down to salmon salad and homemade potato wedges washed down with the white wine Serena had brought. Pimms now showed an interest in Serena, patting her knee with her paw. The cat happily accepted some salmon. Alicia then produced a homemade white chocolate and raspberry cheesecake. She proceeded to cut a huge slice for Serena. This Serena hoovered up in no time.

'Yum, that was delicious. Just what I needed!' Serena licked crumbs of white chocolate from her lips. 'Thank you.'

'Glad you enjoyed it. I was thrilled when you agreed to visit me.' Alicia bit her lip. 'You see I always wanted a sister and I hoped we could become friends…' She glanced at Serena. 'One day…'

Serena had been touched by all Alicia's efforts to make her feel welcome. She began to thaw towards Alicia. Slightly. After all it wasn't Alicia's fault, the manner of her birth. She didn't ask to be born.

'We are friends,' Serena said. She squeezed Alicia's hand.

'I'm so pleased. And thrilled.' Alicia was delighted and then blushed. 'Now I'll go and get us a glass of madeira.'

When Alicia returned, she motioned to Serena to move over to the swing seat where they both sat down. Sipping their drinks, they sat enjoying the exquisite garden while watching the sun beginning to set.

'Something is obviously bothering you. I hope you don't mind me saying.' Alicia scanned Serena's face, anxiously, and her almost empty glass.' You know you can tell me about it.'

Serena shrugged her shoulders.

'Is it to do with work?'

'Sort of work related,' Serena said putting her hands over her face.

Then it all came out about Amy. How Serena had encountered her at the stables where she kept her pony Cola and that Amy had taken a real dislike to Serena for some reason. The only thing she could think of was that she owned a pony and Amy didn't.

'Well, it certainly could explain why she behaved as she did. She was jealous of you. Then because she didn't like you she turned all the other liveries and stable girls against you spreading lies and making up stories about you. You and I know how cruel teenage girls can be. Sadly. I'm guessing she would also hate the fact that you were prettier and slimmer than her. From how you've described her she sounded like a large beachball on two legs!' Alicia deduced. 'Is that about right?'

'Well, maybe. Sort of,' Serena laughed, despite how she felt.

'Which won't help, given how you look. But I'm guessing the story doesn't stop there, does it?' Alicia searched Serena's now tear-stained face.

'No. I'm sorry I'm being such a drip, but Amy really gets to me at times.' Serena blew her nose noisily and wiped the tears from her face.

'I might be overreacting, but Amy now also works at the bank. She's in a department my team closely deals with on almost a daily basis. I have also become friendly with a boy or youngish man, I should say, called Robin on whom she is very keen.'

'We're just good friends, that's all,' she added as Alicia smirked. He's devilishly handsome, very tall and has quite a way with him. I've given him the nickname the Earl of Leicester.

Why do you call Robin the Earl of Leicester? What's that all about?'

Serena dabbed her mouth delicately with her napkin.' Well, you probably won't know of my interest in Tudor history?'

Alicia shook her head.

'No, I didn't think so. Robin or Robert Dudley, a sixteenth century courtier, was Elizabeth I's Master of the Horse and a superb dancer. He was given the title Earl of Leicester. Being good with horses is certainly not true about this Robin, I doubt he's been near a horse in his life. Still, there's plenty of time to rectify that!' She grinned, displaying slightly uneven teeth. 'And *his* dancing's pretty good!'

'Do you think he likes you... in *that* way?' Alicia asked.

'Hard to tell. It's just he is so pleasant and charming with everyone. Does he really like me or is just being polite. Who knows?' Serena shrugged her shoulders.

Noticing Serena's empty glass, 'more madeira or wine?' Alicia asked.

'Silly question. Wine please?'

Alicia opened another bottle of wine and poured Serena a large glass.

'I know it's a silly comparison, but Robin does bear more than a passing resemblance to the real Earl and has something of his confidence and perceived arrogance.'

'You're not selling him to me.'

Serena recounted the story of Midnight the kitten to Alicia. 'That really touched my heart. You know how much I love animals.'

Alicia looked slightly mollified.

'Well, why don't you reserve judgement until you meet him. I'm thinking of asking a group of friends along to a Christmas Ball. Though would he turn up?'

Looking at Serena's flushed face and trembling lip Alicia thought she had got it bad. 'I'm sure he would.'

'Well, to return to Amy. She is obviously crackers about him. Constantly chatting him up at work and draping herself over his desk,' Serena groaned. 'So, regarding him liking me, I think he does slightly, but it doesn't help the situation.'

'Great!' Alicia wrinkled her nose.

'She is always very unpleasant to me when we're alone looking at any work issues she's raised,' Serena said pushing her fringe back from her forehead. 'Whereas when we are in a group of people, she is almost civil. Mary, my best friend at work, has noticed this too.'

'But there's more to this, isn't there?' Alicia said. 'What is it? Why are you so afraid of her? You don't strike me as someone who gets easily upset. Is she trying to blackmail you?'

Serena lowered her eyes to the cushions on the swing seat.

'What *on earth* makes you say that?'

'Just a feeling I have.'

'If I tell you, you'll not like me anymore.'

'Don't be stupid – of course I will. I can't imagine it's anything that bad?' Alicia stared at Serena's face. 'Is it?'

'Will you keep it to yourself? No one apart from Mum knows.'

'Yes, yes of course I will,' Alicia said. She was concerned what the problem was with that clearly odious woman Amy. What was it that Amy knew about Serena?

'Take your time and tell me. Then if I can help in any way I can, I will.

Serena took a deep breath, exhaled lengthily and turned to face Alicia on the swing seat. The sky was turning crimson. Alicia clicked her fingers and Tosca came to sit beside them. Tosca rested her head against Serena's legs, nudging Serena's hand with her nose. Absent-mindedly, Serena began to stroke Tosca's ears.

'Did you ever hear from Mum about the time we went on holiday to Devon?' said Serena.

'I don't think so.' Alicia shook her head.

The last few rays of the sun, remaining from the spectacular sunset had begun to disappear. An afterglow remained.

Serena turned a reddened, swollen face towards Alicia and she started to talk. 'OK, I'll start at the beginning. When I was sixteen, we went for a holiday in Devon. Just me, Mum and Dad. When you said you lived in the village of Kingston, I recognised the name. That wasn't far from where we stayed nearby, Queenston. Mum loved Agatha Christie and begged

Dad to take us there for a week. She had always wanted to stay in Burgh Island hotel. There was that heavenly beach there. I was so jealous of those staying on Burgh Island and travelling on the Sea Tractor to get to the hotel when the tide was in. I had to make do with walking across at low tide and enjoying a crab baguette at the Pilchard Inn. Of course, you must know how enchanting it is around there?' she added.

Absolutely blissful.' Alicia smiled.

'The week passed quickly, we spent our days at the gorgeous beach, visits to Torquay and Plymouth. The weather was sublime. On the Wednesday night as a special treat for Mum, Dad booked a one-night stay at Burgh Island Hotel for the dinner dance. It was a total surprise for her. I secretly packed a small suitcase containing one of Mum's Joseph Ribkoff evening dresses carefully, so as not to get it crushed and, of course, her favourite ruby earrings. You can imagine how ecstatic she was when Dad sprung the surprise on her on the Wednesday morning. Early afternoon, I saw them off onto the Land Rover which was taking them across to the island. They were incredibly happy that day. Mum was over the moon; she had always wanted to stay at Burgh Island. A dream had come true for her. Unfortunately, a nightmare followed the dream soon after.'

Serena took several large mouthfuls of wine. 'At sixteen, I was happy to stay in the self-catering cottage by myself,' Serena continued. 'There was going to be a sort of beach party later that afternoon. I had become friends with a girl called Belinda who was sixteen, like me. She had a younger sister. June. She would be about nine years old. We arranged to meet up on the beach.'

Alicia topped up Serena's glass with more wine. 'What happened?

'It's not easy to talk about this. It's so awful and terribly sad,' said Serena.

'Do you want to stop?'

Serena shook her head and continued. 'After Mum and Dad had left, I headed down to the beach. It was another beautiful warm and sunny day. Not a cloud in the sky. The golden sand warm. The sea sparkling and inviting. Belinda and June were there chatting to a group of teenagers I didn't know. Someone had erected a net and we started to play volleyball. Belinda and June were on the opposing team from me. I remember June's little blonde pigtails flapping in the wind as she leapt about, trying unsuccessfully to reach the ball. She was such a sweet little girl. About half an hour later, the three of us were fed up playing. We then sat about on the sand. A long-haired boy called Josh joined Belinda. He was obviously keen on her. Josh retrieved a bottle of vodka from his rucksack, drank deeply from it and passed the bottle to Belinda. She took a couple of swigs and offered the bottle to me – I refused it. I wasn't keen on vodka at the best of times and this didn't seem a good time or place to be drinking alcohol,' Serena explained to Alicia.

'We went and mucked about around at the water's edge. You know that silly game where you run forward when the water runs back and when it flows towards you run back onto the sand? All of us played this for a while. Presently we grew bored. Josh proposed we swim out to a rock which was only a short distance away. I asked Belinda if June could swim could very well. I had only ever seen her splashing about in the shallow water. Belinda assured me that June could and that she had been having swimming lessons for a year or so.'

'I remember Josh saying, "Race you to the rock!" again and again.' Serena took another gulp of her wine.

'In a line, we all sprinted into the sea and started swimming. I wasn't a fast swimmer and the other three forged ahead. Even June, who was gripping onto Belinda's arm. I started to swim and swim and swim. It seemed to be taking forever to reach the rock... The rock which I thought was close before now seemed much further away. I shouted to the others that I was heading back to the beach. Belinda was treading water, she turned and waved. I don't know if she heard me or not. June was now on Josh's back. That was the last time I ever saw her.' Serena shuddered.

'When I reached the beach, I flopped down beside a sand dune, wrapped my towel around me and fell asleep. The next minute or so it felt, Belinda was shaking me,' Serena said. 'Belinda started to scream wanting to know where June was. I said that I thought she was with them. Nearly at the rock.'

Alicia sipped her wine. Her eyes focussed on

Serena's face.

'I stared at Belinda. I was sure June was with Belinda and Josh. The last time I saw June she was on Josh's back. I'm sure they were almost at the rock. I told Belinda this. Again. And again. Belinda went white. She said she thought June had come back with me. And that one minute June was on Josh's back, the next she had disappeared.'

'Oh, that's awful.'

'I know it is.'

'Go on. If you can.'

'I guess so. I had swum back by myself. Thinking that June was with Belinda and Josh. Belinda kept saying, "What are we going to do?"'

'There was a lifeguard sitting in one of those highchairs on the beach. We bolted over and Belinda told him June was missing. The coastguard was phoned and we hurried down to the water's edge. Fog had descended obliterating the clear blue sky and visibility was now poor. The lifeguard swam out towards the rock. It felt like ages until he returned.'

Serena polished off her wine and resumed talking. 'Belinda raced over to him. The lifeguard explained that he couldn't see June and that hopefully the coastguards would find her. When Belinda heard that she burst into tears. She kept repeating that she thought June was with me. I wish she had been. The lifeguard assured Belinda that the coastguards would contact her parents as soon as they had any news.'

Alicia topped up Serena's glass. She was shocked. This story was so unexpected and harrowing.

'We stayed on the beach until darkness descended. Cocooned together in beach towels. No one spoke. All of us hoping against hope that June would be found. Alive. We then returned to our separate holiday homes. I was the first home. Belinda and Josh, holding hands, stumbled on towards her house. Once inside I poured myself a large gin and tonic. Then I broke down and cried. Poor, poor little June. Please God make her OK, I said to myself.' Serena fiddled with her watchstrap as she stared down at the picnic table.

Alicia waited for Serena to continue. 'What happened? Was June ok?' She touched Serena's hand.

'Sadly, June wasn't OK. The next morning, I headed to the beach and arrived there just after nine. Two coastguards were coming out of the sea. They carried a tiny body with its pink and white spotted swimming costume and laid it on the sand. The blonde pigtails, intact, still neatly tied with pink ribbons. June looked like a little doll. Fast asleep.'

'Belinda was there, in a sea of tears, with her parents. Josh was nowhere to be seen. She saw me and screamed at me. Belinda accused me of leaving June alone in the water and letting her die.' Serena said. 'Which I didn't do. When I last saw her, she was on Josh's back, her hands clasped around his neck, with Belinda swimming alongside. That was the last time I saw her alive. I told Belinda again *and* again.' Serena thrust her palms upwards. 'I felt awful and didn't know what else to say. It was the truth. On the wet sand, Belinda crouched down beside June's body.

I joined her, we both stared at the once perfect vibrant little girl. I turned round and placed my hand on Belinda's back but she pushed me away. I said I would return later and then I sprinted back to our cottage. I hoped my parents would be home soon. They were already home. When they opened the front door, they were still happy. Not for long. They were appalled and upset when I told them about June. My dad said I would have to attend an inquest.'

Alicia's eyes never strayed from Serena's face.

Serena carried on talking. 'The inquest was held soon afterwards. It was horrendous. So terribly sad. June and Belinda's parents arrived with haunted eyes. They were heartbroken at June's death. Belinda couldn't look me in the eye. In my mind I kept seeing June's lifeless little body on the beach. What did come out at the inquest was what *had* happened to June. Belinda, Josh and June *did* reach the rock. They didn't hang round for long as the water was very cold. Josh had said "race you back", and that the last one back was "a smelly kipper". They all proceeded to swim back towards the beach. Belinda got there first, followed by Josh. They began fooling around, smooching on the beach. They forgot about June. When they remembered about the girl, she was nowhere to be seen.'

'What a ghastly thing to have happened, that poor little girl,' Alicia said.

'I do blame myself. However, when I last saw June, she *was* on Josh's back as Belinda treaded water. I *did* shout to them that I was going back. But did they hear me? I don't know. I kept thinking about it again and again. Over and over. The memory haunts me still. If only I had stopped them or taken June back to the beach with me.'

'Well, if anyone was liable for June's death it was Belinda and Josh leaving her to swim back by herself. Not you,' Alicia reasoned.

'Belinda blamed herself for what happened and never got over June's death. I never saw her again after the inquest. A few years ago, I read in a newspaper she had tragically taken her own life.'

'That's heartbreaking. Poor Belinda and June's family to have suffered so. One tragedy is bad enough, let alone two.' Alicia retrieved a crumpled tissue from her pocket and blotted the tears on Serena's face. 'Look you can't keep torturing yourself forever about this. They're dead. Nothing can bring them back. Don't let this poison and ruin your life.'

'I know you're right. But that's easier said than done,' Serena said. 'And there's another connection to me too. Amy,' Serena admitted.

'Amy? How come?' Alicia asked.

'Amy was Belinda's and June's cousin, so she holds me accountable for both their deaths,' Serena said.

'Right, I see. That makes sense. After what you've told me about her. So, another reason to hate you,' Alicia said.

'Regretfully yes and I'm just waiting for her to tell everyone at work about it. Although this happened more than ten years ago, she'll still try her damnedest to convince them that I'm responsible for June's death.'

'Great!' Alicia frowned.

'She has hinted that much to me. At work when we have been reviewing system issues together,' Serena said.

'Surely, they won't believe what she says?' Alicia questioned.

'Well, Amy can be pretty persuasive at times,' Serena said, 'and has also suggested to me if I make it worth her while she'll keep quiet about it. She's intent on ruining the good reputation I have at work.'

'That's blackmail!' Alicia said. 'You must stand up to her, after all it wasn't your fault what happened.'

'It's just she seems to hate me so much, starting with when I owned Cola. Then June. And then Belinda. Now you know,' Serena yawned and decided against mentioning the nightly visitations. They could keep for another day.

Seeing how tired and washed-out Serena appeared, Alicia screwed the cork back in the wine bottle. 'Now Serena – I really think it's time for bed. You're exhausted. Things will seem better in the morning. They always do.'

Serena climbed the creaky wooden stairs leading to the little bedroom. The window was slightly ajar. Serena looked through it at the view over the river Tweed. The stars were starting to emerge in the night sky, Serena could see the silhouettes of cows along with their calves, grazing contentedly on the other side of the river. She didn't think she would fall asleep easily. But she did. For once she didn't have the recurring nightmare that June was in the bedroom with her.

The next morning Serena left early. She had to ride Rose who was entered in a show jumping competition the following weekend. There was a course of jumps set up at the livery yard and Rose needed a practice session.

'Don't leave it too long till you visit again,' Alicia urged. She hugged Serena. 'Please don't worry about Amy.'

'I'll try,' Serena said.

'I don't think anyone would believe her and anyway it's not your fault what happened in Devon. Just remember that,' Alicia reiterated.

Once Serena left Alicia sat down at the kitchen table with a fresh mug of coffee. Secure in herself and her ability as a painter, self-doubt wasn't something she subscribed to. But she was worried about Serena. This woman, Amy, seemed bad news, she appeared to be conducting some kind of vendetta against Serena. Understandably Amy was upset about the deaths of her cousins but was using Serena as a channel for her grief. And a touch of the green-eyed monster where Serena was concerned didn't help either.

She wondered if she could do anything to help. It was obvious Serena wasn't a terribly confident person. According to Phyllis, when Serena rode a horse, it was a different story. Serena and the horse were a team and to watch them together, poetry in motion. Just a shame she couldn't be like that around people. Alicia drained her coffee, stood up and clicked her fingers at Tosca.

'Come on we're going for a walk,' she said to the now jubilant whippet that was wagging her tail from side to side, as if it were a conductor's baton.

Chapter Thirteen
Edinburgh

Music played tranquilly in the background of the minimalist sitting room. The Thomas Tallis CD ended and Robin switched the CD player off. It was a lazy Sunday for Robert or Robin to his friends. He had arranged to meet Graham for brunch at The Standing Order pub in George Street. Robin's elegant mews house was situated in Stockbridge, so he didn't have far to stroll through the beautiful Georgian New Town.

A biography of Robert Dudley, Earl of Leicester, with its well-thumbed pages had been carelessly thrown onto the glass coffee table. From Graham, (*heaven knows how Graham knew this*) Robin only recently discovered that Serena had secretly christened him Robert Dudley, Earl of Leicester. On hearing this, he couldn't resist purchasing a biography about the Earl. He couldn't quite see the resemblance. After reading the book several times, he did concede to himself that, like the Earl of Leicester, he was considered a superb dancer, although, unlike the Earl, no good with horses.

He rearranged the framed photographs, one of a tiny black kitten wearing a cerise velvet collar, the remainder featuring his brothers, on the grand piano. The sole adornments in the room. Poignantly, only one of his brothers still lived. Focusing on his career to distract him from the loss of his brothers, he had reached dizzying heights in his career at an early age.

One day, he promised himself, Serena's likeness would be displayed alongside the others too.

A vision of Serena drifted into his mind. He thought she was a gorgeous girl with her pinned flame red hair which flowed down her back like a banner. She vaguely reminded him of someone he knew. From his not too dim and distant past. Although she was always friendly towards him, he sensed something was troubling her. Something holding her back. It didn't help that that pain of a woman Amy was always hanging around him. Never leaving him alone. Nor were matters improved by Amy continuously bitching to him about Serena. Why was Amy so mean about Serena? They must have some history. One day he was going to ask Serena what that was all about. He liked her very much.

There was a work night out in a few weeks which he hoped Serena would be attending. Perhaps they could have a chat there, although if Amy were going, she would probably stick to him like super glue all night.

Robin glanced at his watch. Just before ten-fifteen. Eggs Benedict and a large cappuccino beckoned. He threw on his yellow puffer jacket hanging in the hall and jumped down the steps of the spiral staircase. His long, lithe legs jumping two steps, at a time. He was going to be late. Tonight, he would give serious thought to how he could speak to Serena properly. Alone.

Chapter Fourteen
The Bank, Edinburgh

It had been a long and tiring day at the office. Thursday, the penultimate day of the working week. Serena checked her watch. Six pm. She was desperate for a drink. The previous implementations she had worked on had all been successful. If slightly nerve-wracking at times. Now considered an important member of the IT department she had been promoted to senior developer and all the responsibilities that entailed. Including quality assuring the junior developers coding. Newly out of university, some of them thought they knew it all. They needed to learn how to ensure their code was efficient and that it was thoroughly unit tested before handing it over to the system testers. Not full of bugs. Serena liked things to go smoothly. The earlier defects were discovered the easier and cheaper they were to fix.

Mary stopped by Serena's desk. 'Fancy a drink?' she said.

'Goodness I'd thought you'd never ask!' Signing out of her laptop, Serena then pulled her navy blazer on over the chartreuse linen dress.

'Where shall we go? Bellinis?' Mary suggested.

'Let's go to the Club.'

Mary glanced at her 'You mean the one you're a member of?'

'The very same. Thought I'd taken you before. Obviously not.'

'Well, yes, maybe last year?' Mary conceded.

'Probably. You've got a mind like a sieve at times!'

'I know that!' Mary smirked. 'I'll go and get the boys.'

'Which boys? 'Serena asked.

'Well, just Graham and Robin,' Mary said.

'OK, if you must.' Serena grinned.

Mary rounded up Graham and Robin. Both were easily persuaded to go the Club for drinks.

'Quick, come on let's get to the lifts before Amy spots us,' Mary said.

Amy's desk was just along from the lift, on the other side of the office.

'I don't mind if she joins us,' Serena said.

Mary shot her a look. 'Yeah, right!'

The four of them sped to the lifts and jumped inside as soon as it arrived. Out of the lift on the ground floor, giggling like a bunch of naughty children they sprinted out of the building.

Strolling round onto Princes Street they enjoyed the remainder of the Indian summer. Then heading along Princes Street and then up onto Frederick Street before turning into George Street. Entering The Meridian Club via the revolving doors, Serena stopped briefly at the reception area.

'Good evening, Miss Kennedy,' the former sailor behind the reception desk said.

'Good evening, Tom. It's lovely to see you. I'm here for drinks with my friends,' Serena said.

'It's very pleasant on the balcony this evening.'

'I'm sure it is and that's precisely where we're heading.' Serena smiled.

Divested of their coats and jackets in the cloakrooms, the four of them marched up the flights of stairs until they reached the balcony floor. Pausing at the bar adjacent to the balcony, Serena ordered four large gin and tonics.

'It's so nice to see you here again, Miss Kennedy,' the pretty blonde waitress said.

'And lovely to see you too, Jane,' Serena said.

'In no time the Ball will be upon us,' Jane said. 'I know how much you enjoy it, Miss,' she added.

'Yes, that's very true,' Serena laughed. 'And I'm going *this* year!'

Serena brought the drinks over on a tray. They all sat down on a rattan sofa and chairs on the balcony. Everyone raised their glasses in a toast. There was silence for a minute as they enjoyed their drinks. Serena presently stood up and walked over to the balcony balustrade.

'I never tire of this view. I could sit here and watch it all day,' she said. Looking out over George Street, from the balcony, the New Town could be viewed in all its splendour. And in the far distance, the sparkling blue water of the river, the Firth of Forth.

Mary joined Serena and said, `What a glorious evening. You're so lucky to be a member here.'

'I know I am. Well, it was down to my dad. He had been a member for years and thought I would meet interesting people. Which I most certainly have! When I younger I thought about doing law.'

Instead of IT?' Mary asked.

'Yes,' Serena grinned. 'I wasn't clever enough.'

'Still, you've not done too badly,' Mary laughed.

'Yes. Not THAT badly,' Serena said, patting Mary on the arm. 'Come on let's go back and join the others. They'll be ready for a top-up.'

Graham, cheery and thirsty as ever, had already finished his drink.

'Same again?' Serena asked. 'Stupid question!'

She went back inside to the bar. Waiting there was a man she knew. Hamish. Fortyish, flamboyantly and stylishly dressed as usual. A black and emerald-green striped blazer, well-cut twills and black shoes with green detailing completed his outfit. *A very modern-day Beau Brummell,* Serena thought. She always looked forward to seeing Hamish's attire.

Gesturing extravagantly with his right hand towards Serena, Hamish said, 'My dear, I haven't seen you for so long. You look divine. Are you well?'

'I'm fine thank you,' she said. 'And you? And Flora?' Flora was Hamish's successful fashion designer wife.

'We're both splendid. Thank you. Thinking about attending the festive Ball this year? We are. It does seem a long time since you graced the Ball with your presence.'

'Yes, contemplating it,' Serena said.

'Delighted to hear that. Now, please excuse me, my dear, I mustn't neglect my guests. Super to see you again. You must pop down to Zeals for a visit.'

'I would like that very much,' Serena replied.

Hamish then wandered off with two bottles of champagne. He re-joined the group of men seated round a table of empty glasses at the far end of the balcony.

Serena headed back to her table with four gin and tonics.

'Did I hear mention of a Ball?' Graham sharp ears had overheard Serena's conversation with Hamish 'When and where?'

'Yes, there is a Ball here at Christmas every year,' Serena confirmed.

'Can we go?' Graham said, cheekily.

'Wait till you've been asked!' Mary said.

Serena wondered if it would be enjoyable, the group of friends going along to the Ball. She hadn't been for a couple of years or so.

'You mean the four of us here plus Mary's husband?' she said.

Mary looked pleased at the idea. 'And what about your long-lost sister Alicia?' she asked.

'*Half-sister*,' Serena interjected. 'Good idea, And I'll maybe ask another couple along,' she was thinking about her horsey friends Ginny and Rory.

'What's the format of the evening?' Graham asked.

'Well, it starts around seven pm with a champagne reception, followed by dinner, then dancing and there's a break around midnight. Then more dancing and an early breakfast – for those with stamina!' Serena explained.

'Sounds like my kind of party,' Graham said. 'Of course, you'll be going, Robin – you're an expert dancer after all,' he nudged Robin in the ribs.

'Count me in.' Ignoring Graham, Robin grinned at Serena.

'I didn't know you danced, Robin?' Serena said.

'Well, yes, I was a member of a reeling club when I was at university. 'It was great fun, along with the swimming and shooting clubs which I enjoyed very much.'

'Well, you learn something new every day,' Graham said. 'I didn't have you down as a shooter though?'

'Yes – shooting clays is my thing, I attend a clay pigeon shoot in Fife.' He glanced at Serena.

'The dress code is black tie.' Serena's face reddened under Robin's gaze. 'So, you'll all need to dress up!' Serena said looking at Graham.

'Don't look at me like that! I do own a kilt and a jacket and all the paraphernalia that goes with them, you know!' Graham glared at Serena.

Serena shook her head apologetically. 'Oh, sorry Graham, I didn't think!'

'Apology accepted,' Graham said.

'Ok, if you're all up for it I'll apply for tickets,' Serena said.

Everyone nodded several times.

Robin looked pleased. Maybe he would be able to properly speak to Serena alone. For once.

Mary mentally went through her limited wardrobe, to think what she could fit into and more to the point what would Henry her husband wear.

Graham thought it sounded great fun with gallons of alcohol to drink. Plus, loads of yummy food to eat.

What more could anyone ask for?

'More drinks anyone?' Robin said brandishing a twenty-pound note.

'No thanks. I think I'll need to be going,' Serena shook her head and stood up.

'Guess I'll need to make tracks too,' Graham said.

They all left the club. Mary and Serena in one direction. Robin and Graham heading off to their regular pub, just along George Street. Graham having successfully convinced Robin to have 'one for the road'.

'You know, this could be your big chance to get together with Robin?' Mary suggested to Serena while they were waiting for a taxi. 'He's obviously mad on you.'

'I don't know whether he is or not. After all, Amy's always hanging around him.' She turned her bright green eyes to Mary. 'Anyway, I'm not sure if I'd want to go out with anyone who works in the same department as me. It could cause problems. And I have enough of these with Amy.'

Mary shook her head merrily. 'But that's the thing I don't think Robin will be at the bank much longer. He has been offered a consultancy job at an insurance company. He will take it. I heard this on the grapevine.'

'You mean the Graham grapevine?'

'Yes, OK, the Graham grapevine,' Mary confirmed.

That would simplify matters, Serena thought.

'When is he leaving?'

'The end of January,' Mary said.

Something to bear in mind, Serena pondered.

A taxi showed up. There was no more talk of Robin. Their conversation turned to what they were doing at the weekend before they were dropped off at their respective homes.

Chapter Fifteen
Edinburgh

Two days later, Alicia paid a rare visit to Edinburgh. She had arranged to meet Serena for lunch. Leaving Tosca for the day at Phyllis's house, she drove to the Borders railway station at Tweedbank. The train was waiting at the station, and after parking her car, Alicia ran to the train. The train left shortly afterwards. Alicia always enjoyed the hour or so journey to Edinburgh. The scenery was so picturesque.

A raucous group of girls, obviously on a hen party, joined the train at Galashiels station. Waving their fairy wands and adjusting crooked rhinestone tiaras they staggered up the corridor into Alicia's carriage. Swaying as she went, the 'hen' with her 'L' plates attempted to press the button to open the door into the adjoining carriage. There were loud whoops of laughter as the girls collapsed into their seats when the train, with a judder moved off. Pulling out an A4 sketch pad, Alicia tried to capture the countryside as it flew past. In no time the train stopped at Newcraighall station on the outskirts of Edinburgh. She put her sketch pad away and applied a much-needed bright coral lipstick. She felt nervous about meeting Serena and telling her, her news. When the train arrived at Waverley, Alicia headed quickly out up the ramp onto Princes Street. Not too quickly though. She had caught a final glimpse of the hen party, clearly the worse for wear! Arms linked in a row they were swaying in the direction of Princes Street.

They moved slowly and cautiously, tottering about in their impossibly high heels. The *hen's* tiara was now skew-whiff on her head and had fallen over her right eye. Alicia hoped one of her friends would rectify it, but doubted they were in a much better state than her.

A chilly breeze caught Alicia unawares and she drew her loose-fitting jacket tighter around her. She plodded along to the far end of George Street. Not far to Tiger Lily now. Slightly panting after ascending the short flight of steps, Alicia entered the sophisticated and stylish restaurant. A waiter stood talking with the bartender while simultaneously tidying his hair in the reflection from the large gothic mirror behind the bar. He noticed Alicia.

The waiter stepped forward. 'May I help you, Madam?'

Alicia said, 'Yes, thank you. I've a table booked for twelve-thirty for two, under the name Fairfax.'

The waiter checked the bookings and promptly escorted her to the table.

Serena was there already. Wearing a scarlet silk shirt and dark green velvet jeans. She gave Alicia a hug when she arrived at their table.

'It's lovely to see you,' Serena said.

'And you,' Alicia replied. Alicia removed her jacket and slumped in her chair. The vivid purple Cashmere polo neck jumper, although very baggy, complimented her auburn hair. Serena thought she looked skinnier than ever and worryingly even thinner in the face. However, Alicia's eyes still sparkled with pleasure at seeing Serena. Alicia glanced round the restaurant, admiring the artistic decor and opulent velvet seating. 'I love it in here,' Alicia said. 'Thanks for suggesting meeting up here.'

'I'm glad you like it; Mary and I enjoy lunching here.'

The waiter returned shortly afterwards to take their drinks order.

'A lime and soda for me please,' Alicia said. Serena glanced at Alicia. 'I'm driving later,' she explained to Serena.

'I'll have a large glass of pinot grigio please,' Serena said.

'So how are things?' Alicia asked.

I'm fine, thanks,' Serena said. 'I've been busy competing my horse Rose in local show jumping competitions. With some success,' she added. Rose, the feisty chestnut mare was extremely competitive at shows and sailed effortlessly over the highest of jumps. There was a sea of red rosettes on Serena's kitchen wall from all of Rose's wins. 'I'm just amazed at how well she is going this season,' Serena added.

'That's great. You must both be so talented. I would love to come to the stables and meet her,' Alicia said. 'And paint her too. If you would like me to?'

'That would be brilliant. Thank you!' Serena smiled.

Flicking through the menus, they chose their starters which arrived promptly.

Alicia devoured the king prawns lathered in butter. She offered one to Serena who had settled for an avocado and quinoa starter.

'No thank you,' she said, 'although they do look delicious. Anyway, you haven't told me much about yourself. I just seem to talk about myself when I'm with you.'

'What do you want to know?' Alica asked.

'How did you get into painting?'

'Well, where I lived as a child, there was a farm nearby which bred pedigree cattle and sheep. I was sent up there every week to buy eggs and used to wander past the fields in which the animals grazed. In one small paddock the orphaned lambs lived and Juno, a brown and white calf. She was very friendly and loved me to rub her forehead which had an unusual white marking, snaking down her face to her nose. When Juno was born, her mother rejected her – she was a twin you see, but the kindly farm manager hand-reared her. She never lost her affection for people and remained a pet for the rest of her days on the farm.'

'That's such a sweet story,' Serena said.

'I love farm animals and seeing them properly cared for.' Alicia smiled. 'One day, I took my pad of paper and I sketched Juno alongside the lambs. The farm manager loved my drawing, gave me some money for it and hung it in his living room where it took pride of place. So that was my first commission.'

'Are you still painting? Animals?'

'Yes and yes. Mostly horses and dogs. The occasional prize-winning sheep or bull. And enjoying it. I've had several commissions to paint from people living round about.'

‘It sounds like things are going well for you, living up here.’ Serena said. ‘And what are your adopted parents like, what did they think about you moving to Scotland? Have they visited you yet?’

Alicia stared down at her bony fingers. She rotated the gold Russian Wedding style bangle round and round her wrist. Should she also tell Serena about her treatment and how she was feeling now? What to leave out? Alicia thought for a moment.

‘My adopted parents, Joyce and Bob are now both in their eighties. They also had a son – Geoff – who lives in South Africa. They were well into their forties when they adopted me and had always encouraged me to look for my birth parents. They never kept it a secret that Phyllis Kennedy, the landscape painter, was my mother. However, they were unsure who my father was. Several years ago, I heard Bob had developed a heart condition and might not have long to live, although he’s still hanging on. Joyce said I should contact Phyllis. I never did so previously as I felt I would upset them despite them saying to the contrary. I contacted Phyllis; she was thrilled to hear from me – after nearly thirty years of silence. She realised I wanted to be nearer to her and to meet you. She was the one who suggested moving to the Scottish Borders.’

‘I still wish my mum had told me sooner about you. I can’t understand why she didn’t and how she kept you a secret from Daddy. All these years. Living a lie.’

‘I know Serena, but things were different when I

was born. Different times. And the lecturer had made it clear to Phyllis that he wasn't going to leave his wife. It can't have been easy for our mum.'

The 'our mum' expression still annoyed Serena but she knew she had to get over it.

'Joyce and Bob encouraged me to move and gave me their blessing – I keep regularly in touch with them. They feel they're too old to make the journey up here. Our mum found a flat for me to rent in Melrose and I moved up from Devon a couple of years ago. Then I found the house of my dreams and having nothing to sell, was able to snap it up. I was so lucky.'

'You *were* lucky – places like that rarely come on the market,' Serena said.

'Unfortunately, the day I signed the missives on the house was also the day on which I was diagnosed with an aggressive form of breast cancer.'

The blood drained from Serena's face, she reached for Alicia's left hand. 'That's terrible news. I never knew. Mum never said. I hope the treatment was successful?'

'Yes. Yes, it was at the time.'

'But that's awful!' Serena exclaimed. 'How could you go through all the treatment by yourself?' The waiter breezed over and took their empty plates away. She waited for Alicia to continue. 'Did you?'

'Well, I didn't. Thankfully. Our mum knew and was a tower of strength for me,' Alicia said.

'Tell me what happened to you?' Serena asked.

'Not long after I was diagnosed with cancer, I had a mastectomy. It went well with no complications apart from a haematoma which took it's time going away, but we got there,' she grinned. 'And of course Mum looked after me when I came out of hospital.'

Ah now that explains why Mum said she was busy, and was so secretive, about two years ago, Serena thought.

'This was followed by eight sessions of chemotherapy.' Noticing the grim expression on Serena's face, she added, 'It wasn't that bad and I got off lightly.'

Serena screwed up her face. 'But all those needles. Yuck!'

'Yes, well, that was made better by the nurse who before she inserted the cannula into the vein in my hand, soaked my hand in a bowl of hot water so that the needle went into the vein more easily. And less sore, too.'

Seeing Serena now looking a bit green, Alicia continued. 'When the chemotherapy was being administered to me, in a large sunny room, I sat in a circle with other people also receiving chemotherapy. Some read, even knitted, most just talked. I remember one lady extolling the virtues of mushrooms for boosting her immune system to a nurse. I've always enjoyed people watching. Plus, the friendly nurses are always bustling about, seeing if you'd like tea, coffee, hot chocolate and/or biscuits in that order! I was very well looked after!'

Serena smiled at Alicia; she was so positive about her experiences.

'Snooping in on other people's conversations is

always interesting. There was one man in for his last session of chemotherapy. Lucky thing, I thought at the time! He said to the lady seated next to him that one thing he would never be was a drug addict.'

'Why?' Serena asked.

'The whole room waited to hear the reason why,' Alicia said.

'"Because I never want to see a needle again in my life!" the old man replied,' Alicia chuckled.

Serena laughed too.

'Seriously though, you got through it OK?' Serena asked.

'Yes. With a never-ending supply of ginger biscuits to hand in case I felt sick and a vigorous walk in all weather – every day. What choice did I have anyway?'

'I get that, but it still must have been pretty grim at times.'

Alicia shrugged her shoulders and continued. 'The course of radiotherapy that followed the chemotherapy was a breeze. Although the tissues where the mastectomy had been done, got stuck, so to speak, under the skin. However, the physios at the hospital soon sorted that out and I regained full movement of my right side and my arm,' Alicia said. She then proceeded to do a perfect ballet movement with her right arm.

'What I'm afraid of is I think that the cancer has come back.' Looking down at the bruised veins on her hands, Alicia added, 'I'm not sure I could face any more chemotherapy.'

Serena was horrified. 'But that's terrible news. How do you know for definite it has come back?'

Alicia turned worried eyes to Serena. 'No, I just have a bad feeling about myself. I've felt like this since before I moved to Scotland. That's why I wanted to be closer to Phyllis and to meet you. I'm going for a check-up at the end of November and will know for definite then.'

Serena was distressed to hear this and didn't know what to say. But what could she say? Nothing. Poor, poor Alicia. 'Well, if there's anything and I mean anything I can do, please let me know.'

'Thanks, that's really kind. Just having you around for support is marvellous,' Alicia said. 'What you can do is tell me about that dance you and your friends are going to. Mum mentioned it to me that you were thinking of going.'

Serena looked at Alicia questionably. 'Yes I'm hoping to. The Ball is in December and being held in the Meridian Club. The Club is just along the street from here.

'I need a distraction,' Alicia said. Placing her knife and fork on the empty plate, she smiled at Serena.

'Look why don't' you join us? I'm sure it'll be a fun evening. Robin is going.' Serena blushed when she said this.

'Sounds like an amusing evening and I get to meet ALL your friends,' Alicia mused.

'Well, there are five of us going so far. Me, Mary – you've heard me mention her before – she's so kind, always up for a laugh and mad on animals -like me,

Mary's husband Henry whom I've only met once, Graham, a fun guy from work I'm friendly with, and Robin too.'

'Naturally.'

Serena silenced Alicia with a look. 'I haven't asked Ginny and Rory yet but I'm sure they'll come along. They're keen dancers. You've heard of Ginny who helps me with Rose?'

Alicia nodded. 'What are they like?'

'Ginny... I first met her when I owned Jubilee. She's now a close friend. Helps me out tremendously with my horses and so supportive in other ways. Her husband, Roderick, or Rory as he prefers to be known, is a quite a character. Just wait till you meet him. It would be lovely if you were able to join us. That would be a party of eight?' Serena said. 'I'm sure it'll be a fun evening.'

'OK, I'll think about it. I would love to meet Mr Perfect... or should I say the Earl of Leicester?' Serena threw her napkin at Alicia. A tight-lipped couple on the opposite table turned and glared at Serena.

'That's me told!' Serena said, muttering under her breath.

The waiter arrived with their main courses. He placed them down on the table with a flourish. Steak burger with fries for Serena and grilled seabass for Alicia.

'Will that be all ladies?' he asked, gazing into Serena's green eyes.

'If you could please bring us another one of these,' she said pointing to her empty wine glass. 'And a large coke and ice too, please?' she asked.

The waiter returned in no time with their drinks. They started their main courses.

'It would be brilliant if you came along,' Serena persisted. 'Why don't you?'

'Well, I'm older than all of you,' Alicia reasoned. She decided not to spoil the now happy mood by asking if the dreaded Amy might be present too.

'So? You're only a few years older,' Serena pointed out. 'Next, you'll be saying you don't have anything to wear!'

'Well, you're wrong there. I do have. When in Devon I painted a couple of horse portraits for friends and ended up attending several hunt balls with them. So, I'll be suitably dressed. Don't you worry, I won't let the side down!'

Serena laughed. 'What are you like? I'd say a bit of a dark horse?'

'Well, just because I don't ride doesn't mean I don't like horses or horsey folk.'

'So, you will be joining us?' Serena looked hopefully at Alicia.

'Oh, very well. If it makes you happy.' Alicia smiled and tucked into her fish.

*****

Around the same time at which Serena met Alicia for lunch Amy paid a visit to her only great-aunt.

Neither time nor teaching had been kind to Miss Fenton. Her glory days of teaching were well past. She had stayed on as long as she could until forced to take retirement. The deputy head teacher at Corbie

Primary School, she still taught the 'littlelies' as she sarcastically called them. That is until the day she was caught wrapping a five-year-old boy over the knuckles with a metal ruler. His knuckles had bled copiously. The head teacher who had caught her in the act of doing so, had remonstrated with her.

'Now, now Miss Fenton, I know you only want to make sure children learn to read properly, but there are ways and means of doing so. Ways and means,' he said to her, when they were sitting in his office that sunny afternoon.

Pushing her greying frizzy mop out of her Samson strength glasses, Miss Fenton retorted, 'He was an annoying little so and so. He never tried. Not at all. His parents should never have given him a mobile phone. I tried to confiscate it from him numerous times, but he wouldn't hand it over to me.'

The head teacher glared at Miss Fenton.

'I was struggling to take his mobile phone off him. He kept holding it behind his back. All the class were laughing. At *me*.'

'All the same, Miss Fenton you shouldn't have hit him over the knuckles with a ruler in the first place,' Mr Black countered.

Miss Fenton's face turned tomato red and to her horror she felt tears welling up in her eyes. Nobody had *ever* spoken to her like that in her nearly fifty years of teaching. Who was this so-called head teacher to speak to *her* like that? At least twenty years younger than her and obviously not as bothered with making sure the children should be able to read well as much as she was.

Mr Black looked slightly sympathetically at her. He arranged the jotters into a neat pile on his desk. 'Maybe it's time you should consider retirement. Imminently?' he questioned.

So that was what had happened. The school board was entirely in agreement that Miss Fenton should leave. Soon. Little Johnny Barker's parents had complained to the school about their son's treatment. They were only slightly mollified to hear Miss Fenton was going to retire in a week's time just before the start of the Easter holidays. Miss Fenton would never teach Johnny or any other child again. Naturally, Mr and Mrs Barker weren't the only parents or first parents, to complain about Miss Fenton. There was a multitude of children who had been bullied by Miss Fenton, humiliated in front of their classmates, their confidence in themselves shattered. She was a monster, a well-meaning one in her goals, but a tyrant all the same. One who wrecked children's lives.

The following year, she suffered a small stroke. She put this down to the lack of mental stimulus in her life, which teaching had given her. Crosswords and attending medieval lectures at Edinburgh University were a poor substitute for her active mind.

Miss Fenton lived in a thirties-built bungalow on the outskirts of Edinburgh. On arrival, Amy noticed the sparseness of the small garden in front of the house. She had never observed this before. A small square of grass previously surrounded by rose bushes, was now overgrown with weeds and, where roses would have been in full bloom, in summer, neglected; just stumps with thorns protruding from the small branches.

She knocked on the peeling paint door. Aunt Betty didn't believe in doorbells. Anyway, who *would* want to see her? True there were visitors, her niece Amy sporadically, and ladies who were participants of the local Women's Institute branch. Invariably some of these were members of the blue rinse brigade. They bored her. She had long given up frequenting their meetings where the highlight of the evening was winning first prize for the best bird ornament, brought along by the attendees. Really. All that fuss about winning someone's un-wanted Christmas present. Betty had once won first prize, everyone enthusiastically applauded – a set of men's deodorants. She gave up going shortly after that. A highly intelligent woman, she needed to keep her brain energised. This visit from her great-niece, Amy, who was as spiky as the thorns on the decaying rose bushes in the garden, was just the tonic she needed. Thinking of tonic, she hobbled as fast as she could into the untidy kitchen to check she had fresh tonic for Amy's mandatory large gin.

Miss Fenton, Betty to her few friends, opened the door and glared disapprovingly down at Amy's barely there denim mini skirt and black opaque-encased meaty, chunky, sausage-like legs.

Miss Fenton muttered an abrupt 'Good morning' to Amy.

'Hello, Aunt Betty. How nice to see you,' Amy

replied in response.

Amy stomped through the narrow hallway lined with bookcases (which contained mostly non-fiction books) and into the spacious living room with its magnolia woodchip walls and numerous upright chairs dotted round the room. Looking round the room, *so this is how a resident's lounge must look in an old folks' home*, Amy thought. She sat down on a green chair which gave the impression of being the most comfortable. A faint smell of cabbage met Amy's nostrils, pulling her face into a habitual grimace. The room was freezing, so Amy flicked the switch on the portable electric fire to make it warm. Standing in front of it she rubbed her hands together and wished she had worn her fingerless gloves.

Aunt Betty vanished into the kitchen reappearing shortly afterwards with the obligatory (large measure of) gin and tonic. Pulling the green tweed skirt methodically around her, she seated herself opposite Amy in a high-backed wooden chair. Her posture was ramrod straight. Unlike Amy's, she noticed who was slouched in her chair like a giant amoeba. Had Aunt Betty deigned to watch the film 'The Empire Strikes Back', she would have likened Amy to Jabba the Hutt. T*hat girl should really have more self-discipline*, Aunt Betty thought. Helping herself to a cup of cold tea from the teapot on the chipped coffee table She squinted at Amy through her pink plastic-rimmed glasses. *Goodness, I must get a new pair of glasses, things weren't as clear to see through them as before*, she thought.

‘Are you well, Amy?’ Aunt Betty enquired.

‘I’m well, thank you. What about you?’ Amy replied.

Aunt Betty launched into her litany of ailments, most of which came with age. A very disciplined woman, she had never touched a drop of alcohol in her life nor smoked. She ate a diet of home-cooked plain food. A perennial favourite was mince and tatties. Her idea of a treat was a sparsely-buttered, home-made plain scone.

‘My doctor is also concerned I might have another stroke and now says I have to take pills for…’

‘What did you just say, Aunt? I didn’t quite catch what you said?’ Amy’s mind had strayed off by this point, apart from making appropriate sympathetic sounds, as and when required by way of a reply.

‘I said I’m not happy taking apixaban tablets to thin my blood. The doctor put me on quite a high dose.’ Aunt Betty repeated. ‘I hate taking any form of medication but they were prescribed a few months ago, because I have an irregular heartbeat. I’ve been getting increasingly breathless this year and my doctor sent me for an ECG. That’s when they discovered the problem with my heart.’ Looking at her hands she pointed out to Amy the small flat red spots under the skin which had flared up recently. ‘I don’t know if I should speak to the doctor about these or not. Are they a side effect of the medication? I really must read the leaflet that was in the box the pills came in.’

‘Well, I’m sure the doctors know what they are

doing. They wouldn't have prescribed them for you otherwise,' Amy said. She wasn't particularly perturbed by her aunt's health. After all, she was a tough old bird. 'It's probably nothing to worry about,' she added.

'I hope so too. And sometimes I don't even remember whether I've even taken the tablets or not.' Aunt Betty sipped her tea. 'Now what about you. How is your love life?' She enquired.

Amy startled at that. Aunt Betty was as blunt as an unsharpened pencil at times. It was really none of her business. Still, it would while away the time before she could leave at, after what would be considered an acceptable period to do so. Running her fingers through her neatly bobbed hair, Amy contemplated mentioning Robin to her aunt. A vision of her nemesis surfaced in her mind. Serena.

'There's a man at work I'm very taken with,' Amy said.

'Indeed! I knew it!' Aunt Betty smirked.

How could she think that? What did Aunt Betty know of men? Of love? Amy thought. She had never heard of any men connected to her aunt. Would any man want to be?

Aunt Betty sat there looking expectantly at Amy. She picked her ear, discovered some wax, inspected the brown substance now on her finger and promptly placed it into her mouth. Amy retched. She felt nauseated, although that was probably more caused by the effects of drinking five large glasses of red wine with Graham at the pub the previous night than to do with Aunt Betty's minging behaviour. Amy swallowed and forced herself to take a large gulp of the industrial strength gin and tonic in front of her. The hair of the dog. That *should* help.

'So, there's this man called Robbie who I like. I *really* like. He works at the office too. He's very charismatic,' Amy's eyes misted over, 'But, I think there's someone else he's keen on. Her name is Serena. Serena Kennedy,' Amy said. 'I hate her!'

Aunt Betty stared at Amy. She crossed and uncrossed her legs at her ankles, her posture remaining as straight as a poker. She had never seen Amy look so animated. Her face had gone pale, but two red spots of anger had appeared on her cheeks. Normally when she visited, she sat lifelessly in an armchair, uttering monosyllabic replies to her aunt's questions.

Vitriol spouted from Amy's tongue as she went on and on like a record stuck on the same tune about Serena. How she had been the bane of Amy's life and was still trying to spoil it. And she would have to work at the same place as Amy. How inconsiderate. Things were going to change, though. Soon. Serena was going to get her comeuppance. At the Meridian Club Ball.

'And, of course, she was responsible for my cousin June's drowning, a number of years ago,' Amy continued. 'Serena should have got in trouble for that, but she managed to wriggle out of it. I don't know how she managed to,' she squawked.

Aunt Betty's ears pricked up at the mention of this name.

‘What did you say the girl’s name was again, dear?’

‘Serena Kennedy.’

‘Serena, Serena Kennedy,’ Aunt Betty mused to herself. ‘Now I know that name.’ She was particularly good with names. Must be around the same age as Amy. And then it came to her, a child with green eyes of an unusual shade, the promise of beauty in her heart shaped face. The child begging and crying and begging and crying to go to the toilet.

Amy then recounted the various occasions on which if Serena was present Robin only had eyes for her. It was all so annoying.

‘She’s like a stick insect, a playing card, to look at. No curves. Whereas I’m just like Marilyn Monroe,’ Amy sat up straight for once and thrust her voluptuous chest forward.

Aunt Betty couldn’t concentrate on what Amy was saying. Her eyes glazed over. Everything was spinning in front of her. She shook her head. The dizziness stopped. She forced herself to think. Her recollections came flooding back.

‘Now, I knew that girl. I taught her at primary school. A regular little cry-baby she was.’

Amy was ecstatic. A smile brightened up her nondescript features, making her look almost pretty. ‘What was she like then?’ she said.

Aunt Betty settled back in the chair. She related how Serena had been terribly ill, off school for weeks and made to take an antibiotic, which had a laxative side effect.

'So of course, she was desperate to go to the toilet and I wouldn't let her go. She had had her chance to go at break time and she was back in class time. My class time. I couldn't let children in my class do what they wanted to do. They had to be disciplined. The belt came in handy. There was barely a day went past when at least one child was punished for their misdemeanours. I was in charge and my word was law. Absolute law. Although I never had to use the belt on Serena.'

'So, she messed her pants.' Amy drawled. 'Poor, *poor little baby*!' Amy was delighted. Smiling so much that all the metal fillings in her teeth could be clearly seen. Another thing to taunt Serena about and tell all her friends. This titbit could be kept for the Ball. She hooted with laughter.

Aunt Betty grinned. She was glad to see Amy smiling. Let alone laughing. Neither were a regular occurrence.

'I can't wait to remind Serena about this. It'll make my day or should I say night at the Ball!'

The smell of cabbage seemed to have diminished by the time Amy left. Fortified by another strong gin and tonic everything felt brighter. The sun had come out metaphorically and physically for Amy when she waved goodbye to Aunt Betty, promising not to leave it too long before her next visit. That extra morsel about Serena from her aunt made her smile and Amy almost whistled as she departed from her aunt's house.

Chapter Sixteen
The Bank, Edinburgh

A few days later at work, Serena was loitering at the drinks machine waiting for the tea she had selected. Amy noticed her and tottered across in her skyscraper heels to Serena. Smoothing down her red cord pelmet skirt, Amy turned round to face Serena. Serena snatched her cup of tea up and began to stroll back to her desk.

'Hey, wait a minute – I want to talk to you,' Amy said. Picking her nose with her left index finger, she then used it to select the hot chocolate option from the drinks machine.

Yuck! Remind me to never choose hot chocolate or, if I want to do so, find another drinks machine, Serena thought. Fixing a smile on her face, she turned to face Amy.

'How are you, Amy? Having a good day?'

'I'm going to the Meridian Club Christmas Ball too. I thought you'd love to know,' Amy smirked. 'So, you'll have the pleasure of my company there. All night.'

Serena was almost speechless, 'That's nice for you. Who are you going with?'

Amy grinned. 'With Jinty Mackay who works in the marketing department here. I've known him for *years*! As well as some other friends. Several of them are members of the Meridian Club. Just like *you*.' She laughed. 'So, you see, *you* think you are special but you're *not*!' Amy's father was a member of White's

Club in London, which she never tired of telling people. According to Amy, only those such as *her* friends and *her* relations were members *there*.

Serena's heart sank. Jinty's wife was a member of the Meridian Club, like herself. She was a successful lawyer, who on the occasions, they had met at the Club, had been very pleasant to her.

'I knew you'd be over the moon to hear my news,' Amy sneered, baring capped even white teeth.

'Yes, I'm sure it'll be a wonderful evening,' Serena forced herself to say. 'I really must go, I have tons of code to write,' and with that she scurried down the office.

'Yes, I'm sure you do. Rewrites!'

Amy started to laugh. She couldn't wait for the Ball. For two reasons. One to get her claws into Robin Dudley and secondly to discredit Serena in her friends' eyes and show them what she was really like. A woman not worthy of anyone, nor of any importance. Someone to the ignored. And despised. That was Amy's plan.

Serena sat down slowly at her desk. The day was stretching ahead of her like a ball of wool which had been unravelled. Lots of background coding was required for the new equity release functionality to be present on the mortgage website. *I'll have my cup of tea, sit quietly for a moment, and then start work,* she thought. An hour or so passed, nothing much inspirational flowed from Serena's fingers onto the laptop keyboard. *I must get on*, she thought.

Daisy stopped at Serena's desk. 'So, how's the new

functionality coming along? Have you finished it yet? Is it ready for handover to system test?' she inquired.

Serena ceased typing. 'It's getting there. Parts of the code are incredibly complex and I want to make sure it's spot on and working properly before it's available to the system testers,' she explained.

'Well so long as it's ready for system testing in two days' time,' Daisy said. 'We're relying on you, Serena. It *must* be ready for then.'

'It will be ready for then,' Serena replied. She crossed her fingers under her desk.

'Cool. Nine am on Wednesday and no later,' with that Daisy, who had noticed the IT director was in the office and hastened after him.

Just like a matron on her rounds checking up on her patients, Serena decided. She'd get this screen done, even if it killed her. Today. Her phone pinged. A text from Mary. Gosh that girl *is* psychic, she thought. She read the text.

'Chin up,' it said.

Serena sent a thumbs up by way of a reply.

Then another text arrived. From Robin. A smiley face emoji That was all. Still better than nothing. She dispatched a cheesy grin emoji back.

The day dragged on. Serena had no meetings for which she was grateful. Meetings were only useful, she felt if she'd nothing better to do. In her mind, any meetings which went on for longer than half an hour, diverged from their agendas and lost their original purpose.

Lunchtime. All too soon. Exhausted and feeling in

need of inspiration, Serena resolved to venture out for a walk. The frozen leaves crunched under her feet as she wrapped the woollen scarf tighter around her neck. Five minutes later, Serena sat alone on a wooden bench facing the fountain in the sunny square along from the office. Watching running water always soothed her. The fountain consisted of a large bronze wave surrounded by four leaping dolphins. Water drops glistening like diamonds flowed from the dolphins' open mouths. Rapidly eating her cheese savoury roll, which she ate without tasting and after gulping down a bottle of mineral water, she then perched on the stone rim surrounding the fountain. She had better go in soon. Splashing her fingers in the cool water to wake herself up, staring down into the clear water, her tumbling loose hair almost reached the water. The water changed, becoming dark. A shadow loomed behind Serena. Robin. Shielding her face against the sun, with her hands, she turned round to face him.

'May I join you?' Robin asked. He sat down beside Serena.

'Well, only briefly. I was just going back in. I've got heaps to do,' Serena said. 'I'm hoping the icy water will stimulate my flagging brain!'

Robin dangled his fingers in the cool water. 'I'm sure it will. Goodness, this water is freezing!' he said.

Robin was silent for a minute or so. He studied Serena. 'You know, you shouldn't let Amy bother you. Even if she's going to the Ball too. There'll be plenty of fish for her to catch there and I'm sure she'll take a huge net with her!’

Serena laughed so much her shoulders shook. Although she was convinced the only fish Amy wanted to land was Robin, the vision of Amy casting a large fishing net around at the Ball to catch an eligible, wealthy and possibly titled young bachelor *was* hilarious, though.

‘That’s better,’ Robin said. ‘It’s so nice to see you laugh. You’ve been looking peaky recently and your sparkle has vanished.’

‘Not now,’ he said as Serena smiled at him.

‘Why should you care?’ Serena questioned. Her mind was turning somersaults at the discovery that Robin considered she sparkled.

Robin was still dangling his fingers in the water beside Serena’s. His fingers briefly caressed hers. Glowing green eyes met smoky brown ones. His eyes as warm and inviting as a swimming pool on a sultry day. Serena dropped her eyes.

Abruptly, Robin stood up from the fountain and checked the time on his Rolex. ‘See you soon,’ he said and marched back towards the office. A rainbow-like smile enveloped his face.

Minutes later, Serena waltzed back to the office. She felt she must have imagined Robin’s fingers caressing hers. Hammering away at her laptop, she concentrated on the code she was developing. The afternoon flew by. The JavaScript flowed from her fingers as fast as an upturned bottle of wine on a table. Towards the end of her working day, Serena started to unit test the code. From what she had seen, it was working as expected. Time to leave. Serena slammed her laptop shut and stored it in her rucksack. She left the office with a jaunty spring in her step. It had been a *most* productive day.

Chapter Seventeen
Edinburgh

No stars shimmered. A midnight blue blanket smothered the night sky. The wind howled like a banshee. It was threatening to rain, Miss Fenton noticed, as she drew the bedroom curtains tightly shut. Settling down in her metal framed single bed, she sipped her sugary hot chocolate. Her new indulgence. Pulling the blankets on the bed closer around her since she felt shivery, she noticed the small red spots remained on her hands. *I wonder what caused these,* she thought. *Come to mention it, did I take my pills at seven pm tonight*? This concern fully occupied her mind. Daily. Just recently she had taken to leaving her shopping outside for hours, only to be tidied away late in the day. The milkman now needed to knock on the front door to ask for his money. Previously it would be waiting for him, in a neatly scribed envelope, on the doormat.

She concluded it would be better to take her prescribed dose of pills on the off chance she hadn't done so. Envisaging further problems with her heart filled her with dread. She hated going to hospital. Reaching out for her glasses on the tea-stained bedside table she couldn't locate them. How annoying. Scrabbling around with her right hand she located the bottle of pills. *Four? Or was it two? Four, yes that's the dose I'm sure I'm meant to take,* remembering what the doctor had said. She popped them in her mouth, downing the remainder of her hot drink. Finally, locating her glasses, she opened her book, one of her favourites, *The Prime of Miss Jean Brodie*. Three chapters later she was ready for sleep. The room was warmer now. Images of her happy teaching days swirled through her mind. Sleep came.

Miss Fenton awoke unexpectedly. Her heart was banging against her ribs and her head throbbed. *I'll get a glass of water, that'll make me feel better*, she decided. Now. Unable to locate her bedside lamp, she stumbled out of bed in the blackness.

Once out of her bedroom she crept along the dark hallway. In her urge to get a glass of water she had forgotten to flick the hall light switch on. Concentrating on where she was placing her feet, she failed to notice the bag of shopping she had forgotten to put away the previous day. Tripping over the bag, she smashed her head against the edge of the old oak dresser. With a howl of pain, she crashed to the floor.

Her head spun and she tasted vomit in her mouth. After falling to the floor, she lay motionless for several minutes. She attempted to move her legs. They still moved. Thank goodness. Patting her forehead, she discovered it was warm and sticky. Feeling light-headed and giddy, she attempted to push her legs together, so she could stand up. Clinging onto the side of the dresser, she endeavoured to pull herself up. The effort made pains shoot through her chest. She sank downwards again. *I must phone for help,* she thought. A red mist descended in her head. Her breathing became laboured. Minutes passed. Miss Fenton remained immobile. In a daze. *Could she hear children laughing? A group of school children were sniggering at her*. They were jabbing freshly sharpened pencils into her brain. Darkness fell, like the curtain descending at the end of a play.

Chapter Eighteen
Edinburgh

The day of the Meridian Club Christmas Ball arrived. The weeks had galloped past. The code and screens developed by Serena for the bank's tight deadline were now a distant success.

Inside Mary's house in Inverleith Row, all was tranquil. After finishing work at five, (which was exceptionally early for her) she then languished in a hot bath. After a leisurely cup of tea and a piece of toast she considered it was now time to get ready.

'When's the taxi booked for?' Mary asked Henry, her husband. A plump balding, fortyish man, he wasn't particularly interested in attending the Ball. He would rather stay in and read his newspaper. However, he knew Mary was and he also was used to her hit or miss timekeeping.

'Six thirty, so you'd better get a move on,' Henry replied. 'We don't want to be late. Not for this.' It was almost six pm.

In their bedroom, Mary pulled the two evening dresses out of her wardrobe and held them up in front of her. One at a time. Hoping they would still fit. She didn't get dressed up very often. The long, jade green silk dress was her preferred option, more forgiving and suited her better, but there was a red wine stain on the front. It would have to be the turquoise damask midi dress. At least it complimented her copper hair. Zipping herself with an effort into the dress, it must have shrunk at the dry cleaners, she decided. She surveyed her reflection in the full-length mirror. It would do. Sitting at her spotless dressing table, devoid of any lotions and potions, she applied mascara and tawny-coloured lipstick. She wasn't really a make-up person. Ready. Mary went downstairs and poured a small glass of white wine. She was very much looking forward to the Ball, but hoped Amy wouldn't cause any trouble for Serena. Amy still appeared to hold a grudge against Serena. What the grudge was, Mary didn't know, even though she'd been friends with Serena for several years now. The fact that Robin was fond of Serena had made Amy even more antagonistic towards Serena. Mary resolved to make sure Serena stayed out of Amy's way.

'Come on Mary, we're going to be late. The taxi is here,' Henry tapped his velvet evening slipper on the hardwood floor. He neatened the winged collar on his evening shirt before putting his overcoat on. Mary grabbed a lavender pashmina. One quick glance in the coat stand mirror. Her customary low bun updo was tidily pinned, as usual. Henry paused to let Mary pass outside before he locked the oak front door.

*****

Nineties dance music reverberated around the Marchmont flat. The neighbours had long ago given up telling Amy to turn it down. But on the plus side, she was helpful at collecting their mail if they were out.

Amy surveyed her bedroom. Dresses and shopping bags littered the carpet and bed in the pink and lime bedroom. Nor was there was space on the antique dressing table for any new purchases. Partly opened expensive cosmetics and perfumes were scattered everywhere on the glass top. The dressing table drawers bulged with lacey underwear.

Dressed in a black silk wrap following a hot shower, Amy sat on the edge of her bed. She started to paint her toenails a deep purple colour. An unwelcome vision of Serena materialised in her mind. Annoyingly, the vision would not disappear. Amy began to think back to when she had first started to dislike Serena. She couldn't quite recall. The hate came later. She recollected incidents which had happened over the years in her mind. Thinking back, the aversion she had felt towards Serena had begun at the riding stables where they first met. Serena riding around on that flashy chestnut pony of hers. The pony had such a stupid name. Coca Cola. It had all been so easy for Serena. True, she had a rough time at the stables where the other girls egged on by Amy were mean to Serena and at times took it out on Serena's pony too. If Amy was being honest with herself, her feelings stemmed from jealousy on her part. Amy didn't do self-honesty. It was of no significance to Amy that she attended a private school in Edinburgh from the age of eleven and annually enjoyed summer holidays at Disneyland in Florida or in the Caribbean. Her posh clothes, (mostly from Harrods) were bought by her doting mother. Diamond studs, weighing several carats each, adorned her fourteen-year-old ears. She wanted a pony. The one thing she didn't own was a pony. She had to make do with leasing a pony at the stables which was ridden by other children too. Grass green with envy, she watched Serena effortlessly elegant on her pony cantering round show rings, Cola's bridle festooned with rosettes by the end of a show day. What made it worse was that Serena had tried to be friends with her until she caught Anny slagging her off and telling lies about Serena and Cola to the other pony owners. From then on Serena was polite but distant. Thankfully, Cola was moved to another livery yard, so Amy didn't have to endure Serena's presence anymore. She assumed she would never meet Serena again. Regretfully, this was not to be.

When Amy heard about poor little June drowning in Devon, she immediately accused Serena. Venom dripped from Amy's lips, disclosing to everyone she knew that Serena was responsible for June's death, until she received a stern telling off from Belinda and June's heartbroken mother.

The years passed and Serena no longer featured in Amy's life and mind. Until she joined the same bank that Serena worked at. Amy was a business user tester. She observed the high regard Serena was held in by the IT department where she worked. Matters were made worse by the fact that their paths now crossed frequently. Professionally. Serena did walkthroughs of the new functionality she had developed, which would be passed over to the business users to evaluate before going 'live'. These unfortunately included Amy. Serena's presence grated at daily morning progress meetings. Always so enthusiastic and happy to help. Amy felt sick thinking about this. Naturally, Amy was ignorant about the sadness's in Serena's life. Of her dad who had unexpectedly died nine years ago from a burst aortic aneurysm. A heavy smoker, he had started to complain of pains in his back but by the time he was in hospital it was too late and he had passed away shortly afterwards. This was devastating for Serena and her mum. Her father was a very sociable man for whom a night spent at home was a night wasted. An aspect of character inherited by his daughter. Following his death, Serena had concentrated on studying for her degree and her mother on her painting. Nor did Amy know of the demise of the beloved Jubilee and of the horrific accident Serena had experienced on the horse she had owned prior to Jubilee. Few people would have got back on a horse after a fall of that magnitude. Amy still rode, she could have afforded her own horse, but her enthusiasm had dwindled towards owning one. It galled her to hear that Serena still owned a horse, a large chestnut mare, which she show-jumped with much success.

Amy finished painting her toenails, stood up and stretched. Enough thinking about Serena, she decided. There were more important things to be considered. What to wear tonight? She was convinced this was the night she was going to get her long damson claws into Robin. Forever. She knew he liked her and always laughed extremely heartily at her jokes. Going through her cosmetics, she picked up her favourite Bobbi Brown smoky eye shades and proceeded to apply them with an expert's skill. Concentrating for the next hour or so on her face, Amy then glanced at her watch. Only five pm. She had taken a half day holiday from work to pick up a new evening dress from Harvey Nichols and give herself loads of time to get ready. After all, tonight was *the* night. It was regrettable that the dress code dictated long evening dresses only. Her favourite evening dress was of wild black silk, short and with a V-neck at the front that plunged to her waist. Trust Serena to be going to the Meridian Club Ball, although Robin being there made up for that. Somewhat. But tonight, she was going to be classy. She knew Robin liked classy birds. Like that skinny cow Serena. A wannabe Audrey Hepburn. Well, she would be Marilyn Monroe to Audrey Hepburn and Amy knew which one would win. After pouring herself a large vodka and tonic, she surveyed the carnage of dresses and bags. Her large white poodle, Mr Boye, launched himself onto the chartreuse green and shocking pink satin bedspread.

'Get off, you!' Amy yelled, affectionately pushing Mr Boye off the bed.

She chose her new dress which would show an expanse of her generous cleavage. It fitted her like a second skin. She had read Marilyn Monroe was sewn into some of her dresses and wished she could have been. Tonight. Fastening her twenty-first birthday present, a diamond riviere necklace round her neck, Amy admired herself in the cheval mirror. Perfect. One more thing. She unlocked the bottom drawer of her bedside table. Reaching tentatively inside, she pulled out the small pearl encrusted pistol. She squeezed the gun into her silver sequinned evening bag. Amy had inherited the pistol from her grandmother, who had lived on a farm in Kenya during the nineteen thirties, in addition to the white mink stole which she now wrapped around her bare shoulders. The taxi tooted outside. Planting a kiss on Mr Boye's head, she left the flat, hobbling in her high heels, down the tenement stairs, ready for the night ahead.

*****

Robin drummed his fingers on the meeting room table. Time was marching on. He glanced up at the large clock on the wall. The afternoon meeting had overrun by an hour. He was going to be late. Extremely late. He *hated* being late. Especially, when he wanted to make a good impression. Tonight. Of all nights. On Serena.

'Robin? Robin...?'

Robin blinked his eyes and refocused with difficulty on the high-level design document which lay in front of him. The IT department was developing a new loans product for the bank, for which he was the lead solutions architect.

'Robin, Robin. Sorry – what I'd like to ask is, I don't get why this process happens here?' Derek, the senior developer drew Robin's attention to a diagram with his index finger.

'What part of the process don't you understand?' Robin turned murky brown eyes on his subordinate.

Why did he have to work with such stupid people? Not for much longer though. Thankfully. 'It's pretty obvious, how it all hangs together, if you had read the document *before* this afternoon's walkthrough of the design.'

Derek's face reddened under Robin's gaze. 'I mean the release funds process – here,' he jabbed the page with his finger. 'I don't think it works. Sorry.'

Robin pursed his lips and stared at the other developer, Paul.

'Paul, are *you* happy with what we've covered this afternoon? I thought it was pretty cut and dried what was explained here. Are you clear about what part of the design you'll be working on?'

'Erm, yes. I think so,' Paul pushed his glasses back on his nose. He wasn't sure he was but didn't want to rattle Robin any further this afternoon. Goodness – he was in a foul mood. Paul sensed waves of anger emanating from Robin. He had been on the receiving end of Robin's temper before and had no desire to experience it again.

'Good. That's reassuring to hear,' Robin beamed at Paul. At least *someone* understands what is written here,' he frowned at Derek.

Derek scanned the document. 'Look, I'm sorry Robin. Really sorry – I'll go over it at the weekend. Just to make sure I'm clear what I'll be developing. I promise.'

'Good. You do that,' Robin snapped. 'We've a tight deadline here and I can't afford any slackers on our team. Guys – time to wrap this meeting up. It's gone on way too long.' Robin slammed his laptop shut and stood up.

'Oh, and Derek – I expect better from you! You're the *lead* developer on this project. *Try* to act like one!' And with that he swept out of the meeting room.

Derek and Paul stared at each other. They left the meeting room together, saying nothing. Paul judged it was safe to speak when they could see Robin at the far end of the office.

'What a guy,' Paul whispered. 'Derek – are you OK?'

Derek sighed. His hands shook as he fastened his rucksack.

'You better do what he says,' Paul said.

'I know. I'll try.' Both men grimaced.

'What's gotten into him today? He's getting worse.' Derek asked.

Paul pointed towards the desk with the horse and cat photos displayed on it. 'I think I can hazard a guess.'

Both men nodded.

Robin returned home after six. What a hectic day at the office. Being an important member of the department, he was much in demand. Especially today, having to explain how the infrastructure of the bank's mortgage website hung together to a group of obviously disinterested and non-IT literate staff. And then, last thing, having to deal with the airheads in *his* own team. That was the final straw!

Draping his wool overcoat over an armchair, he wished he could just go out for a pint instead of attending this Ball. He needed to forget about those halfwits at work today and focus on tonight.

Perhaps a strong cup of tea would revive him? The twill sofa looked very appealing. Eyeing the comfortable sofa regretfully, he decided he'd better lay out his clothes for the evening ahead. Passing the glass cabinet beside the sitting-room door, Robin glanced at the numerous sporting trophies and accolades displayed in the glass cabinet. He had won these at university and at his private school. The prize he now yearned most to win was Serena.

Rifling through several suit bags in his wardrobe he retrieved the one containing his bottle green velvet smoking jacket, with the Black Watch tartan trousers hanging underneath. Time for a snooze. Bringing a cup of tea through to the bedroom, he lay down on his bed and promptly fell asleep.

Robin awoke with a jerk; he had been dreaming of Serena. Her long hair rippled over her shoulders as she sat wiggling her fingers in the water of the fountain near the office. He remembered how his fingers, also in the water, touched hers of their own accord. Sparks of electricity emanated from the encounter. They looked at each other. Properly. For the first time. He had abruptly withdrawn his fingers away from hers. The spell had been broken. By him. He hoped it hadn't for Serena. Robin knew she considered him to be arrogant and a ladies' man. Like his namesake Robert Dudley, his dancing was exceptional. Although unlike his namesake, he wasn't exactly an expert with horses. Non-existent in fact. He wouldn't have liked to have been caught between Elizabeth I and his second wife, Lettice. Maybe there was a parallel here between Serena and Amy. Robin laughed out loud. He could certainly see Serena as Lettice but Amy most definitely *not* as Elizabeth I.

What he was dreading tonight was the possibility of any altercations between Serena and Amy. Fingers crossed that their parties wouldn't be sitting close together at dinner tonight. What to do about Amy? Robin had indulged Amy. Once. A big mistake. To his cost. Never again. He knew she was a tricky character and needed to be managed with kid gloves. Be polite but distant and discourage any advances on her part. He knew she was mad about him; her feelings would soon turn to hate if he spurned her. As luck would have it, he was leaving the bank in the New Year after being head hunted by an insurance company, the offer being too good to refuse.

Now Serena. The critical issue was what to do about Serena? In his mind's eye he could conjure up a vision of her. Now. The stunning flame red hair cascading down her back, the shining peridot eyes, the way she floated, not walked, as gracefully as any model. The apparently confident woman with an air of vulnerability about her. Mary was always harping on about Serena's exploits. Her well-known kindness towards other people and animals. The way she was fearless riding that wild mare of hers which went by the gentle name of Rose. Hurtling on Rose's back around the countryside rescuing sheep with their heads stuck in wire fencing or lying cast on their backs. Feeding stray cats, befriending wild birds which fluttered around her shoulders and flew to her when she whistled for them, writing letters about animal welfare to MPs. The list went on and on. He desired her. And what Robin wanted, he usually got. Tonight, he would let her know how he felt. If only that meddling and jealous bitch Amy would stay out the way.

Dressing quickly, tying his black velvet bow tie, no ready tied ones for him! The taxi was outside. Robin slipped into the taxi which then headed towards the Meridian Club.

*****

Breathless, after climbing up the one flight of stairs, Graham forced the key into the lock of the dented orange door of his Ednam Street flat. Once inside, he chucked his leather jacket on the hall carpet and kicked off his shoes in the dingey hallway. In the kitchenette, where a week's worth of dirty dishes were piled up in the sink, he deliberated whether to have a drink? After turning on the radio, he grabbed a can of beer and knocked it back. Enjoying listening to 'Don't you want me' by The Human League, he glanced at the Donald Duck wall clock. It was half past six, so he was going to be late – extremely late. Well, he'd still better have a shower, he wanted to look his best for the ladies. Serena *and* Amy.

Scurrying into the bathroom, he turned the shower dial on full. After what seemed an age, the water was finally warm enough to get in. Graham hummed to himself in the steamy shower cubicle.

Work had certainly become interesting since Serena and Amy had joined. New eye candy. And both single. In his eyes, Serena… well Serena, she gave off an air of being unobtainable and off limits. In that way. To him. If he was being honest with himself, she probably only regarded him as a work buddy. Nothing else. Someone to attend work events alongside and have a laugh with. Amy. Well Amy was another matter. Her tongue was as spikey as a hedgehog's back, frequently entertaining – usually at someone else's expense. And a looker to boot. Now, there was the possibility of success with her. Graham licked his lips, his tongue removing the remaining residue of beer. He WAS looking forward to tonight.

Loathe to leave the warmth of the shower, Graham wrapped a towel around himself and headed into his bedroom. Looking in the mirrored glass wardrobe doors, Graham examined his body. A bit chubby. Maybe? He prodded his tummy which was spilling over the top of the tightly wrapped towel and attempted, unsuccessfully, to hold it in. There was no point. Too many beers and whiskies. If only he was as tall as Robin and not just on eye level with Serena. Combing the sparse brown hairs across the centre of his shiny forehead, he wished he possessed a full head of hair. Like Robin. And to be handsome. He didn't know quite what to make of Robin and was unsure of whether he liked him or not. Still, it suited him to chum Robin along to work get-togethers and the possibility of attending events at which Serena might be present. Such as this evening. Thinking about tonight, Graham paused as he unearthed his kilt outfit from the wardrobe floor. Flinging all the outfit's crumpled components onto the bed he contemplated the predominately black and yellow tartan kilt. Would he look good enough in this getup for the Ball? Particularly as he was trying to impress those two ladies. Fortunately, or possibly unfortunately, the decision was taken out of his hands. The last time he had worn the kilt was to his cousin's wedding, over two years ago. It had been a snug fit then. Now he was unable to fasten the kilt even in its loosest fitting. Well, that was that. Plan B. A more recent acquisition was his black dinner suit which he had worn a few months back to accompany Amy to a charity dinner dance at the Sheraton Hotel. Amy had made it clear that the dress code was black tie and that only a dinner suit would suffice.

Graham jerked the dinner suit from its hanger and grabbing the trousers, tugged them on. He struggled to fasten the waist button, but managed to do so by breathing in. Then he splashed a liberal amount of Calvin Klein's 'Obsession' onto his chest and around his neck. The creased, white evening shirt with the ready tied black polyester bowtie followed and he hauled on his black dinner jacket. Thankfully he was able to do up the jacket buttons. Now, shoes? Where were his only pair of black formal shoes? Scrabbling around under the bedside table, he found them. Dusty and covered in hairs. Nothing that a bit of spit and polish wouldn't sort out. Graham spat on his shoes and rubbed them with the sleeve of his dinner jacket. They would do. Would *have* to do. Surveying himself, now fully dressed in the mirror, pleased with the results, he decided if this getup didn't work tonight, then nothing would.

Back in the kitchenette, he took another can of beer out of the fridge and gulped it down. Dutch courage *was* required. Relaxing in the small sitting-room, slumped on the grubby cream fabric sofa, with his feet propped against the drink-stained coffee table, he felt very well disposed to the world. He picked up his packet of cigarettes lying on a sofa arm and lit one. Blowing smoke circles, he began to think about his chances with Serena and Amy. Serena? Perhaps not? He considered himself an average person compared to Robin and it was obvious, to him anyway that Serena only had eyes for Robin. So, Amy it would have to be. There was just the small matter of getting though the Ball and meeting Serena's friends. That horsey woman Ginny sounded formidable from what he'd been able to discover from Serena and goodness knows what Rory, her husband would be like.

It was gone seven. Graham debated whether to have another beer or not. Probably best not to. He needed a (reasonably) clear head for the Ball and to avoid doing any dancing. Which he hated.

*****

In the Trinity flat's living room, Serena lounged on the sunflower yellow chenille sofa. A smoked salmon and scrambled egg bagel while watching 'The Booze Cruise' (again!), had made for a very relaxing lunch and afternoon. Shadow, her darling rescued cat, stretched out luxuriously beside her, the cat's steel grey furry body no less plush than the sofa.

Serena reluctantly stood up from the sofa. 'Well, I really need to go and get ready,' Serena said to Shadow who now had a huffy expression on her face. The cat leapt down and proceeded to sharpen her claws on the frayed and scratched end corner of the sofa.

'Stop that!' Serena yelled at Shadow. 'It's bad enough without you making it any worse!'

Shadow ignored Serena and continued clawing the sofa. She then stared at Serena, a defiant look on her leonine features.

Serena sighed. The sofa was new only a few months ago. 'You can come through to the bedroom and help me choose,' *I wish you could*, Serena said to herself. Finishing at lunchtime had been a great idea and allowed plenty of time to prepare for the Ball.

In her bedroom, Serena, after carefully applying her makeup, plucked out her chosen dress from her large wardrobe. The dress was black and sophisticated. Putting on the Joseph Ribkoff chiffon halter neck, she felt she was ready to face the evening ahead.

Pushing open the door, with her paw, Shadow made her way into the room and appeared to survey Serena's choice. Shadow sat down on the dressing table stool and proceeded to wash herself. Bending down to stroke Shadow's velvet head, Serena caught a glimpse of herself in the dressing table mirror. She was dissatisfied with her appearance. The reflection revealed a severe-looking female, like a black beetle in a dress that was now too baggy on her. It didn't do her any favours. She applied a darker lipstick and heavier eye makeup. An austere and gothlike image stared back at her. The contrasts between the black dress and darker makeup made her look almost ghost-like. Or ghoul-like. She giggled to herself. That wouldn't do. What now?

The dark lipstick was tissued off. Putting the black dress back on its hanger, she reached into her wardrobe. Next. The mermaid dress, a long aquamarine shimmering sheath of sequins, beckoned. *Excellent choice,* she thought trying it on. In the dressing table mirror reflection, the sequins glistened like the sea on a sunny day. Shadow glanced up at Serena and concentrated on washing her front paws.

'What do you think?' Serena said to Shadow. *I really must be turning into a crazy cat woman*, she thought. Shadow glanced at Serena and seemed to shake her head from side to side. As if to say no. *I'm going mad,* Serena deliberated 'OK you win,' she said to Shadow. The unzipped dress slid to the floor in a glittering heap.

Her most recent purchase enticed. A slinky red Gina Bacconi number with a gold beaded bodice and a mermaid skirt. This would have to do. Wasn't there a famous fashion designer who had said when in doubt wear red or words to that effect? Serena slipped the dress on. It fitted her perfectly and clung in all the right places. Looking in the mirror she felt elegant and almost Audrey Hepburn-like. In her dreams. Hopefully, Robin would think that too. Albeit he had been distant, remote since the episode at the fountain. It was possible she had read too much into what transpired then. Of course, Amy would be attending the Ball too. Serena resolved to stay away from her. With luck, Amy's party wouldn't be sitting close to hers during dinner. Anyway, tonight regardless of Amy, she was going to have a fun time. Time to apply a more subtle lipstick. Rummaging through the top drawer of her dressing table, she found what she was looking for, a tiny jewellery box hidden in an old sock. This was one item she had no hesitation whatsoever in choosing and wearing. Her diamond earrings. The best diamond earrings in the world. Serena smiled at herself, remembering how they became hers. All thanks to her mother.

The auction was held in a small Borders town. Phyllis parked her tiny car near the entrance and proceeded as quickly as she could inside. After registering for bidding, she examined the earrings Serena wanted. Geoffrey, Serena's dad, had passed away the previous year leaving Serena a small amount of money. Phyllis had remonstrated with Serena arguing that didn't she need a new saddle, a new bridle or some other horse paraphernalia. But, after seeing a photograph of the earrings on the front page of a local paper advertising the auction, Serena brushed aside her suggestions, adamant she wanted them. And was going to get them. Hopefully. The lighting inside the room where the jewellery was displayed in locked cases wasn't excessively bright but there was no mistaking the sparkle of the earrings. Phyllis noted down the lot number and registered for bidding.

The auction began. A variety of items were sold, vintage decanters, a Georgian tallboy, an Edwardian silver candelabra, several gem set rings. Presently, it was time for the earrings. Phyllis sat down on a wobbly chair in the hall where the items were being auctioned. Along the row of chairs from Phyllis was a smartly dressed lady of a similar vintage. Phyllis felt downright scruffy beside her after barely having time to exchange her paint-splattered trousers for clean ones before leaving. She had been running late, as usual. The other woman expertly applied fuchsia pink lipstick and glanced at Phyllis.

'Interested in the earrings, are you?' she raised a well-groomed eyebrow.

'Well, I'm going to bid for them,' Phyllis said. She didn't give much for Serena's chances here. The figure Serena had instructed her to bid wasn't very much given how dazzling the earrings were. Plus, that woman was obviously well heeled. The superbly cut camel cashmere coat and what looked like a Cartier watch on her right wrist. The manicured and varnished nails. Looking down at her own reddened hands and chipped nails, Phyllis's heart was pounding. She knew how desperately Serena wanted those earrings.

'Ladies and gentlemen, can I now have your

attention please?' the auctioneer announced. 'Lot fifty, a pair of diamond drop earrings, unknown diamond carat weight, possibly Edwardian. Now the bidding will start at five hundred.'

'Who'll give me five hundred and ten?'

'Six hundred.'

'Six twenty.'

The bidding went on and on. Up and up. Phyllis raising her hand to bid each time.

'One thousand.'

Phyllis crossed her fingers; they were sweaty, as were the palms of her hands. The amount was getting close to Serena's limit. It was now a two-horse race. There was only Phyllis and the smartly dressed lady seated along the row from her who were now bidding.

Serena's maximum was reached. Phyllis put up her hand. *That's it,* she thought. *Finished.* She turned round and realised she was now the only person bidding.

'Sold to the lady sporting the mustard coat in the front row,' the auctioneer said.

Phyllis's heart did a somersault. She couldn't believe she had managed to secure the earrings. Serena would be over the moon.

'You can't possibly want those earrings?' the smartly dressed lady sneered.

Phyllis came back down to earth with a bump. She stared at the irate woman.

'Why did you bid for them? What would *you* do with them? Where would someone like you wear them? Or have an opportunity to do so?' the lady challenged, looking Phyllis up and down. 'Look, I'll make it worth your while if you sell them to me. For cash? Five hundred more?'

'They're not for me. They're for my daughter,' Phyllis explained. The cheek of that woman! Phyllis' s temper started to ignite. 'And *she* has places to wear them!'

With that Phyllis swept out of the auction hall and proceeded to pay for the earrings. To celebrate, she allowed herself a small port at the nearby pub.

Serena arrived later that day to pick up the earrings. She had been competing at a dressage show with Rose. A successful show. Showing her proof of identity, and after paying, she was handed the earrings by a member of the auction house staff.

Her eyes shone when she examined the earrings. They were even more fabulous. And they were hers.

'They're magnificent!' she said to the auctioneer who had sold them.

'You're a very lucky girl,' he said.

'I know! Thank you. I can't wait to wear them!'

Serena's attention returned to the dress. The red dress was stunning. The gold bugle beads on the bolero bodice glittered just the right amount. Shadow caught Serena's eye. She was delicately washing her face by licking her left front paw and then patting her face with it. Shadow stopped washing herself and her yellow eyes coolly stared at Serena. She blinked her eyes at Serena's dress or so it seemed to Serena, as if to say that's better. Serena tickled the steel grey chin of Shadow who purred ecstatically. Serena then turned her thoughts back to her appearance.

Securing the diamond earrings, she checked her image in the mirror. Better. In fact, loads better. The diamonds caught the light on the dressing-table mirror and glistened like raindrops back to her. She always felt glamorous wearing those earrings.

Serena deliberated about which perfume to wear, finally choosing Coco Chanel, her favourite. That would most certainly do. Sitting down at the dressing table down she put her elbow on the glass surface and resting her chin on her hand gazed into the mirror. Her eyes misted over at the thought of seeing Robin at the Ball. She could visualise him in her mind. Arriving at the Ball. Tall, elegantly attired in black tie, a veritable James Bond in appearance and manner. The soft, deep brown eyes in which she could drown, the muscular arms wrapped around her, Robin's head lowered – his lips seeking hers for their first kiss... Enough of this! Serena shook her head to dispel these pleasant images. Perhaps this would be her opportunity. Tonight.

Serena wasn't good at romance. She had neither the ability to flirt nor able to recognise when being flirted with. Awkward with members of the opposite sex, especially those she was captivated by, she just clammed up inside. The couple of boys she had gone out with previously paled into insignificance compared with Robin. She was terrified of the emotions he aroused in her. Somehow, she felt they had met before. In another lifetime.

The big question was how to behave towards

Robin during the evening? Should she play it cool? Be distant. Bold? Making it clear she was interested in him? But how to be bold? Like Amy? No! An inner voice interrupted and terminated these deliberations. *Be yourself. And if he doesn't find that attractive, he's not worth the effort.*

The doorbell rang and Serena leapt up from the dressing table stool. Shadow glanced towards her as if to say, 'Are we expecting visitors?' Alicia would be staying the night after attending the Ball. Now firm friends, Alicia was latterly the reliable older sister that Serena always wished she had. She was good for Serena, banishing disparaging thoughts about Amy and encouraging Serena to be more confident and believe in herself.

Serena let Alicia in. Alicia had already changed. She was wearing a black velvet dress with a boat neck. A single string of lustrous pearls fastened with a sapphire clasp, her only adornment. Heaving her overnight bag up the tenement stairs, into the flat, had been an effort for her and resulted in a prolonged coughing fit. She was far too thin, her shoulder blades protruding up above the neck of the dress. A bit bleak, too, Serena noticed, and not just in appearance.

'Here. Let me.' Serena took Alicia's bag from her and carried it through to the spare bedroom. They then went into Serena's duck egg-blue living room.

'Gosh. You look fabulous!' Alicia gasped. 'Give us a twirl then?'

Serena attempted to pirouette, lost her balance and almost fell over. 'And that's with no drink!' she said. They both laughed.

The same couldn't be said for Alicia's appearance, Serena thought. The gloomy wraithlike dress was baggy and sack-like. The pearls hung loosely around Alicia's neck which was as scrawny and red as a turkey's.

'So how are things?' Serena asked, staring at Alicia's pale and drawn face.

'I'm OK,' Alicia said, her eyes not quite meeting Serena's.

'Really? The cancer has come back, hasn't it?' Serena said studying Alicia's face. 'Please – please tell me I'm wrong?'

'Unfortunately you're not wrong. It's now in my lungs. There's a tumour there. I developed a persistent cough which wouldn't go away. My back is painful, too, most of the time,' Alicia admitted. The cancer had spread in such a way that it was now incurable. She *wasn't* going to let on about that. Not tonight anyway.

'So, what happens now? Please, please tell me.'

'I went for a scan a couple of weeks ago and the results were back, very fast – two days later. Not sure what happens next,' Alicia said, concentrating on Shadow who was overjoyed at having her tummy tickled.

Serena didn't know what to say. What *could* she say? She enveloped Alicia in a bear hug.

'I'm so, so sorry to hear this. I wish I could be your fairy godmother, wave my magic wand and make it go away.'

‘I wish you could too.’

‘You would tell me if it’s incurable, wouldn’t you?’ Serena pushed Alicia slightly back so she could look her straight in the eye.

‘Yes. Yes, I’m sure it will be fine,’ Alicia lied, crossing her fingers. ‘Anyway, it’s your big night tonight and I’ve been looking forward to it immensely. I wasn’t going to tell you until next week that the cancer had returned. Let’s enjoy ourselves tonight and see if you can finally get your claws into Robin. Figuratively speaking!’

Serena shrugged her shoulders. ‘I’ll try and put your awful news out of my mind. Tonight. Only.’ She flopped down on the sofa and stared down at her hands.

‘Anyway, I brought you this,’ Alicia said. She was eager to change the subject. She handed Serena a small tissue wrapped package.

Serena opened the present. Inside was an exquisite miniature portrait of Shadow painted by Alicia from a photo Serena had sent her.

‘Its’ gorgeous,’ Serena gasped. ‘You’ve *caugh*t Shadow’s expression perfectly. And her mismatched eyes! Thank you so much – I love it.’ She hugged Alicia and stood the miniature on the fireplace mantelpiece.

‘Now, let’s have a champagne cocktail to get us in a cheerier frame of mind. For tonight,’ Serena said. ‘What do you think?’

‘Yes please, ‘Alicia gesticulated a tiny amount with her fingers. ‘Only a small drop of brandy. I want to enjoy the evening and not drift off to sleep during dinner!'

After Serena had mixed champagne cocktails, with a modest amount of brandy, they lounged on the sofa. Sipping their cocktails, they sat in a companionable silence. Lost in their thoughts. Alicia was the first to speak.

'So, I'm really looking forward to tonight and of course dying to meet Robin,' Alicia said. 'It sounds like he's keen on you.'

Serena laughed despite her sadness about Alicia. 'What makes you think that?'

'By what you've told me and call it feminine institution!'

'Well, let's see what happens.' Serena frowned.

'You mean with Amy? Are you nervous about Amy being there tonight. What is it that bothers you?'

'Probably that she'll confront me about June drowning again, tell everyone about it and say it's all my fault. Not to mention Belinda too. Blacken my name and reputation *and* make my friends hate me and Robin!' Serena began to shake violently. 'Amy has a great capacity for hate.'

'Aw, come here,' Alicia said, she hugged Serena until her body stopped trembling. 'Just keep out of Amy's way tonight as much as you can. Regarding your friends, if they're loyal friends they won't believe anything Amy says. Chin up and let's enjoy tonight!'

Serena didn't look convinced. 'You're right of course regarding my friends – that is, if they are loyal and faithful friends. Although I'm sure Mary and

Ginny are.' Serena took a gulp of her drink. Alicia noticed she hadn't mentioned Graham and Robin. Serena continued, 'Nor are matters helped by Amy being mad about Robin either. And I think she'll go out of her way to ensnare him in her trap tonight. She's never liked me ever since we met at stables all those years ago.'

'Well, she wanted a pony and didn't get one. Whereas you who had been a helper at the stables deigned to then get Cola. Getting above your station in life, or so it must have given the impression to Amy. Fanning the flames of envy,' Alicia reasoned, pushing her short spiky hair off her forehead. 'It seems to me to be a case of sour grapes now on Amy's part.'

'Yes, it all stemmed from there, then poor little June, Belinda, then working in the same office and of course Robin being there too didn't help. She's mad about him. Although he's leaving soon to work at a top insurance company,' Serena explained.

'You've got to stop this! Forget about Amy and concentrate on yourself,' Alicia retorted. 'And enjoy yourself tonight!' She was perturbed. It sounded like Amy could and would attempt to cause trouble for Serena. Unlike Serena, Alicia wasn't much of a dancer; she would be able to watch what antics Amy got up to at the Ball.

'I'll try.' Serena smiled.

They finished their cocktails, the brandy adding fire to the Moët and Chandon champagne.

Alicia checked the time on her gold wristwatch. 'Isn't it almost time to go soon?'

‘It is. Time to knock ’em dead, tiger!’ Serena said to Alicia who high fived her in return.

Five minutes later the taxi turned up. Serena planted a kiss on Shadow’s velvet head and then pulled on her black faux-fur bolero jacket. Alicia draped a crimson pashmina over her shoulders and they were ready to go.

Chapter Nineteen
The Meridian Club, Edinburgh

The Meridian Club was decorated for Christmas. In the marble reception hall beside the silver staircase, a strikingly embellished Christmas tree stood. Resplendent with gold and silver baubles, interspersed with twinkling tinsel, the tree glittered in the muted lighting.

After depositing their wraps and pashminas in the ladies' cloakroom, Serena and Alicia headed towards the blue drawing room. Champagne corks popped and there was an expectant air within the room. With Alicia trailing slightly behind, Serena made her entrance. Green-eyed women clocked her evening dress...

Serena and Alicia drank the champagne which was handed to them by a passing waiter. Surveying the room, Serena took a large gulp of champagne.

'That's better,' she remarked to Alicia.

A rainbow of colours surrounded them on three sides. Ladies in long evening dresses, of varying styles and materials. Shot silks with metallic hues, shimmering, iridescent satins, floaty, pastel chiffons and a plethora of velvet in rich jewel colours could be observed. Diamonds and other precious stones, adorning the ladies sparkled. Blue and pink fire emanating from diamonds. Serena was glad she had worn *her* diamond drop earrings. The men were no less resplendent, she noticed glancing round. Full Highland dress, white tie, black tie, men sporting tartan trews and the occasional soldier or ex-servicemen in their dashing dress uniforms.

Ginny and Rory were among the first to arrive. They were undoubtedly the most glamourous couple in the room. Both tall and impeccably dressed.

Ginny offered a pink satin gloved hand to Alicia.

'I'm thrilled to meet you; I didn't realise Serena had a sister until earlier this year,' Ginny smiled.

'Well, a half-sister. Neither did she! It's lovely to meet you, I've heard lots of good things about you. And I know *you* are referred to as the horse goddess!'

They both laughed. Ginny turned a shade of pink matching her rose pink one shoulder dress. 'I wish!' she said.

Rory marched up to Alicia and introduced himself.

That's some uniform,' she said. *Wow,* she thought, her eyes out on stalks. *I'd love to paint him. If only I were a few years younger and Rory was unattached.*

Rory puffed up like an adder. 'I don't get that many opportunities to wear it since I left the army.' He removed a microscopic speck of dust from the facings on his mess dress jacket. The miniature medals gleamed.

'What regiment were you in?'

'The Royal Scots dragoon guards, formerly the Royal Scots Greys. A cavalry regiment. We were the ones with the grey horses. Purely ceremonial these days, I'm afraid. Although I still play polo which I did while in the regiment,' swinging his right arm. 'And of course – second to none.' Rory grinned, displaying perfectly even white teeth. 'The regiment, I mean!'

Alicia looked at Rory and shook her head.

'That's one of the regiment's mottos.'

'Ah, I see.'

'Naturally, it could apply to me too,' his black curly locks shook, as he roared with laughter when Serena lightly slapped his arm with her evening bag.

'Oh you! You – you're so vain!'

Rory smirked. 'My darling, you don't want to damage my arm tonight. Think of all these fancy turns we can do together on the dancefloor,' this directed at Serena who loved nothing more than being twirled faster and faster when dancing reels.

'Yes, that's true,' Serena thought she'd better go easy on the full-bodied champagne. This was especially hard for her. A glass of *plain* champagne being her favourite drink. She smiled at Rory.

'Anyway, you look as debonair and dashing as ever tonight!'

Rory reached for Serena's hand, raised it to his lips and kissed it. 'Madam, you flatter me – but I love you for it!'

Serena laughed and turned round to see that Mary and Henry had arrived. Henry waddled into the room behind Mary.

They were both introduced to Alicia.

'I'm so pleased to meet you at last. I've heard loads about you,' Mary gave Alicia a hug. Like Serena, she was dismayed by Alicia's appearance.

'It's so nice to meet Serena's best friend from

work. Although I heard Serena's bête noire will be here tonight?' Alicia's bruised hand trembled when she shook hands with Mary.

'Yes – you heard right. Regrettably so. I just hope she doesn't intend to cause any trouble,' Mary scoured the room, searching for Amy. 'There's always trouble when she's around.'

Ginny introduced her flamboyant husband to Mary and Henry.

'Charmed, I'm sure,' Rory lifted Mary's hand to his lips and kissed it. She snatched it away. Rory winked at her. What *would* Henry think? Taking a swig of her champagne she was conscious that her face was burning. *What a hunky man,* Mary almost swooned. *Lucky, lucky, Ginny. Rory would be perfect for the role of Sergeant Troy, in a film adaption of Thomas Hardy's novel 'Far From the Madding Crowd',* she thought.

Rory laughed – he had enjoyed seeing (and knowing) the effect he had on Mary. Locating his next target, he swaggered over to Henry.

Henry briskly introduced himself. Smoothing his receding greying hair back from his forehead, he decided this evening really wasn't quite his cup of tea. Especially that ex-cavalry officer fawning all over the ladies. Even Mary.

'I must say I think you're looking super tonight. Absolutely supah,' Rory drawled to a still crimson-faced Mary.

What a flirt he is, thought Mary, lowering her eyes and finding her silver strappy shoes fascinating.

Still, it was nice to be flattered. Especially by such a gallant and raffish ex-cavalry officer. And one so handsome. That didn't happen every day. Or many days. Compliments weren't really Henry's thing and were almost extinct from his vocabulary.

Henry cringed and tightened his lips. He forced himself to speak. 'Yes, she does look nice tonight.' Not to be outdone by Rory, Henry smiled at Mary.

'Thank you, Henry,' Mary beamed, surprised. *This was going to be a fun evening,* she thought.

The group looked round as they heard a loud peal of laughter. A chubby man in a dinner suit sauntered across the room clutching a glass of champagne. A waft of 'Obsession for men' greeted them.

'Graham! You made it!' Serena hugged Graham. 'Love the greased back hair. Very thirties matinee idol looking.'

Graham simpered and ran his fingers through his specially oiled hair back over his ears.

'So, where's the kilt? I thought you were wearing a kilt tonight?' Serena pursed her lips and put her hands on her hips.

Graham tittered away and patted his tummy. 'Too many beers recently, I'm afraid. You'll just have to make do with a James Bond lookalike. Daniel Craig,' he joked.

'Yes, you'll do.' Serena wrinkled her nose at him.

Graham spotted a tall woman who resembled Serena. `Pleased to meet you, you must be the mysterious sister,' he said, perceiving the facial likeness between Serena and Alicia, although Alicia could have done with more flesh on her. *She resembles a skinned rabbit*, he thought.

Graham noticed a raven-haired man swaggering over in his direction. The man towered above Graham, the side stripe of his trousers lengthening his impossibly long legs. Flinging out his right hand to introduce himself.

Taking the hand offered to him, Graham introduced himself feeling like a common crow in comparison with this fiery peacock of a man.

'I'm Rory Favell. Charmed to meet you, I'm sure,' Rory gazed downwards at the stocky little man in black.

'Any friend of Serena's is a friend of mine.' Thrusting his hand into Rory's, to receive in return a bone-crushing handshake, Graham was determined to keep his end up. He glanced upwards at Rory, however Serena noticed, the smile didn't quite reach Graham's eyes.

Thankfully for Graham, an altogether more pleasant sight beckoned. A vision in floaty chiffon, glided over towards him. A be-gloved and be-ringed hand disguised an unexpectedly steel grip as she shook Graham's hand. *Ginny... must be controlling all those spirited horses,* Graham reasoned.

'Ginny. Ginny Favell, how do you do? You may have heard of me as Serena's horsey friend?'

Graham vaguely remembered. He always switched off when Serena rabbited on and on about horses and how marvellous Ginny was with them. Ginny was certainly a beauty and didn't remotely resemble one of those weather-beaten outdoorsy women. 'I'm Graham. Nice to meet you. Yes, I've heard all about you and how marvellous you are with horses.'

'Thanks. And I've heard you referred to as *cheery* Graham? A veritable ray of sunshine. Or so I've heard. Are you? Cheery – I mean?' Ginny observed him, her auburn fringe almost obscuring her blue-green eyes which darted from side to side. She pushed a loose hair into her French twist.

Graham smiled his cheeriest smile. It opened his face and his eyes twinkled, he appeared almost good-looking, but not quite.

'I'm sure we're going to be great friends. Look, the gong has gone for dinner?' Taking his arm, Ginny guided Graham towards the dining room.

Graham smirked to himself. His frosty blue eyes thawed. He felt he'd got one up on that dandy ex-cavalry officer. Who on earth did he think he was? Flashman?

Serena was distracted by one of her lady friends at the Club. Louise strolled over to Serena. A regular Club attendee, she was stylishly dressed as always, in a plum velvet cowl neck dress, her platinum blonde hair arranged in a neat chignon.

'Evening Serena, good to see you here again. It must be three years or so since I remember you gracing the Ball with your presence?' Louise said.

'Yes, at least three years. It's good to be back.' Serena beamed.

'Looking forward to the dancing?'

'Of course. My favourite part of the Ball,' Serena said.

'Not mine especially. I just enjoy people watching and catching up with my friends. Speaking of friends – may I introduce you to Brad? He's staying with me over Christmas. He's a retired detective over from Michigan.'

Brad shook hands with Serena. His eyes gleamed when he noticed her ears. 'Lady, you wouldn't wander down a dark alleyway where I live wearing those earrings!'

Serena laughed. 'I bet! And probably not here either!'

'Anyway, it was lovely to meet you. Can we get together for a dance? Later?' Brad asked smoothing his close-cropped blonde hair with one hand.

'Of course,' Serena said. 'Louise, I'll catch up with you after dinner for a chat?'

'That would be super. I'll look forward to then,' Louse replied. After a passing glance at the table plan, Brad and Louise sauntered into the dining room to join their party.

'Hang on a mo. I know you're all starving but where's Robin?' Serena scanned the room searching for the familiar lanky figure. Her heart started to beat faster against her rib cage. He should have been here by now. Where was he? Out of the corner of her eye, she saw him. A tall, commanding figure, the luxuriantly plush jacket offset by the well-cut, tartan trews. Ladies' heads turned as he hastened across the room towards them, a glass of champagne in his hand.

In no time he was at Serena's side. His eyes lingered appreciatively over Serena's appearance. It surpassed his expectations. She was taller than the other girls in their party and stood out from the crowd in her slinky scarlet dress.

'Wow! You look a million dollars!' Robin admired and approved of the elegant dress. A total contrast to the demure shift dresses Serena usually wore in the office.

'Thank you! And you don't look so bad yourself!'

'Guys – I'm sorry I'm late. The taxi driver took his time getting here,' Robin said.

Serena grinned at him. 'But you are here now and that's what counts.' She looked round, were they all ready to go in?

Noticing the groups of people heading towards the dining room, Serena said, 'It's time to go into dinner.'

Without being asked Robin took Serena's arm.

After checking the seating plan, Serena was thankful to see they were sitting nowhere near Amy's party. Serena spotted their table in the oak panelled dining room. Pictures of 'worthies' stared down at them. Reading her hastily scrawled seating plan, Serena pointed out where everyone in her party should sit.

'Ginny, you're opposite me.'

'Graham, come and sit beside me.'

Graham smirked, delighted to hear he would be sitting beside Serena. He was also happy to be sitting far away from that proud peacock of a man and pleased to have Robin opposite him.

Waiters came round and filled their glasses with white wine almost to the brim.

'Cheers everyone – here's to a fun evening!' Serena said. They all raised their glasses.

The party demolished their seafood starter. It was delicious. Ginny glanced round the room to see if she could find where Amy was seated. This wasn't easy as all she knew about Amy appearance was that she was blonde and not very tall. Though she had her suspicions she might have seen her before they went in for dinner.

'Where's Amy sitting?' Ginny asked Serena.

Serena quickly found Amy's table. Amy turned round unexpectedly sensing she was being observed. Serena swiftly looked away.

'Amy is sitting at a long table, roughly in the middle section, towards the back of the room. There's a large candelabra directly in front of her on the table. She's dressed in a white, strapless dress and is dripping with diamonds.'

'I can't really see her.' In the candlelit room Ginny was unable to see Amy clearly. 'Still from what you've said about her, I'm sure she'll pop over to see us later.'

'Yes, I expect she will. She won't be able to help herself.' *Hopefully not, I could do with an Amy-free night. Tonight, of all nights,* Serena thought to herself.

The main course arrived in tandem with the wine waiter who assiduously filled their glasses with claret.

The friends talked and ate and drank and talked.

Graham felt he was making a bit of headway with Ginny. She was a smashing girl, he concluded. The next thing she said knocked him for six though.

'Graham – you're quite fond of Amy, aren't you?' Ginny said,

Graham was momentarily speechless. 'Whatever makes you say or think that?'

'I saw you talking to someone earlier and I wondered who it was.'

'I see.' He played for time. Second-guessing what was coming next.

'That was why I asked Serena what Amy looked like. She was the girl in the tightly fitting dress you were talking to before you joined us for champagne.'

'Yes, well, for a bit. Maybe.' Graham wriggled in his chair.

Ginny stared at Graham and narrowed her eyes. 'That means yes, then. Doesn't it?'

'I suppose so.'

'You.. you suppose so? I thought you were friends with Serena. *Not* Amy?'

'I am friends with Serena and she asked me to join the party. I knew Robin was also going. You've got to appreciate that I was in a difficult position...' Graham glanced round at where Serena was sitting. He hoped she couldn't hear his conversation with Ginny.

Ginny ploughed on relentlessly. 'Did Amy ask you to be her partner tonight?'

Graham flushed, he took a gulp of wine and looked away.

'She did, didn't she? Gets even better.'

Graham hung his head.

'Just make sure you don't do anything to spoil Serena's night.' Without waiting to hear Graham's reply she turned to her left and proceeded to engage Henry in conversation.

Robin had overheard snippets of this discussion. He couldn't believe his ears. Graham usually had plenty to say about Amy and most of it unpleasant. Graham and Amy. Graham *and Amy* it made no sense? Or did it? He remembered there had been occasions when Amy had unexpectedly arrived at which Serena was present as well as Graham. How had Amy known to come along? Graham. It must have been. Clearly Graham was deluded if he thought he was the object of Amy's desire. She was just using him as an excuse and a source of information. To be close at hand where Robin himself was going to be too. Marvellous. He turned narrowing eyes onto Graham.

'Having a jolly evening, Graham?'

Graham picked up his empty wine glass and attempted unsuccessfully to catch a nearby waiter's eye. 'Yes, quite pleasant. That champagne – I could have drunk a magnum! The sirloin beef just melted in my mouth. I could have eaten it again. Not to mention the salted caramel chocolate torte with the vanilla ice-cream. And of course, that red wine.' He tittered. 'What about you? Did you enjoy it? The dinner I mean?' Graham waffled on and on. Reading Robin's mind, Graham squirmed in his seat. He looked over his shoulder to check where Amy was.

'As a matter of fact, I did. Though obviously not as much as you.' Robin glanced in Amy's direction. A frown creased his forehead.

The volume in the room was rising. A club member held in low esteem, could be heard complaining about his party being seated at the table next to the kitchen doors.

'Serves him right! Nobody really likes him, the silly sod. Issuing orders to the staff as if he's still in the army!' Hamish, a friend of Serena's passing by Serena, glanced over at the man with the crew-cut nut brown hair.

Placing a hand momentarily on her shoulder. 'Catch you later for a waltz?'

'Yes, I'd love to.'

Mary and Alicia had been having a marvellous time with Rory. Compliments tripped from his tongue as freely as the wine he drank.

Gosh that man must have hollow legs. I don't know he does it, Mary concluded, sipping her wine. The wine waiter noticed and immediately topped her glass up. Mary inwardly groaned. She'd better pace herself.

'It's all that army training.' Henry had read her mind. 'Attending those regimental dinners, I suspect,' he wasn't having quite as good a time as Mary. Still, it was nice to see her enjoying herself and smiling even if it was directed at the gallant ex-cavalry officer.

Sipping their teas and coffees at the end of the dinner, Serena remembered the dance cards.

‘Oh, I nearly forgot. Everyone here are your dance cards.’

‘Serena – you and me – Duke of Perth?’

‘Yes that’s fine, Rory.’ Serena wrote his name against the dance.

‘Mary, now you and Ginny and I will do the Dashing White Sergeant.’ That was a command from Rory. Not a request. Mary hadn’t planned to do any dancing. She went tomato red in the face and simpered. Her cheeks dimpled. What a man!

Rory roared with laughter. ‘That’s a ‘yes’, I take it!’

Mary giggled and beamed at Rory.

Henry felt a bit put out. No one had asked him to do a dance yet. There was a swish of chiffon beside him as Ginny crouched down next to his chair.

‘I knew you wanted to do The Eightsome Reel, so let me fill in your dance card.’

Henry smiled gratefully at Ginny. ‘I’ll look forward to that.’

Graham appraised Alicia. She was as delicate as a crystal flower. How would she stand up to a night’s hard dancing? That black, velvet dress didn’t do anything for her. More like a shroud than an evening dress. He turned and smiled at her. ‘Now, Alicia, what about the first waltz?’

‘That would be lovely. Thank you, Graham.’

‘Serena, would you like to do the Reel of the 51st Division?’

‘Love to Robin.’ She filled in her dance card with the little attached pencil.

In the distance, the band was playing a waltz to warm up.

Serena glanced at her watch. 'Ladies, if you want to sort your hair or anything we'd better go. The dancing will be starting soon and we don't want to miss the first dance.'

Serena, Alicia and Ginny proceeded to the ladies' cloakroom to freshen up before the dancing started. Standing in front of a mirror, concentrating on smearing vermillion lip gloss across her lips, was Amy. The diamonds twinkled like stars in all directions round her neck. Catching sight of the trio in the reflection from the mirror, she turned and faced them.

'Well, if it isn't the three musketeers.'

'Amy, this is my half-sister Alicia and my friend Ginny,' Serena said.

Amy adjusted the bodice of her dress and inspected Alicia. She ignored Ginny.

'A bit too restrained for me.'

'Your dress reminds me of the one Marilyn Monroe wore to sing "Happy Birthday" to President Kennedy.' This was *not* a compliment coming from Alicia.

Regrettably, nothing Alicia could have said could have pleased Amy more. Amy smiled a Cheshire cat grin, the grin making her plain face almost interesting. Alicia's jaw dropped when Amy reached out and grasped her arm. Serena covering her mouth with her hand, managed to suppress a fit of giggles.

'I *do* like your sister. I'm sure we're going to be the

best of friends,' then releasing Alicia's arm she gave herself a final once over in the mirror and flounced out of the ladies.

'I guess that was Amy?' Ginny said.

'Yes, *that* was Amy.'

The three of them burst out laughing.

The Meridian Club's celebrated white and gold ballroom did not disappoint. Built in the late eighteenth century it featured a perfectly sprung wood floor for dancing. Four magnificent crystal chandeliers, which dominated the room hung down the middle of the gold-leaf gilded ceiling. Along one side of the room, great white marble fireplaces festooned with garlands of holly and mistletoe were positioned. Above the mantelpieces, palatial gilt-framed mirrors glistened. On the opposite side of the room, elegant Georgian sash windows looked out, over onto George Street.

Serena's party entered the ballroom and made a beeline for the far end where a line of gilt and maroon velvet cushioned chairs were positioned near the bar. Henry immediately headed to the bar and returned with a tray groaning with generously filled glasses of white wine.

Rory sat down on the chair next to Mary. Admiring Rory's long, lean, muscular thighs, she suppressed an urge to stroke them. *Stop it*, she told herself. *I'm an old married woman*. Rory sensing what thoughts were passing through Mary's mind, grinned at her. Mary's face scorched and she pretended to study her dance card.

The band played the opening tunes for the Dashing White Sergeant. Serena sat down beside Alicia. It was Serena's least favourite reel and she had intended to miss this one out.

Rory pulled Mary and Ginny up from their seats.

'Come on, ladies. On the double. Quick march!'

'Righto, sergeant!' Mary looked regretfully at her replenished glass of white wine as Rory heaved her up from her comfy seat.

'I was a colonel, ladies, and don't you forget it!'

'As if I would ever be allowed to,' Ginny muttered to Mary.

Amy unexpectedly showed up. She grabbed both Robin's and Graham's hands. Serena watched with dismay at what was happening and gritted her teeth.

'Gents, I knew you were waiting for me. So here I am.' Gripping tightly onto Robin and less tightly to a more willing Graham she spied another three people to start the dance with. Fortunately, Mary, Rory and Ginny were at the opposite end of the room.

The dance commenced. People circling speedily round for eight and back for eight. Serena sat in stony silence beside Alicia, her eyes riveted to where Amy was. Amy unfortunately lived up to Serena's expectations. She loved dancing in the middle of the circle. Showing off. Her setting steps exuberant and completely over the top. Being the centre of attention as usual, Serena grimly thought.

'Chin up.' Alicia turned and watched the dancers. 'It's not as if it was a waltz or one of your favourite dances.'

'Yes, I know you're right and the night is young.' Serena sat up and squared her shoulders.

The dance ended. Rory trooped back to where the friends were sitting. Still holding onto Ginny's and Mary's hands. Very firmly in Mary's case, to ensure she remained upright. Her head was spinning. Rory escorted Mary to her chair. Mary collapsed onto it; grateful the dance was over.

A smirking Amy, her arms locked through her partner's even though the dance had finished, strolled up to Serena.

'We had a marvellous time, a fantastic time. Didn't we, gents?'

Graham in his element being praised even if it was from Amy. 'Of course, Amy.' He smiled broadly.

Amy gazed up into Robin's eyes. 'Robbie, Robbie – what about you?' Robin managed a slight smile.

'Yes it *was* fun,' he scowled.

'Robbie, Robbie – I'll see you later for the Reel of the 51st Division?' Amy regretfully let go of Robin's arm.

Robin grimaced. He turned and stomped off in the direction of the bar.

That's my dance, we'll see about that, Serena thought.

The night flew by. The music speeded up. Serena, Ginny and Mary had a lively time dancing with Rory, Graham surprisingly too, and even a reluctant Henry. Alicia was persuaded up for a waltz, otherwise she was content to just sit and enjoy watching the dancing. To Serena's disappointment, Robin, after catching up with friends he hadn't seen in a while, had now disappeared. She reasoned that at least he wasn't with Amy.

'Ladies and gentlemen, the next dance will be the Duke of Perth,' the band leader announced.

'Come on Serena. It's *our* dance.' Rory held out his hand to Serena who responded with an equally firm grip. Rory pulled Serena to her feet and they strode towards the top of the room close to where the band was situated. They were the first couple, at the top of their set. Rory counted down the set marking the remaining couples on the floor, off in groups of four couples. To Serena's horror, Amy had managed to sneak in with her partner to be the fourth couple in their set.

Amy scowled when she spotted Serena. Jinty, Amy's dance partner, bellowed a greeting. Serena couldn't quite hear what he said and then they were off.

After curtseying to a bowing Rory, he turned her by the right hand at a rate of knots. Turning again and setting to the man in second place, Rory then double-handed twirled her. Serena was exceptionally relieved she had gone easy on the wine at dinner. She was also glad she didn't have particularly high-heeled shoes to dance in. They repeated the dance from the second couple's place and then it was fortunately time for a breather. But this was not to be, the band played an encore. The music quickened.

'More, more, more!' Stamping their feet, the exhilarated dancers on the dance floor demanded of the band.

Serena hoped this would be the *last* time.

A kind of madness descended on the couples in Serena and Rory's set. Everyone was dancing faster and faster. Spinning and turning Serena ever quicker, Rory's double-handed turns had accelerated. Serena glanced down briefly; the floor was revolving. She concentrated on keeping her balance and trying to anticipate where she would end up next after being propelled across the dance floor by Rory. Amy was having quite a time of it too with Jinty. He had entered the spirit of things and was trying to outdo Rory's double handed turns.

The dance was reaching the last sixteen bars, when Jinty spun (or rather hurtled) Amy across the floor. In a move reminiscent of Jayne Torvil with her partner Christopher Dean, at the climax of the Bolero freestyle ice dance, but by no means as elegant, Amy ended in a crumpled heap on the floor. Everyone in the set stopped dancing, then turned and gaped at Amy. A distraught Jinty scurried over to where Amy had fallen and pulled her shakily to her feet.

'Amy? Amy – are you alright?' Jinty babbled. He was worried. 'What about your ankle? You took a terrible tumble.'

'I'm fine, thank you. Remind me not to ask you to dance Posties Jig.' Amy smoothed the wrinkles out of her dress. She gave Serena an evil look when she noticed Serena staring at her. 'What are *you* gawping at?'

'That's the spirit, Amy,' Rory chortled.

'Are you sure you're OK?' Serena enquired. It was a miracle Amy was able to stand and hadn't damaged her ankle more seriously, reeling in those killer heels.

'A fat lot you care.' Amy patted her hair back into shape and without a backwards glance stumbled off in the direction of the bar. Jinty scampered behind her.

'I say, what a fine filly!' Rory looked approvingly in Amy's direction.

'You have such bad taste in women!' Serena laughed.

'Well, present company excepted and, of course – the wife!'

'Naturally.' Serena said, winking in Ginny's direction.

Serena and Rory plodded back to where their friends were sitting.

'I need a drink after that.' Serena held out her glass. Henry, ever obliging whenever alcohol was involved, took her glass and the other empty ones back to the bar to be replenished. 'And a rest!'

'You did well, dancing with that devil!' Alicia said.

'I know! I couldn't believe it when Amy fell.'

'Neither could I! Well, she was fortunate she didn't break her ankle or something,' Mary said.

Robin sauntered over to Serena. 'Look, why don't we take our drinks out onto the balcony. I could do with some fresh air.'

'Yes, that sounds like a marvellous idea. Me too. My head is still reeling.'

Amy had collapsed into a chair beside Graham.

Gulping down a glass of red wine, she reflected she hadn't had a particularly pleasant evening. It was not going to plan. True she had danced with Robin. Once. Then twice with an obviously smitten Graham. She had settled upon hanging around near where Serena was sitting, with any luck Robin would be there too. She narrowed her eyes when she saw Serena and Robin leaving the ballroom.

Graham followed her gaze. 'Look, Amy, there's something I'd like to ask you. Shall we go for a wander?'

Amy had an idea what Graham was about. 'OK, let's go into one of the sitting rooms on the top floor.' Hopefully she would be able to see where Robin and Serena had vanished to.

Looking for somewhere private to talk, they climbed up the flights of the grand staircase which, for Amy, gave the impression of going on forever.

Limping, Amy followed Graham into the small library on the top floor of the Club. There were chairs scattered around the room for people who wanted a break from the dancing, to sit and chat. Brass uplighter wall lamps dimly lit the room casting sinister shadows on the scarlet embossed walls. The room was empty.

Shutting the door quietly, Amy turned and faced Graham. 'So, what was it you wanted to say to me? In private?'

Graham played for time. He went and stood, his back against the shelves of books. 'How are you, Amy? Is your ankle OK? You took quite a tumble?'

'Yes, I'm fine. Thanks for asking, though, Graham. You're one of the few who has. Now what was it you wanted to see me about?' Amy picked at her gel nails.

Graham ran his hands through his slicked, back hair and stared directly at Amy. How to put it, after all he might never have an opportunity like this again… Especially since Robin was obviously sweet on Serena. He thought for a minute or two before responding. 'Well… well, the thing is, I think you're a smashing girl, Amy.' He beamed at Amy. His eyes crinkling at the corners. 'Amy… Amy – how about you and me getting together? Properly?'

There was no response, visual or verbal. Amy continued to examine her nails.

'I hope you like me. I've always tried to be nice to you. Passing on useful information,' he said gazing at Amy, a mute appeal to her in his eyes. 'And I've always been happy to accompany you to events when you didn't have a partner.'

'Yes, yes, you have,' Amy felt she could be generous here. 'And of course, I to you.' She folded her arms.

Graham tried another approach. 'Enjoying the evening? I am, despite not liking dancing. Except with you. But I had a marvellous time with you. I always do.' He smiled encouragingly in Amy's direction.

This was completely the wrong thing to say. Amy's lower lip drooped petulantly. Crossing to beside the bookshelves, she flipped the light switches off and on, off and on. 'Yes, it's not been too bad. I suppose. Although I could have done without being hurled across the floor by that twit Jinty.' Lurching over to Graham, she straightened his bowtie which had spun round all evening like the propeller on a spitfire fighter plane.

Graham gazed at Amy and grasped her hands softly. Equally gently Amy removed them from Graham's hands. 'But I thought you liked me?' He said.

Amy swallowed and forced herself to look into Graham's bulbous eyes. She had kissed lots of frogs in her time hoping they would turn into princes, but not this one. He would always remain a frog. 'Yes, I do like you, you know I do.'

'So, what about it then, Amy – you and me? We could be good together.'

'No, Graham, I don't think so. I don't like you *that* much.' Amy backed away from Graham towards the edge of the room. She selected a book from the bookshelf and idly flicked through the pages.

'Amy, Amy, I've been a loyal friend to you. Spying on Serena, trying to find out from Ginny more about her, more ammunition for you to discredit her.' Graham's bottom lip quivered. He attempted to grab Amy's hand. Amy snatched it away. 'Please, please Amy, don't make me beg?'

'You've been good to me, Graham. I've been good to you. We're friends. That's all.' She slammed the book shut. 'You must be as mad as a box of frogs if you think I could ever love you!'

'Give... Give me a chance – Amy? Please? You

know you'll never get together with Robin! He doesn't fancy you!'

This was the worst possible thing Graham could have said. Amy went white in the face. Her cheeks then flushed crimson red. She hurled the book on the floor. 'How *dare* you say that! Get away from me. Go away. Leave me alone.' It was as it were AD 79 again and Vesuvius had just erupted.

'Please, Amy. *Please.* Robin's mad about Serena. Not you. But what about me?' Graham gesticulated wildly with his hands, in Amy's direction, his eyes blinking. 'I could make you happy – I know I could!'

'You? *You* could never make me happy. Not in a million years! You're nothing to me!'

Lava was now streaming in molten rivers, descending the sides of the volcano...

'All that sucking up to Serena, fawning over her, *pretending* to be her friend.' Amy turned to face Graham. 'You – you ugly little toad, what made you think I would ever like you? *That* way.' She jabbed her forefinger into his cheek. Graham winced and staggered backwards.

'Go on then, crawl back under that stone from which you emerged, back to Serena and see if she likes you now! I'll make sure she hears all about your spying on her. How *you* slag her off behind her back! How *you* describe her as being toffee nosed, a right stuck-up cow!'

'But, Amy...?' Graham gasped. 'I never did...'

The Pyroclastic flow had now well and truly started. 'Just leave me along. you, you lowlife – you're just scum!' Amy shouted at him.

Graham's eyes stung with tears. He caught sight of himself in a mirror. He saw himself through Amy's eyes. A small thirtyish, tubby, balding man. Not much really going for him apart from his cheery nature and kind smile. How did he think he could ever be compared to Robin? He had neither Robin's film star looks nor his rapier-sharp mind. Graham realised he was sorely lacking in both departments. All that time he had been bewitched by Amy and she had just used him. Like she had others. Countless others. And he had never once said things like that about Serena to Amy. Amy had a wicked tongue and he dreaded to think what Amy would now say to Serena. What if Amy got to Serena before him and told her he had said those things? What if Serena believed Amy? This would sabotage his friendship once and for all with Serena...

'Robin will never go out with you!' he yelled back at Amy. 'He fancies Serena.'

Amy's eyes narrowed. She brushed past Graham almost knocking him over. Throwing the library door open, she stormed out as fast as her injured ankle would let her.

Graham wiped his wet face. *I hate her*, he decided.

Once out the library Amy was indecisive about what to do next. Re-join her party in the ballroom? Perhaps. Maybe drink a lavish amount of claret? More likely. Or go and confront Robbie. Tell him how she felt about him and that they were a match made in heaven. First though she wanted to check the neckline of her dress wasn't skew-whiff after her fall. The ladies' cloakroom at the top of the stairs was quiet. She tottered inside, into an empty cubicle. Only two older women were present, redoing their make-up at the dressing-table. They weren't aware of Amy sloping in.

'Fi? *Fi* – did you see that girl in that tarty white dress take a dive on the dance floor? She looked a *right* sight!'

This was followed by braying laughter from her fuchsia-lipped companion.

'My dear, I've not laughed as much since Johnny split his tartan trews pretending to be a stag with giant antlers during the Eightsome Reel at the Berwickshire Hunt Ball!'

'Well, if she would wear such a tight dress, no wonder she couldn't dance properly in it! The stupid cow!' The other woman tittered.

How dare they? Amy thought. Flushing the toilet violently, she threw the cubicle door open. There was a sudden waft of Chanel No5 as the two 'cats' exited the ladies' cloakroom. After reapplying her lip gloss, Amy left too.

While Graham and Amy were having their altercation, Serena followed Robin up the carpeted steps to the top floor of the club. Her feelings were mixed. Wasn't he reputed to be a ladies' man; a story frequently put about by Graham? Graham was Robin's friend but was he, *her* friend? Really? She had caught the end of the conversation Ginny had had with Graham and now she wasn't quite so sure.

Entering the softly lit sunroom Robin pushed open the glass doors which led out onto the balcony. Once outside, Serena moved towards the balustrade and surveyed the view, out over George Street. Robin joined her. Both were silent for a minute or so, enjoying the impressive panorama. The street was beautifully lit for Christmas, stars shimmered overhead in the clear Edinburgh night sky. Beyond, in the distance, flashing lights from ships navigating the River Forth.

'Are you enjoying the evening?' Serena prattled on. 'I am.' She felt awkward out here on the balcony, alone with Robin. Practically tongue-tied.

'How could I not be? It's been a fantastic evening. What about you?'

'I enjoy being anywhere – with you.' Serena blushed. The words mirroring her thoughts had just slipped out.

'Serena, so you *do* like me?' Robin moved closer over and stood beside Serena. She could hear Robin's rapid breathing. Her own heart was beating fiercely against her rib cage.

'Really, Robin, what a silly question to ask!' She pushed stray hairs from her pinned hair back over her shoulders. Playing for time, unsure what else to say.

'Well?'

Serena turned to face him. For once his facial features appeared gentler, the razor-sharp cheekbones in soft focus. His eyes flickered, avoiding contact with Serena's.

'Yes, yes of course I do,' Serena said.

'You know I'm leaving to work at another company? Soon.'

Serena nodded. 'Yes – and I'll be sorry to see you go.'

'Look, we might not see each other again. In circumstances such as tonight. I like you. You *know* I like you very much and I want to go out with you.' He glanced away briefly. His throat was itchy and he had a sudden urge to cough violently. 'Gosh that sounds so corny and trite!'

Serena stroked Robin's hand. 'I'd hate it if you were a patter merchant with an encyclopaedia of chat up lines!' she said.

They both laughed.

'You know I'm not that great with people!'

'I don't think you're that bad.'

'Good! Well, if you can be as fond of me to start with as you are of that large, orange horse of yours, that'll do to begin with!'

Serena smiled and tinkered with the strap of her evening bag.

'Well?' Robin took another step closer to Serena.

Serena let go of her evening bag and it fell to the ground.

Butterflies flew around Serena's tummy. Her heart pounded. She thought, she hoped – *what I've dreamt about and longed for...It's going to happen just as I fantasied it would.*

'Yes,' she said, a bewitching smile illuminating her face.

The sparkle in Serena's eyes rivalled those of her diamond earrings. She gazed up into Robin's shining brown eyes. Her eyes met Robin's and then fluttered shut as his lips pressed lightly against hers. What they had both desired for so long. Robin pulled Serena towards him, threw his arms around her and they kissed passionately. Neither then spoke. They didn't feel like breaking the spell.

'You know, I've wanted to do that since the first time I saw you,' Robin caressed Serena's hair with his left hand.

'I would never have guessed. It's just you've always come across as being so upright and stern – to me! 'Serena snuggled closer to Robin. She turned her head abruptly and stared beyond the open glass doors.

'What is it, my darling?' Robin followed her gaze, 'Tell me?'

'Nothing, I just thought I heard something or someone in the room?'

They both looked round, the room from which the balcony was adjacent, was silent.

'Anyway, Isn't it time for your favourite dance? It's not long until midnight. The last dance just before the break at midnight? We can continue where we left off – later!' Robin gave Serena a quick kiss on her forehead.

'Gosh! Yes. We'd better run!' Serena took Robin's hand. They dashed back into the sunroom and shot down the stairs to be back in time for the Reel of the 51st Division.

Amy had hidden behind the chaise longue on the opposite side of the dimly lit landing so she couldn't be discovered. She then followed Robin and Serena into the sunroom at a distance. Peering out from behind the curtained corner of the glass door, she had seen them kiss. Neither had noticed Amy, in their euphoria, realising how they felt about each other. Amy tiptoed out the room at that point – she couldn't bear to watch any longer. Robbie and that bitch! Going back inside the now empty sunroom, rage pulsing through her veins, swearing irrationally at anything or everything, Amy picked up an antique table lamp and launched it at the large antique sunburst mirror hanging on a side wall. The mirror shattered into a thousand tiny pieces.

Echoing Graham, a short while ago, 'I hate her!' Amy announced to the tranquil room.

She has spoiled my life. Everything I want she has got. Effortlessly. It was SO unfair. And now Robbie. That was the icing on the cake. Time to administer the coup de grace, Amy thought. A red glow appeared in front of Amy's eyes. She opened her evening bag and fingered the dainty pistol.

Meanwhile back in the ballroom the band were limbering up for the Reel of the 51st Division. The tune, *the Drunken Piper* filled the regal room. Serena's feet started to tap of their own volition. Looking round, she was cheered to see Amy was nowhere to be seen. Serena flopped down on a chair beside Mary. Robin sat on the other side of Serena holding her hand.

‘Having fun?’ Mary winked at Serena when she saw Robin’s hand.

‘Oh, yes. I’m having a fabulous time,’ Serena grinned from ear to ear.

‘You and Robin too?’ Mary glanced in Robin’s direction. She had never seen him smile so much.

‘Yes, it has been a most perfect evening,’ Robin agreed.

They were interrupted by Rory who had dragged Ginny onto her feet.

‘Come on, up you get, Mrs Favell. Hope you are ready for ALL those fast turns.’

‘As ready as I’ll ever be,’ Ginny muttered to Alicia who had been sitting beside her sipping a glass of white wine. Alicia rolled her eyes in agreement.

Serena felt guilty. She had been neglecting Alicia. ‘Are you OK, Alicia? I’m sorry but I’ve hardly seen you all evening.’

‘Yes, I’m fine thanks, enjoying chatting to Mary and Henry. Could hardly see Ginny and Rory for dust all evening. And Graham has been keeping me company too. Haven’t you, Graham? Graham?’

‘Sorry, I was away in another world just now.’ Sitting on the other side of Alicia, Graham nodded. ‘Yes, it’s been a super evening.’ His lips said the words, but his eyes didn’t echo his response.

Serena was perturbed, Graham seemed very upset. She wondered what had happened to him this evening. He did not look his usual cheery smiley self.

‘Graham – are you sure you’re OK?’

‘Yes, I’m fine. Thank you.’ His lower lip trembled.

Trying but failing to shut the door on his interrogators.

Ginny was quick on the uptake. 'Has anyone seen Amy, I thought she would be over here asking you to dance Graham. Or Robin?' The last name was said flippantly.

Graham's face turned tomato red and to his horror, his eyes started to water. 'I don't know where she is. And I don't care!' retrieving a yellow and black spotted handkerchief out of the breast pocket of his jacket, he dabbed his eyes and scanned the crowded ballroom.

'Chin up, Graham.' From Ginny, 'your *real* friends are here.'

Graham attempted a smile. 'Yes. Yes, you're right. Of course.' Putting away his handkerchief he gulped down his red wine.

'That's better,' Ginny patted Graham's hand.

'Now this dance ought to be danced by eight men,' Rory declared. 'So, you ladies can all sit down!'

'We're not in a prisoner of war camp now, Rory!' Ginny laughed.

'Come on everybody. Time to go,' Robin clapped his hands. The band is just going to start playing the reel,' Robin was impatient and dying to dance. 'Let's get to the top of the set.' He stood up and took Serena's hand. Alicia winked at Serena who winked back.

The group of four trotted up to just in front of where the members of the band were seated. Robin began to count the standing couples in a long line, in groups of four down the room.

'I've just realised this is the Aberdonian version,' he said, starting to count in groups of two couples instead. 'Are you ready for this?'

'You bet!' Serena grinned.

The music started in earnest.

*****

Unseen by the others, Amy crept into the ballroom. Propping herself against the wooden panelling, Amy watched the dance commence. Only ten minutes had passed since her confrontation with Graham and she still burned with anger. Her eyes glued to the dancers, observing Robin and Serena enjoying themselves on the dance floor. She pursed her lips as Serena faultlessly executed the steps of the reel. A vertical line appeared between Amy's eyebrows as she clasped and unclasped her hands, willing Serena to stumble. To come a cropper. To hurt herself. Badly.

Serena danced the initial setting steps to Robin and cast off one place. After a whirlwind double handed turn from Rory, she was in the middle of the set balancing in line with Robin, Ginny and Rory and so the reel went on. Serena and Robin progressed effortlessly down the line of dancing couples. They were the best dancers in the room. They bypassed a drunken couple, clearly the worse for wear, who were bumbling back and forth across the dance floor doing their own private version of the reel. In no time at all, the dance came to an end. An encore was requested and they then were off, turning, settling and circling again, continuing dancing from where they had just finished. Again, the dancers cried 'more, more,' and the reel was danced for a third and final time. When the reel ended the band were given a standing ovation.

'I loved that!' Serena winked at Robin who took her hand and kissed it.

'Me too!' he said. 'Heavens, it's already gone midnight! Doesn't time fly when you're enjoying yourself. And I most certainly am!' Robin looked down at his watch. 'It must be time for champagne. Let's head through to the music room?'

'I need to wash my hands. I'll be back soon. Grab me a glass of champagne. Please?' Serena proceeded towards the ladies' cloakroom. Seeing there was already a queue of ladies waiting there, she opted to try the ladies' cloakroom on the top floor. Serena rapidly clambered up the stairs, two at a time. She needed that glass of champagne. Unbeknown to her, Amy was pursuing her up the stairs.

Alicia frowned when she saw Amy had taken off after Serena.

'She didn't trust Amy and was sure she was up to no good. She considered following her up the stairs.

Graham glanced ruefully in Amy's direction. He was sorry things hadn't worked out between them and by the sound of things never would. He shook his head and his eyes started to water again as he plonked his wine glass down on the nearest table. He shuffled out of the ballroom.

The ladies' cloakroom on the top floor was

unoccupied. Serena headed for the line of basins and washed her hands. Glancing at her hair in the mirror above, she thought she looked a fright. Her usually tidy hair had slipped out of its clasp on one side, was now loose and flowing down the front of her dress. Not surprising really after all those wild turns during the last reel. Perching on the stool at the dressing table she attempted to repair her hair. The door into the cloakroom was thrown open and Amy stumbled in.

'Hi, Amy! How is your ankle? Are you having an OK time?' Serena could see Amy was still limping.

'Yes, marvellous. The best time ever. Thanks to you.' Amy narrowed her eyes as she stood behind Serena.

Serena observing Amy's reflection in the dressing table mirror had the urge to stand up which she did so. Rapidly. She disliked the expression on Amy's face. The curled lips. The teeth exposed, like the fangs of a cobra ready to attack. A pulse could be seen throbbing on the left side of her forehead.

'Can I do anything to improve it?' she asked Amy. Trying to defuse the ticking time bomb.

'Yes. You can! Get out of my life. Now. Forever!' Amy expelled the words like bullets blasting from a machine gun.

A flame of anger now lit within Serena. What had she ever done to Amy? She had tried to be pleasant to her, despite what had happened to Cola and Amy's accusations about June. Not to mention the recent insinuations in the office that her work wasn't up to scratch.

'Amy, what have I *ever* done to hurt you so much?'

Amy's face turned scarlet. She picked up a half empty can of hair spray and slammed it down on the dressing-table, cracking the glass overlay, 'You? You, have the nerve to ask *me*. How dare you!'

Serena waited to hear what Amy else had to say.

'I hate you! I've always hated you! You've ruined my life!' Amy spat the words out. 'You've made my life hell since the first time I saw you. All those years ago at the stable where you kept that stupid pony, Coca Cola.' Amy's eyes were now so narrow they were almost closed.

'What's that got to do with anything? That was *years* ago?' Serena glared at Amy. 'Anyway, you had a good pony too, on loan from the stables.'

'Cola was a brilliant pony. I would have given anything to own him and being a better rider than you would have won more competitions on him.' This wasn't strictly true. Amy had a reputation for being hard on the pony she loaned from the stables. When mounted, she sat like a sack of potatoes and expected the pony to make up for her lack of talent and ability. Amy was more at ease lounging on the dusty sofa in one of the barns at the stables. Holding court there – slagging off other people's efforts and their ponies than riding regularly. She liked the idea of being an excellent rider but didn't strive to do so like Serena. This was the story of Amy's life.

'I loved Cola. He died in his old age at home. Rolo

was a terrific pony – you just didn't ride her enough.'

'Yeah, well at least your parents bought you a pony. Mine didn't.'

'Well, that was all I had. Any money I earnt, or pocket money, was spent on Cola.'

'You, poor, poor little girl. Your parents couldn't afford to send you to a proper school like George Watson's, could they?' Amy taunted.

'I'd rather have had my pony than been at a private school. Even if we couldn't ever afford holidays abroad, we had some super holidays here.' Serena had heard enough. She rose from the stool, stood up and glared back at Amy.

For Amy this was like a red rag to a bull. Her face was now entirely crimson. She charged towards Serena. Seizing Serena's shoulders, she shook her from side to side.

'Yes, like that holiday you had in Devon. You killed my cousin, June! You drowned her! If YOU hadn't suggested swimming out to that rock, she would be alive today.'

This was too much. Serena yanked Amy's hands from her shoulders. It wasn't easy, Amy's grip was vice-like. Serena backed away from Amy.

'How dare you say *such* a wicked thing! That's blatantly untrue and *you* know it.' Serena stared Amy straight in the eye. 'Your cousin Belinda and the boy she was with decided to swim out to the rock and June wanted to go with them. So, they let June come with them. And *you* know that's what *happened*. Belinda admitted as much during the inquest. It was a heartbreaking accident which should never have happened. She was such a sweet little girl. I still think about her with her pretty, blonde pigtails.'

'*She was such a sweet little girl. I still think about her with her pretty, blonde pigtails,*' Amy mimicked Serena's voice. 'Belinda never recovered from June's death. She took her own life about five years ago,' Amy shouted.

'I knew. I read her obituary in a newspaper,' Serena said. 'It was so tragic.'

'*It was so tragic,*' Amy parroted. 'Yes, it *was* so tragic, wasn't it?' Amy shot back. 'Well, I hold you responsible for Belinda's death too. She walked in front of the ten am Kings Cross express and was killed. 'Death by misadventure' the coroner recorded.'

Serena was aghast. 'That's awful. I never knew the way she died. Poor, poor Belinda.' Tears welled in Serena's eyes and she shook her head to disperse them. Her legs wouldn't work, she was rooted to the spot. Amy was like a cobra hypnotising a mongoose before it strikes.

Amy swayed. From side to side. The lava from the erupted volcano was in full flow again. 'Which brings us up to the present day. When I joined the bank. My dream job. And my dream man, too. Right?'

'Robin?'

'Yes, *Robbie*. Who else? Not that little toad Graham. Although over the years he has been happy enough to do my bidding and tell me what Robin is up to. For the occasional treat,' Amy leered. She ran her hands over the straining bodice of her dress.

Serena now realised this was why Amy invariably knew what she was doing, if there was the chance of Robin being there too. Time to leave and return to her friends, she decided. Tomorrow she would forget this altercation ever took place.

Amy second guessing what Serena was going to do, barred Serena's exit from the cloakroom.

At that moment, a lady in a cobalt blue halter neck dress entered the cloakroom. 'Oh sorry, I didn't realise this cloakroom was busy.' She glanced at Serena and Amy.

'Just having a girly chat,' Amy smirked.

The woman stared at them both again and concluded she really wasn't desperate to 'go' just now. After a final look at the sense of menace emanating from the expression on Amy's face, she rushed out of the ladies' cloakroom.

Voices in Serena's head screamed at *her,* to retreat, to escape while she had a chance to. But she was unable to move, her feet remained rooted to the spot.

'Oh right, so where were we? Yes, Robbie. I knew he was the one for me from the moment I started working at the bank. He always gives me such fond looks.'

Serena wasn't sure they were particularly fond looks, but she didn't want to antagonise Amy any further. Let her continue to rant. Let her get this out of her system once and for all.

'We were getting closer. I could feel it, not just in my bones though!' Amy gloated.

'Then *you* invited him to this Ball. So, I had to get myself invited. Not difficult since Jinty and I are old friends, *incredibly* old friends!' Amy cackled away to herself leaving no doubt in Serena's mind about exactly what kind of 'friends' they'd been. 'So, I could make my move on Robbie. But *you* got there first!'

'Surely Robin has some say in this? Doesn't it matter what he...?'

Amy interrupted: 'Men...' She moved in front of the dressing table mirror to preen herself and admire her reflection. '...Men? What do *they* know of love? If Robbie only realised what was best for him. Me!' Amy's eyes became dreamy as she fondled the diamond necklace around her neck.

'Oh, one another thing – you killed my Aunt Betty,' Amy said.

Serena was very confused 'Your Aunt Betty? What? What did you say? Who are you talking about? I don't know anyone who has an Aunt Betty?'

'My Aunt Betty, or Miss Fenton *to you*. She said you were a real cry-baby, who messed up her pants in the classroom. Everyone laughed at you.' Amy cackled.

A long-ago hazy vision materialised in Serena's mind. A woman in a habitual green tweed suit, large, pink-rimmed spectacles and short, corkscrew brown curls for hair. She spoke without thinking. 'That evil woman. She bullied me and my best friend. I even heard of a child who had an asthma fit in class because they were so terrified of her. Others wet the bed.'

'That's a lie. All horrible, wicked lies. So typical of you. She was the kindest old lady in the world.'

Serena raised an eyebrow at that. Given *her* history with Miss Fenton she could *never* believe that to be true.

Amy continued. Relentlessly. 'Anyway, she's dead. You cursed her. You caused her death. I visited her a few weeks ago. When I was there, I was talking about you. Mentioning your name, she recollected she had taught you at primary school.'

Serena could imagine the conversation between the two antagonists in her life. The former had eliminated her childhood confidence and belief in herself, the latter was now striving to remove the man in her life she loved. And blacken her reputation.

'She remembered you well, naturally. You made quite an impression. How incredibly pleased and smug you were as a five-year-old. Always trying to get attention and praise for your work. She said you needed taken down a peg or two. So that's why she let you mess your pants in class and told all the pupils about it! They thought it was hilarious and never gave you a moment's respite for weeks. Or I forget exactly what she said, was it months, or even years!' Amy burst into hysterical hoots of laughter, but she remained in front of the door, blocking Serena's escape.

'Shortly after telling me about you, she died. One cold winter's night. At the start of this month. She was found lying on the hall carpet in a pool of blood. The doctor said she had taken too many pills and the bump to her head caused internal bleeding, resulting in her death. So, they said.' Amy glared at Serena. 'I don't buy that. *You* killed her. You jinxed her to die in this painful way. Retribution *you* would say for what happened to YOU as a young child.'

Serena was speechless. She was flabbergasted to hear about Miss Fenton's death and the manner of her death. Many years ago, she had managed to put that evil woman out of her head. A long time ago. She had tried to make light of what had happened to her as a child at primary school. To imagine her teacher as the wicked witch of the west in 'The Wizard of Oz'. To wipe out in her mind what had happened to her as a teacher would erase chalk with a duster from a blackboard. But the wound ran deep, festered and never fully healed. At the time Serena's childhood confidence and belief in herself had been snuffed out like a lit candle. The confidence and self-belief never completely returned. Glimpses of it were present from time to time on certain occasions such as the Meridian Club Christmas Ball and when riding her horse.

'Well? What have you got to say for yourself?' Amy stamped her foot on the floor.

'I'm very sorry for your loss.'

'Liar!'

Amy reached over and gripped Serena's shoulder. Serena struggled. Her right arm was weaker, due to dislocating her shoulder badly in a riding accident. Serena managed to push Amy off.

'Look, Amy – just stay away from me and we'll

forget this ever happened!'

Despite Serena's conciliatory words Amy was beyond reasoning. Her eyes glittered, she glowered at Serena. Her jaw tense and thrust forward. 'You, you have ruined my life. I am going to make you pay for it. *Now*. Tonight!' Amy lunged towards Serena and clutched her by the shoulders again. The rubies in her bracelet were almost visceral in colour Serena noticed, as Amy's fingers dug into the fabric of her red dress. She pinned Serena in the doorway corner.

'I'm going to tell everyone about you. What a revolting, wicked, evil person you are. Killing June. Making Belinda kill herself and killing my aunt. But first, I'm going to kill you! And no one will ever know I did!' Amy cackled.

The flame lit within Serena had engulfed into an inferno. Adrenalin coursed through her veins. Her heart began to beat furiously. Why was she letting herself be dictated to by Amy? She didn't have to put up with this. Any longer. She had taken abuse like this from people all her life, let alone from Amy. It was time she stood up to Amy and allowed her to do her worst. What could she say? If Amy decided to now tell everyone about June, Belinda and other countless lies she could and would fabricate – so be it. I *can* deal with this, Serena determined. *If anyone swallowed and believed Amy's poison – they're no friends of mine. I'm not a scared little girl anymore*. Serena told herself.

'I'm not that child, the girl you bullied and who hid in her pony's stable. Not any longer.'

Amy's grip tightened.

With a herculean effort Serena eventually managed to fling her arms violently up into the air, terminating Amy's pincer-like hold on her shoulders. She then attempted to open the cloakroom door, but Amy blocked her way.

'Leave me alone, Amy. I tried to be your friend years ago. I'm not responsible for the deaths of June, Belinda, or your aunt. I'm sorry they died, even Aunt Betty. But you must stop blaming me for these things and get on with your own life!' Serena tried to prise the door open, but Amy held it firm. She clawed Amy's hand with her nails. Amy screeched and let go of the door, but her body still barred the way out. With her other hand she reached into her evening bag and produced the tiny pistol. Amy pointed the pistol at Serena. Amy then shouted, 'Die bitch!' Took aim and fired. Serena ducked. The bullet struck the cloakroom door. Using her remaining strength, she managed to knock Amy out the way, wrenched the door open and sped towards the top of the staircase. Amy pursuing close behind. A second bullet whistled by Serena's head. She didn't look back and leapt down the stairs. She kept running until she was in the room where champagne was being served. Several of her friends were standing near the bar.

Serena was breathless and with a shaky hand accepted a glass of champagne from Graham. She gulped it down. Glancing around the room she noticed Robin strolling towards them.

'What the hell happened to you? Why are you so

upset?' Robin immediately went over to Serena, deposited her glass of champagne on an occasional table and enveloped her in his arms.

'I... I don't know where to start,' Serena wiped a tear from her face.

Out of nowhere, an alarm rang.

The Club Secretary put down his glass of champagne. 'Ladies and gentlemen, that is the fire alarm. If you could all, please, make your way into George Street via the fire exit on the ground floor.'

'I do hope it's not a real fire,' Mary said, regretfully putting down her drink.

'Surely not? It must be a practice,' from Rory.

'Look we'd better go,' Henry said.

Everyone filed down the stairs in an orderly fashion and out through the fire exit into the chilly December night.

It was incredibly cold. Serena huddled closer to Robin. He placed his cashmere coat round her shoulders. Serena glanced round. Where were her friends? Mary and Henry together with the Favells, headed over to join them. Alicia and Graham then seemed to appear from nowhere.

'Surely it's a false alarm and we'll be allowed back in?' Mary said. 'Are you OK, Serena? You look very pale?'

'I'm OK, thanks, just cold.' *Despite being shot at by a madwoman,* she thought.

At last, the Ball attendees and the Club staff were allowed to re-enter the Club.

'Ladies and gentlemen, please make your way

back inside. Thankfully, it was a false alarm. Tonight, we discovered the new fire alarm system which was recently installed had not been calibrated correctly. A fresh glass of champagne will be available for everyone at the champagne bar,' the Club Secretary declared, smoothing down the satin lapels on his evening jacket.

The group of friends made their way back in. Once again in the champagne bar they enjoyed their glasses of champagne. But not Serena.

'Robin. I really need to talk to you. Now.'

'So, tell me what happened before we went outside,' Robin regarded Serena's pale face and hands which couldn't stop trembling.

'Come upstairs with me and I'll explain. It's to do with Amy.'

Robin held Serena's hand as they climbed the stairs. Up onto the first landing. All was quiet. They then ascended to the second floor and headed towards the stairs leading up to the balcony and the other ladies' cloakroom. The lighting was dim and shadows cast on the red flocked walls.

Serena screamed.

Amy's body lay in a dishevelled heap at the bottom of the third flight of stairs. She looked so peaceful, as if she were asleep and not dead.

Robin glared at Serena. His eyes narrowed. 'Did you know about this? Have you anything to do with this?' His voice was sharp.

'Of course not! How could you possibly think I knew anything about this or pushed Amy down the stairs!' Serena's eyes gleamed, a mixture of anger and tears.

`We need to get help, just in case she's still alive,' Serena hoped Amy was. Despite their recent encounter she wouldn't wish this on her worst enemy. 'I'll tell you later what happened when I... I last spoke to Amy. I'll stay with her if you run and get help.'

Robin rushed down the stairs to alert the Club Secretary. Several minutes passed. He returned with the Club Secretary and a Club member who was a doctor.

The doctor examined Amy. 'Yes, unfortunately she's dead. She must have broken her neck in the fall.' Both men turned and scrutinised Serena. Serena stared back.

'Well, she was alive when I last saw her, when I left the ladies' cloakroom being pursued by her.'

'I think you'd better tell that to the police. I'm sure they'll be here soon,' the doctor said. 'In the meantime, I'll ask everyone to stay in the ballroom.'

The Club Secretary headed downstairs after taking one last regretful look at Amy. *What a waste of a life*, he thought.

*****

The police arrived shortly after one am. Everyone was in the ballroom. People were talking nineteen to a dozen. Jinty was wondering in a loud voice what had happened to Amy. Why wasn't she here? Serena was standing with Mary, Henry, Rory and Ginny. Graham, Robin and Alicia were nowhere to be seen.

The woman who had seen Serena and Amy

arguing in the ladies' cloakroom, moved towards the senior policeman. She pointed to Serena. 'That's her, she was the one who was arguing with that poor lady earlier.'

Everyone, well it felt like everyone to Serena, turned and glared at Serena, whose face now matched the colour of her dress.

The Club Secretary pointed out Serena to the police inspector.

'That is Miss Kennedy over there, sir. The lady in the scarlet red dress.'

Inspector Gibson introduced himself. A quiet self-effacing man, nothing escaped his notice. Known as 'Hawkeye' to his colleagues, additionally he was an afficionado of the TV series M*A*S*H.' He noted that Serena with her striking red hair and vivid green eyes was an attractive young woman. She was also obviously very distressed.

'Miss Kennedy, I'd like you to come with me. I need to ask you several questions?' The inspector gesticulated to a small room adjacent to the ballroom.

'Of course.'

Serena followed Inspector Gibson into the small anteroom. The constable attending left the room and shut the door firmly.

The inspector motioned to two chairs. 'So, I understand you and the deceased were having an argument before her untimely death.'

'Yes, that's correct, she was blaming me for several catastrophes which had occurred in her life.' Serena looked Inspector Gibson straight in the eye.

'I'll start from when I first went into the ladies' cloakroom. This was shortly before midnight.'

Serena related what had taken place. Describing how Amy had dredged up events from their pasts for which she held Serena responsible. She related how she had tried to refute the allegations and calm Amy down. Unfortunately, Amy became angrier and angrier. Eventually trapping Serena in the doorway corner by grabbing her by both shoulders.

'She was so powerful. I found it hard to get away from her.'

'Rage can sometimes give you extra strength,' Inspector Gibson commented. 'Please continue.'

'Amy then produced a small gun from her handbag. She still had me cornered and pinned down with her left hand. At that point I started to wrestle with her and I was able to break free. She pointed the gun in my direction and fired.' Serena pushed her hair behind her ears.

'What happened then?'

'The bullet missed me. Heaven knows how. It must have lodged in the door. I pushed the door open and rushed down the stairs. Behind me I heard a bullet swizzing by, overhead. I never looked back. I kept on running until I was on the ground floor. That was the last time I saw Amy. Alive.'

'Well, it sounds like you were the last person to do so. You'll need to come down to the police station with me to make a statement. Now.'

Serena was flabbergasted. 'What? Why? Are you accusing me of killing Amy?'

Inspector Gibson frowned and with a stern expression on his face peered over his black-rimmed glasses at Serena. 'Well, let's just say we can't rule out the possibility.' He put his arm behind Serena. 'I know there is another exit in the Club, we'll go out that way.'

'Can I please let my sister know what's happened to me and give her my house keys? She's staying at my flat.'

'My constable will make sure she gets them,' and with that he firmly held Serena's arm and led her out of the Club into the waiting police car.

Chapter Twenty
The Central Police station, Edinburgh

It was cold and damp inside the cell at the police station. Serena pulled the old blanket tighter over the thin fabric of her evening dress. Huddling on the bench, she hoped it wouldn't be long until she was interviewed. An hour or so later, Serena was taken to an interview room, where she was asked to provide a statement relating her last encounter with Amy. Serena did so, highlighting on the statement that she was certain two bullets were fired at her from Amy's gun. After that she was escorted back to the cell.

Wrapping herself again in the blanket, Serena lay down on the bench and tried to sleep. Sleeping was impossible. Images kept flashing through her mind. Of Amy and herself at the stable where Cola stayed. Where she had first encountered Amy. How she had persevered to become friends with Amy, but Amy wasn't interested. Jealous, her mother had said when she told her. Serena had questioned why. Amy's parents were rich, she attended a first-class private school, her clothes purchased from expensive London shops, she had a large circle of friends and travelled to exotic locations for holidays. But she didn't have her own pony, the one possession she was denied, Serena's mother had said. Amy had wanted a pony like Cola. Or better still Cola himself. Her mother always said Amy didn't realise all the effort Serena had put into Cola to make him what he was, something Amy wouldn't or couldn't be capable of doing. Everything else in Amy's life had been handed to her on a plate.

June's face swam through Serena's mind. The cute little girl frolicking on the beach, without a care in the world. So did the anguished look on Belinda's face, the last time she encountered Serena at the inquest into June's death. Serena shivered as she remembered what Amy had just told her about Belinda. In her mind's eye she could clearly see the summer's day. The cloudless cerulean sky overhead, horses grazing peacefully in a paddock alongside, the train tracks glinting in the sun. The once happy girl standing beside the railway line, waiting for the train to arrive. Closer. And closer. Faster. And faster. The clickety-clack of the train's wheels beating on the track. Belinda stepping in front of the express bound for Kings Cross Station. Blasts from the horn, emitting from the InterCity 125's locomotive, shattering the tranquillity of the day. The squealing of the brakes. Too late. Far too late. And then darkness.

Belinda. Such a friendly girl. Full of joie de vivre. Serena cast her mind back to those sunny carefree days on the Devon beach. Before June had drowned. Everything was so simple and everyone she knew, happy-go-lucky. Then. Not anymore. Two girls tragically dead. Other people's lives destroyed. Serena tortured herself thinking if only there was something she could have done to help Belinda. Following June's death, her family made it clear that they wanted nothing further to do with Serena. That she was no longer welcome as Belinda's friend. Belinda had ignored Serena's distraught phone calls and the letters she had written were returned, unread and unopened. Belinda was beyond help. Her waking and sleeping hours filled with flashbacks of June's body lying on the sand. Serena hoped that Belinda was now finally at peace...

Serena's thoughts returned to the Ball. Last night, Robin's reaction when they found Amy lying at the bottom of the stairs. The look of disgust on his face: his lips puckered, the cold look in his eyes as he stared at Serena searching for the truth on her face. The cutting tone of his voice when he spoke to her. How could he believe or think that she might have done away with Amy? Serena was certain she would never again feel the same way about Robin.

She curled into a ball and eventually fell into an uneasy sleep. Tossing and turning on the narrow bench in the police cell, her frequent harrowing nightmares returned. Serena was never very sure if it was a dream or if she was awake and the ghost of the girl she knew was standing beside her. This time however Belinda appeared joining June at the end of the bench. Both stared at Serena, both pointed fingers at Serena in an accusatory fashion, their faces waxen. The faces of the undead.

Dawn eventually arrived. The sky was gunmetal grey, with a few rays of light attempting to break through on what was another dreich December morning. Sitting up and stretching Serena could barely move after lying on the bench. A young police constable opened the hatch in the cell door and passed through a disposable cup containing tea.

‘Here you go, Miss.’

‘Thank you,’ Serena raised her drawn and sleep deprived face asked, ‘What happens now. When can I leave?’

‘You’ll be kept here for now.’

‘In that case I would like a lawyer. Please.’

The constable hesitated. He was young and new to the force. ‘I’ll go and speak to Inspector Gibson.’

Chapter Twenty-one
The Meridian Club, Edinburgh

The Club staff hurried about putting the Club back to normal. The last vestiges of decorations for the Ball had been tidied away. The gold and silver balloons lay forlornly at the Club's back door. The floral table decorations grouped together, ready to be sent to an Edinburgh hospital. The area on the second floor where the stairs led up to the third floor, was in the process of being cordoned off by the police. The Ball attendees had been allowed to go home after providing contact details for the police constables on duty.

Inspector Gibson dropped in. The forensics team were in full flow examining the area of the murder. He spoke to the head of the forensic team.

'Good morning, Tim? Have you found anything of note?'

'No. Not yet, Inspector.'

'The person we have in custody insists that two bullets were fired towards her.' Gibson scratched his nose. 'She sounded sincere.'

'Don't you believe it, Inspector – they all do!'

Gibson decided to take a closer look in the ladies' cloakroom. The forensic team hadn't given the room a once over yet. 'I know you could be right, but I have a feeling about this one.'

Tim shrugged his shoulders.

The ladies' cloakroom was deserted. A stale smell of perfume lingered in the air, a relic from last night's

Ball. Gibson sniffed the scent – he was sure it was the one Serena had been wearing. He needed to examine the back of the cloakroom door. Standing on a stool taken from the front of the long dressing table, he ran his rubber gloved hands along the top edges of the door. Methodically Gibson worked his way down the door using his fingers to feel for any protrusions. Then one of his hands came upon a smooth cylindrical object embedded in the door. It was a bullet.

'Tim, can you please come and see this?' Gibson yelled down the stairs.

Tim, complete with a camera, appeared. He took various photographs of the bullet in situ and arranged for another member of the forensic team to extract and bag the bullet for forensic evidence.

'Well, she was certainly telling the truth about a gun being fired. Once,' Tim grudgingly admitted. 'You mentioned she had said another bullet was fired at her. Now, let's see if we can find it!'

Both men proceeded to walk along the third-floor landing studying the walls nearest the staircase which descended to the second floor. Nothing could be discerned, their search hampered by the magenta velvet flock wallpaper. 'Right, I'll need to get the team to examine this wall. Inch by inch. I think we'll start checking from just outside the cloakroom and work along from there.'

'Of course, the question is, where is the gun which fired the bullet? There wasn't one in the deceased's hand or close to her body,' Gibson said. Looking down the stairs he noticed the heavy Victorian sideboard on the second-floor landing. 'Tim – what about below the sideboard, have you checked there?'

'Inspector, if you'll let me get on with my job and I'll leave you to yours – catching criminals!' Tim snorted. The grey-haired forensic officer had been examining crime scenes for thirty years or more. He was slow and methodical.

'Point taken – buzz off! Well, please keep me abreast of any developments, won't you?' Gibson said.

There was no reply from the head of the forensics team.

Gibson jogged down the remaining stairs and then exited out onto the chilly Edinburgh Street. He hoped the pathologist would have news for him soon regarding Amy's death.

Back at the police station the pathologist had recently completed Amy's post-mortem. Dr Bond, or Mae to her friends, and Gibson stood at head of the cold metal table on which Amy's body lay. Mae ran a tap and proceeded to scrub her hands.

'I've just finished. Pretty young lady. No health concerns at the time of death which I'd say was around midnight. Agree with you that she broke her neck falling down the flight of stairs.'

'The question is why did she fall? Or was she pushed? Any indications of a fight leading up to her death?' Gibson asked.

'Well, I did find red fibres under the nails on both hands and some gunshot residue was present on her left hand. I'd say she fired a gun shortly before she died.'

'Can you be more specific relating to the type of gun?' Serena was wearing a red dress, Gibson recalled.

'No but the firearms experts might have a better idea, at least identifying the type of bullet fired, if I can get them a sample of the gunshot residue.' Mae cracked her knuckles and grinned a toothy smile. 'I'll keep you posted if I find out anymore.'

'Well, we uncovered a bullet in the cloakroom door so it will be sent onto them,' Gibson added. 'Thanks, Mae,' and wandered back into his office.

It was now time to question Serena. Gibson raised the hatch on the cell door and peeked in. Serena was wrapped up in the blanket, her hands cradled round yet another plastic cup of tea. 'Miss Kennedy, will you please come with me?' he asked.

Serena rose from the bench. She was stiff with cold; her evening dress wasn't designed to be warm. She slipped the blanket from her shoulders.

Gibson glanced at her pale, tearstained face. He opened the door to the interview room and motioned for Serena to take a seat.

'We've recovered a bullet in the cloakroom door,' he began. Serena raised her eyebrows and stared at him.

'So, you believe what I said? Now?'

'Well, we haven't found the second bullet you said was fired, nor the firearm it was shot from.'

'I'm sure it was a small gun, very dainty, which was secreted in Amy's evening bag.'

'Or so you say,' Gibson countered.

'I do say!'

Gibson ignored this comment. An expert of the human nature and all its fallibilities, he had listened to many lies like this before. But on the other hand, going by his gut instinct there was a sense of decency, of honesty about Serena. She came across as a woman of integrity. Incapable of telling lies.

'How long do I have to stay in the Police Station cell?' Serena demanded.

'This is why I am here to see you. You are free to go, for the moment. Do not go far away, Miss Kennedy. We may be in touch shortly for further questioning.'

'I... I'm free to go?'

'Yes, yes. For the moment.' Gibson led Serena back to the cell where she picked up her evening bag. She phoned Mary. Within the hour, Mary walked into the reception area at the entrance to the police station. Serena rushed across to see her and Mary hugged her.

'Oh, Mary – I'm *so* glad to see you. It's been horrendous.'

'What happened to you? Why did they bring you here?' Mary patted Serena on the back.

'I don't want to talk about it. Here. I just want to go home!'

'And so, you shall. Let's go.'

Mary drove Serena back to her flat. They sat in silence; Serena didn't feel like talking. Shadow her cat, was waiting for her at the door. *Where have you been, I've missed you?* she seemed to say, rubbing her grey furry body against Serena's legs. Serena sprawled on the sofa, Shadow jumped up and sat beside her, purring loudly. Mary produced two mugs of steaming sugary tea and sat down on a chair opposite her.

'So, why did the police take you away?' She studied Serena's face. 'Did they think you had something to do with Amy's death?'

'Not you as well.'

'What do you mean by that?'

'Robin was very suspicious of me. He thinks I murdered Amy.'

'Look, just start at the beginning and tell me what on earth is going on.'

'Ok, I'll explain why the police took me away.' Serena took a large mouthful of her tea and put the mug down. Lying back on the sofa, she recounted the evening's events starting with her encounter with Amy and subsequently being detained at the police station.

'Well, I would never *ever* think YOU could ever do such a thing. Let alone contemplate it!'

'Thank you,' Serena said, 'You have no idea how much it means to me to hear you say that.' She briefly patted Mary's hand.

'Not your style anyway. I think for you it would be success is the best form of revenge. You, being Robin's girlfriend would have been the ultimate reprisal. And that's...'

'Not that that's likely to happen now,' Serena

interjected. ‘Anyway… So, it sounds like they don’t have enough evidence to charge me with Amy’s murder. But I’m not to go far away!’ Serena was determined to steer the discussion away from Robin.

‘Like leaving the country and going to the Caribbean.’

‘Or such like. The Caribbean sounds very attractive right now.’ Serena smiled despite how she felt. It seemed such a long time ago since she last smiled or even laughed.

‘So, what happens now?’

‘I just continue as normal or as normal as I can be in the circumstances.’ Serena checked her phone. There were frantic texts from her mother and Ginny. Nothing from Robin or Graham though. ‘I’m assuming Alicia’s gone home and no doubt I’ll hear from her later. I’m not looking forward to work on Monday.’

‘I bet! Why don’t you take some time off and stay with your mum or Alicia?’

Serena shook her head slowly. She thrust her chin upwards. ‘That would look like running away. I’m not a coward and I don’t run away.’

‘Cool! Of course I know that. Look, I can stay until Sunday afternoon. To make sure you’re OK.’

‘Thanks that would be super. I’m afraid I won’t be much company though.’

Serena wiped a tear from her face. ‘Poor, poor Amy. I can’t believe she’s dead. Surely this must be a bad dream and I’ll wake up from it and she’ll still be alive.’

'I know – it's ghastly. Hard to believe that she's dead. Poor Amy indeed.' Mary leant forward and took Serena's hand. 'Sadly, it's not a dream. I don't think work will be very pleasant for you on Monday. Are you sure you're up to going in?'

'Well, the sooner I face it the better.'

Chapter Twenty-two
The Central Police station, Edinburgh

Unbeknown to Serena, who had been taken for questioning to the police station, Alicia had returned to Serena's flat to feed Shadow. She wasn't entirely sure what had happened to Serena. The others weren't clear either and Robin was nowhere to be seen. Graham thought he had headed off home shortly after they were allowed back in the Club following the false fire alarm. She knew what she had to do. After putting her overnight bag in the car, she drove to the nearest police station.

Alicia asked the duty sergeant if she could speak to someone in authority there. She had some information in connection with the murder which had taken place at the Ball. Alicia flopped onto a plastic chair; her breathing laboured. She easily became so short of breath these days. The duty sergeant phoned a colleague and requested that Alicia follow him into an interview room.

Inspector Gibson entered the interview room and regarded Alicia. He saw a tall, gaunt, middle-aged woman, who looked as frail as a poppy swaying in the wind. After introducing himself, he motioned for her to take a seat.

'Now, what is it you want to speak to me about? Ms?' he queried.

'My surname is Fairfax. Alicia Fairfax. I killed Amy MacDonald.'

'When?'

'Last night. At the Meridian Club Ball.' Alicia stared straight into Gibson's eyes.

Wrinkles creased Gibson's forehead. 'And why would you do this?'

'She tried to kill my half-sister and I stopped her.'

'And who is your half-sister?'

'Serena Kennedy. She can't be blamed for what I did. I…'

Gibson sat down opposite Alicia at the table in the room. 'Right, I want you to start at the beginning of the evening and tell me what happened.'

'Last night, I went to the Ball, the Meridian Club Ball, with my half-sister Serena Kennedy and several of her friends.' Alicia glanced at Gibson for a sign of recognition at Serena's name but the expression on the inspector's face was inscrutable.

'We were having a fun evening dancing and drinking.' Alicia leaned forward and made a bridge with her hands on the table. 'Serena had pointed Amy out during dinner. She had previously told me about how unfriendly Amy was towards her and that she bore a grudge against her. This dislike of Serena had commenced in their teenage years and had continued to the present day. I resolved to watch what Amy was up to just in case she should try to do anything malicious to Serena this evening. That woman was bad news for Serena.' Alicia then folded her hands onto her lap and focussed on the inspector. 'She had even threatened to blackmail Serena. I had to stop her – to prevent her wrecking Serena's life.'

'So, tell me what ensued?'

‘I had been sitting beside the others in Serena’s party who then danced the last reel before the break at midnight. Serena and Robin were together. I remember Serena’s eyes shining like the diamonds in her ears. They were so happy.’

Gibson’s eyes never left Alicia’s face.

‘After the dancing had finished. I noticed Serena saying something to Robin and she headed off alone. The others, including Robin, made their way to the champagne bar. I sat there for a couple of minutes or so contemplating whether I should join them or not.’ Alicia started to cough. ‘I guessed Serena was going to the ladies’ cloakroom and thought I’d have a quick chat with her about Robin. Then, out of the corner of my eye I noticed Amy following Serena not far behind.’

‘May I please have a glass of water?’ Alicia asked.

Gibson filled a plastic cup of water and placed it in front of Alicia.

‘Thank you,’ Alicia took a sip of water and then continued. ‘Five minutes or so passed and I needed to check if Serena was OK. ‘The hall was deserted. There was a lengthy queue outside the cloakroom on the first floor, so I made my way up the stairs until I reached the top floor. Listening outside the ladies’ cloakroom I could hear voices from within. The voices were raised and angry. They belonged to Serena and Amy.’

‘Were you sure Serena and Amy were arguing?’

‘Yes, I could hardly not be! Bellowing at each other, they were going at it hammers and tongs! At some point, a lady in a bright blue dress rapidly entered and then equally rapidly exited the ladies' cloakroom. I waited until she had descended the stairs. A few minutes later the sound of a shot filled the air.' Alicia sipped her drink. 'Serena came flying out of the cloakroom, hotly pursued by Amy. She had a gun in her hand. Pulling the trigger on the gun, another bullet was fired in what looked to me like Serena's direction. Serena managed to duck and started to jump down the stairs. Amy was now going in for the kill. She tinkered with the gun, getting ready to take aim and fire again. You should have seen the look of pure malevolence on her face. The evil glint in her eye.'

'What did you do next?'

'I edged over to the top of the stairway. Amy was ready to fire her gun. I couldn't let her kill or maim Serena.' Her eyes in mute appeal focused on Gibson's. 'Amy saw me. Just. I think.'

'And then?' Gibson asked.

'I had to stop her. Whether it was by accident or design I stuck out my left foot. Amy was too busy concentrating on the gun and didn't notice this. Amy's ankle gave way and she plunged down the stairs. Tumbling repeatedly. I watched in fascinated horror. I couldn't move. My feet were glued to the spot. Amy fell to the bottom of the stairs. She didn't stir. She was motionless. Then the fire alarm went off.'

'Where was Serena at this point?'

'Serena had just kept going. She never looked back. When outside in the lane we were separated.'

‘What happened next?’ Gibson focused on Alicia’s face. ‘What about Amy. Didn’t you think to alert someone? In case she was still alive.’

‘Descending to the bottom of the stairs, I checked to see whether Amy was dead or alive. She was dead. I knew she was dead. Previously I had worked as a paramedic. There was nothing I could do for her. If the fire alarm turned out to be a false alarm, I was going to let The Club Secretary know when we were permitted back in.’

‘But you didn’t, did you? Serena got there first?’ Gibson added.

‘Yes, and I’ll regret not doing so, until my dying day. She had nothing to do with Amy’s death. Amy would have shot Serena if she’d had the chance to do so. And killed her. I’m a coward but not such a coward. I won’t let someone else be accountable for what I did.’ Alicia raised her eyes to Gibson. ‘That’s why I’m here now.’

‘Well, you’ll be pleased to know Serena is going to be released today subject to being available for further questioning.’

Alicia slumped in her chair and smiled with relief. ‘Thank goodness for that.’

‘You, on the other hand will provide a written statement of what you’ve just said and I’ll take it from there,’ Gibson said, handing Alicia a sheet of lined paper and a biro pen.

Chapter Twenty-three
The Bank, Edinburgh

The Monday morning after the Ball was as bad as Serena had predicted it would be. And worse. People could hardly bring themselves to say good morning to Serena. Most walked briskly past, averting their eyes from her as they did so. There were groups of people whispering in huddles at the drink machine on the rare occasions she ventured there. They ignored her.

Serena tried to concentrate on the code for the web page she was developing but it was hopeless. Staring at the blank laptop screen didn't provide any inspiration. She stopped by Mary's desk. Mary glanced up from the document she was analysing.

'Morning, Mary – can we talk?'

'Morning, Serena. Sorry but I'm very busy just now,' Mary said. 'I'll catch you later.'

Serena slunk away from Mary. Trudging back to her desk took forever. She was conscious of everyone's eyes watching her. She sat at her desk and tried to do some work. An hour or so later a message appeared. 'Lunch?' It was from Mary. Thank goodness for that. Serena immediately replied and headed down to Mary's desk.

Serena crept into the canteen. Finding a quiet corner away from other members of the development team, Serena was aware of disapproving looks. Everywhere. Mary eventually joined her.

'I'm sorry I took so long. Daisy was asking me about the latest set of requirements.'

‘No probs. Well, you’re here now.’ Serena raised puffy eyes to Mary. ‘I feel like a pariah.’

‘Try not to. Look, I know you didn’t kill Amy and more importantly so does Inspector Gibson. If he thought you had, you would still be in that police cell. No doubt about that.’

Serena massaged her temples with her fingers. ‘I’m so glad you think so. Although Amy has never been pleasant to me – I’d never wish her dead!’

Mary patted Serena’s hand. ‘I know that. Hopefully, they’ll discover what happened soon and let you know. And what about Ginny – what does she think?’

‘The same as you. Ginny’s been so kind, offering to go and ride Rose and check she’s OK, if I’m unable to do so. She even invited me down for the weekend – I might take her up on that.’

‘Alicia?’

‘I’ve not heard from her since Saturday – I hope she’s OK.’

Mary asked the question she’d been dreading. The person Serena hadn’t mentioned, the elephant in the room. ‘Now, have you heard anything from Robin?’

‘Neither sight nor sound. I got the impression he thought I’d killed Amy. You should have seen the way he looked at me before the police took me away. Part disgust, part horror at what he must have decided I had done. I did text him but he never replied to any of texts and I phoned him – once, but he never got back to me. I think I should forget about him. I don’t think

I'll ever be able to forgive him for thinking I could have killed Amy,' Serena toyed with the food on her plate. She had no appetite. 'Anyway, he's leaving soon. After all, there's plenty more fish in the sea!' she said giving Mary a tiny smile.

Mary wasn't convinced. She had seen the way Serena and Robin looked at each other. Serena was radiant that night at the Ball. Robin too. 'Speaking of fish in the sea, have you seen Graham today?'

'No. I figured he was probably still the worse for wear after Friday night.'

'Well, it's not like him. I was speaking to Ginny at the Ball and she *sussed,* as she described it that Graham was keen on Amy.' Mary said.

'OMG!' Serena was shocked to hear this. 'Actually, I was thinking about this at the weekend and it did seem odd that Amy turned up at places, I was at. Unexpectantly.' She grimaced at Mary. Her money was on Graham.

'I know I couldn't believe it either. Well to start with. Though I'm sure Graham was also fond of you.' Serena raised her eyes to the canteen ceiling and shook her head. 'Very fond,' Mary reiterated.

'Well, I'm fond of him of him too. Or rather I was. I wonder where he has got to?'

The day dragged on and on. The hands on the clock at the end of the office barely seemed to move. Four pm. Serena decided to leave work early. Arriving home, she tossed her bag down on the sofa. It had been a horrible day. No one apart from Mary had spoken to her and she had barely moved from her desk for the remainder of the day. She settled down on the sofa with Shadow on her knee and a cup of Earl Grey tea. Food could wait.

After an hour or so, deciding she better eat something, Serena started to boil some pasta.

The phone rang. It was her mum.

'Hi, Mum – how are you?' Serena said.

'Darling, you must prepare yourself for a bit of a shock. A terrible thing has happened.' She hesitated for a couple of minutes. 'Alicia has been taken into custody for killing Amy.'

'What!?' Serena removed the pan of boiling pasta from the hob.

'Alicia made a statement saying so at the police station. The one you were taken to. She phoned me on Sunday.'

'I can't believe it!'

'No, neither can I, she confessed she had killed Amy by tripping her up. This resulted in her tumbling down the flight of stairs to her death. Alicia wanted to prevent her from shooting you.'

Serena collapsed on the sofa. 'She sent one text on Saturday morning. Apart from that, nothing. So that explains why I've been unable to contact her. But why didn't you tell me before? What happens now?'

'I was in shock – I couldn't take it in. Serena, I'm so sorry I didn't tell you sooner. There will be a trial and she will probably be found guilty. Although I'm not sure if the verdict would be murder or manslaughter. Amy was attempting to shoot you.' Phyllis reasoned. 'I didn't tell you before because

Alicia said not to.'

'Why ever not? I'm her half-sister, aren't I? I can't believe it. Poor Amy she didn't deserve this.' Tears descended Serena's face. 'Thinking back, I just hurtled myself down those stairs. I was oblivious to anything apart from putting as much distance between myself and Amy. Alicia must have been standing in another doorway close to the ladies' cloakroom. Hanging around to see what Amy was going to do.'

'I know it's hard to believe – Alicia was such a kind-hearted girl.'

'She must have heard the gun going off in the ladies' cloakroom and in the hallway too,' Serena concluded. 'But still, how could she have done this to Amy? This is awful!'

'Alicia was adamant that if she hadn't prevented Amy from doing so, she would have killed you. So, we must wait and see what happens about Alicia. She wasn't feeling particularly well before the Ball. Did you know about that?'

'Yes, it sounded like the cancer has returned. Poor Alicia.' Serena nodded her head. 'And poor Amy too.'

*****

Later that week Graham returned to work. He had come down with some sort of bug or so he said to his line manager. Thoughts of Serena and Amy whirled through his head. Although Serena had been released by the police with no further questioning required, he avoided her. He was positive she had nothing to do with Amy's death. He knew he had been unfair to Serena. A loyal friend, she had gone out of her way to be friendly, inviting him along on several occasions to functions and he had betrayed her. By spying on her and informing Amy of any arrangements which involved Robin. Why? Foolishly thinking that doing something for Amy would make her fonder of him. He had been insane to do so and would always wonder if he had unwittingly provoked Amy into what transpired on that fateful evening.

*****

Friday. The last day of the working week. The week had been dreadful and surpassed even Serena's expectations of how awful it could be. Graham, her so-called erstwhile friend had not spoken to her nor wandered towards her desk. Thank goodness for Mary. Her one loyal friend. She hadn't seen Robin all week. No texts either. She was sure he had been avoiding her. This was easy for him to do; he rarely attended the same meetings which she did.

Serena checked the time on her watch. Two pm. The canteen would still be open. She was famished, after barely eating anything all week she now felt hungry for the first time in days. Deciding to quickly nip down to the canteen, before her next meeting, Serena took the back stairs down to the basement floor for a change. Thinking that she had neither seen nor heard from Robin all week, there he was in the flesh advancing up the stairs towards her. Gazing at Robin, Serena's heart leapt. He was as handsome as ever and had not realised it was Serena who was descending the stairs in his direction. Feeling

Serena's eyes on him Robin looked up. For a second there was a flash of compassion, of fondness, of love. Then the shutters descended.

Robin stared at Serena with wintry eyes. The same smoky quartz eyes in which Serena felt she could once drown in. She noticed the immaculately cut navy chinos and red cashmere quarter-zip jumper reflecting the fact Friday was casual dress day at work. She was only too conscious of her old, faded jeans and creased flowery shirt.

'Robin, I, I...' Serena said. Her lips froze and her feet refused to move. She couldn't speak. She stared back at Robin. He looked briefly at her, glancing up and down, his eyes narrowing.

'Robin, how are you? I've not seen you all week,' Serena managed to say, trying to gaze into his eyes, appealing to him. She put out a hand to towards him, then seeing the look in his eyes, withdrew it. He recoiled from her touch as if she was a venomous snake.

Robin's lips remained firmly sealed. He stared up and beyond Serena. Focusing on the upstairs doorway. Without uttering a single word in response, he brushed past Serena and hastened up the remaining stairs.

Serena was speechless. The exquisite agony and the dawning realisation that the man she loved no longer loved her. Tears sprang to her eyes. She wiped her face. That was obviously that, then. She was glad he was leaving the bank soon. Shaking her, she squared back her shoulders, thrusting her chin forward and upwards. She was damned if she was going to cry. His loss. She had come to a decision. It might be time to look for a new job. That could wait though, until she found out what would be happening to Alicia.

Chapter Twenty-four
The Scottish Borders

At the weekend Serena visited Phyllis. On a cold, clear day she drove down to the Borders. The trees stripped bare of their leaves, the landscape was bleak and unforgiving. Almost Christmas. What kind of Christmas would they have Serena wondered? Phyllis was watching for Serena arriving. She opened the cottage front door and clasped Serena's hands. Looking closely at Serena, she noticed the purple shadows under her eyes, the dullness of her skin.

Darling, you're freezing. Come into the living room and sit beside the fire.'

Serena did as Phyllis said and pulled up an armchair close to the roaring fire. She glanced round the room. A pot of Earl Grey tea and some cheese scones oozing butter enticed on the oak coffee table. Serena shuddered. She had no appetite.

'How are you, Serena?' Phyllis asked.

Serena wasn't interested in social niceties and ignored Phyllis's question. 'So, what's the latest on Alicia?' Serena said. 'Have they let her go?'

'No. She's been remanded in custody. Probably will be held in an Edinburgh prison until the trial.'

'I still can't believe she killed Amy. I didn't like Amy, but I wouldn't have wished this on my worst enemy. Why did she kill her?'

'Because she genuinely believed Amy was going to kill you, she felt she had to prevent Amy from doing so and from the evidence found she was trying to do so.'

'What evidence? What else did the police find?'

'They recovered Amy's gun, a small pistol loaded with a bullet ready to fire. The gun was found under a sideboard on the landing near the stairs where her body was discovered.'

'How do you know all this?'

'Alicia told me during her last phone conversation.'

'I wish I could speak to her.'

'She will be able to speak to you soon.'

'I just feel so angry with her, she shouldn't have killed Amy.'

'Well according to Alicia, it was kill or be killed. She had heard Amy talking with her friends at the Ball, boasting about what a crack shot she was. She was a member of a local gun club.'

'I never knew that.'

'Well, why should you have? You two were hardly friends,' Phyllis tartly remarked. 'Alicia saved you.'

'But at what cost?' Serena stood up and warmed her hands in front of the fire. 'Poor Amy. I wish I could wind back time. If only I hadn't purchased tickets for the Ball. Amy would still be alive and Alicia would be here with us now.'

'If only,' mused Phyllis. 'Well, it's too late now. That poor girl.'

'Well, it's not too late to see Alicia again, after prison. Although do I want to – after what she did to Amy? How could she have...?'

'It could be too late,' Phyllis interjected and wiped

a solitary tear from her left eye. One day she would tell Serena about Alicia's past battles with cancer. In Devon. But not today. The cancer had returned. The prognosis was bleak. 'There were two reasons Alicia came to the Borders. One was to meet you.'

Serena frowned at Phyllis. What was she trying to say?

'The other was to die.'

Chapter Twenty-five
The Scottish Borders

What Phyllis said was true. The trial would never take place. Shortly after the New Year, Alicia was released on compassionate grounds to a Borders hospital palliative care ward. She had days, potentially a few weeks at the most, to live.

Clutching an enormous bouquet of flowers, Serena visited Alicia. The ward where Alicia was residing was bright and airy. A cheerful blonde nurse directed Serena to Alicia's bed. Leaving Serena beside Alicia, the nurse bustled away to find a vase. Alicia lay dozing, Serena was shocked at her appearance. Alicia had been thin before but was now emaciated. Her hands protruded from thin sticklike arms. The hands and wrists covered in bruising. The once shiny auburn hair was now dull and hung lankly round her drawn face.

Alicia awoke and dragged herself into a seating position, in the hospital bed. She gestured for Serena's hand. 'Hi, Serena, how are you? Thanks for visiting me.'

Serena didn't know what to say. She shrugged her shoulders.

'Thank you for the beautiful roses. They're my favourites.' Alicia examined the flowers of varying shades of pink. 'Serena, please come and sit beside me. Please.' She patted the plastic chair close to the bed. Serena sat down beside her.

'Look, I'm so sorry about Amy. I was sure she was

going to kill you and I had to stop her. Somehow. I couldn't believe it myself when she lay lifeless at the bottom of the stairs.' Alicia blurted out. 'I would have done anything to prevent her from killing you. Anything. And from destroying your life.'

'I know you did it for me. But how could you do such a thing? She didn't deserve to die. She was much loved by her parents. Did *you* think about that?' Serena stood up from her chair and contemplated the view from the nearby window.

'I'm not sure, if I did. No, I'm not going to lie – probably not. I'm so sorry.'

'Well, I'm sorry too. I don't think I'll ever be able to forgive you.'

'I didn't think you would. But Amy was intent on wrecking your life. Don't *you* get that?'

'Yes. But Amy died. Don't *you* get that?' A passing nurse glared at Serena. Serena lowered her head.

'I wish she hadn't – in some ways. I'll regret it forever.' Alicia attempted to grasp Serena's hand, 'I, I don't have much time and I want you to do something for me. Please.'

'What is it?' Serena asked. 'Is it the animals – about looking after them?' *When you're gone,* she thought. She just couldn't forgive Alicia for killing Amy. It was an effort to speak to Alicia – even if she was dying. Sitting down again, she grudgingly reached over and took Alicia's hand.

'Mum is going to look after Tosca and Pimms. So, I don't have to worry about them. Thankfully.'

Alicia lay back on the bed. All she wanted to do

was close her eyes and go to sleep. She was so tired. 'Serena – I wanted you to have this?' She pointed to the top drawer in the bedside cabinet.

Serena lifted out a small blue velvet purse. Inside was an Edwardian pendant adorned with peridots and split pearls suspended from a gold chain. The stones gleamed in the winter sunshine.

'They match your eyes – leek green,' Alicia commented.

'Thanks!'

'The pendant was handed down to me from my adopted parents' family. It was given as a wedding present to one of them early last century.'

'It's exquisite. Thank you.' Serena fastened the chain around her neck.

'Suits you. Wear it and think of me.'

I'll treasure it.' Serena resumed holding Alicia's hand. 'In spite of what you did – I... I don't want you to go away. I feel I barely know you.' She tried to be nice. After all, Alicia *was* dying.

'I always hoped I would be like a phoenix emerging from the ashes of a pyre. Reborn. But it was not to be.' A lone tear rolled down her face. Alicia brushed the tear away. 'Now tell me what's happened with Robin. Mum didn't say much. Are you two now an item?'

'No, and that's not going to happen. There's not much to tell. He blames me for Amy's death and probably thinks I aided you in causing it. I've never spoken to him again. And he's avoided me ever since the Ball. So that's that. Finis.'

'Aw, no! I'm so sorry to hear that. It's my fault you're not together now. That's such a shame. I know I only met him at the Ball but seeing you together, I thought the pair of you looked like a match made in heaven.' She reached up and stroked Serena's face, 'You're a lovely girl and deserve to meet someone nice.'

'It wasn't meant to be,' Serena said. 'Anyway there's more important things to think about, like you. You need to get better. 'Alicia's eyes met Serena's. Alicia was the first to look away. She withdrew her hand from Serena's face.

The effort of talking had brought on a crescendo of coughing. Alicia rested her head on her pillow. She looked exhausted, her pasty skin the colour of faded white rose petals.

'Shall I get a nurse?' Serena asked. Alicia shook her head.

When the coughing ceased, Alicia continued. 'I'm tired of living like this. There's nothing more that can be done for me. The cancer returned with a vengeance as you know, last year, I hoped it could be defeated but it was not to be. I've been a bad person.' Suddenly, without warning, she retched. 'I think you should leave. I'll see you again. Soon.'

Serena took Alicia's hand, 'Of course. If you want me to?'

'Yes, I'd like that. I'm not in any pain. But it's my time to go. And your time to live.' Alicia smiled wanly at her.

'What was it you wanted me to do? You never

said.'

'Just one thing. I want you to be happy. Forget about me, I've had a great life. Having had cancer, I have a clearer perspective on what's important and what's not. Enjoy each day. Even if it's boring and nothing exciting happens. It's still a wonderful day and take nothing for granted.'

'I know, you're right.'

'Definitely. Look for happiness and making others happy. However, I always think if you go seeking sorrow then sorrow will come looking for you.'

'I'll try to do that,' Serena said.

'One final thing.'

'What?'

'Always remember tomorrow is *not* given.'

The blonde nurse whom Serena met beforehand hurried over. 'Alicia, I don't mean to interrupt, but it's time for your medication.'

Alicia gave Serena a small wave as Serena stood up then left the ward.

Once outside the hospital, Serena allowed herself the luxury of bursting into tears. She didn't know who she was crying most for. Amy? Alicia? Herself? How she had irredeemably lost Robin?

'Here, love, it can't be *that* bad?' a passing friendly paramedic handed her a paper tissue.

'Thank you.' Serena smiled through a veil of tears. The kindness of people, thinking of the line from one of her favourite films. Trudging back to the car park, Serena admired the snowdrops all around which were in full bloom. She wondered if she would see Alicia again. Getting into the car she contemplated which route she should travel to return to Edinburgh.

Time passed slowly. Alicia clung to life.

Serena struggled to behave and live normally. She found it impossible to do so. Amy's death had cast a long-lasting shadow over Serena's life. People who were previously friendly with Serena, now shunned her. Guilty by association, Mary called it. Robin had left the bank and started his new job in another blue-chip financial organisation. He held a leaving 'do' which neither Serena nor Mary attended. Following the night of Amy's death, Robin had never contacted Serena again and, realising, how the ground lay between them, she was too proud to do so.

*****

A windy and chilly March arrived. It was one of Serena's least favourite months of the year. This year it became the worst month of the year.

Alicia died.

It came as no surprise to Phyllis and Serena. They were just waiting for the phone to ring. Of being advised to get to the hospital as soon as possible. One Friday, towards the end of March, a doctor on the palliative care ward had contacted Phyllis and said to come in that very afternoon. Alicia had only minutes, possibly a few hours, to live.

Phyllis phoned Serena. Grabbing an overnight bag and a protesting Shadow in her cat basket, Serena belted down to the Borders. Phyllis was waiting for her with her coat already on.

‘Serena, let Shadow out in the kitchen,’ Phyllis said, spooning cat food into a bowl, ‘then we must go.’

The thirty minutes journey to the hospital took forever. They sat in silence. There was nothing to say. After parking the car, they both raced into the hospital and then to the palliative ward. The doctor attached to the ward was waiting for them. He asked them to step into the ward *quiet room* and suggested they took a seat. The doctor tapped the door shut.

‘Mrs Kennedy and Miss Kennedy,’ the doctor glanced at Serena as he spoke, noticing the pale complexions and watering eyes. ‘I’m very sorry to have to tell you that Alicia passed away twenty minutes ago.’

‘Was... was anyone with her when she died?’ Phyllis managed to say.

The doctor consulted his notes. ‘No. No one. A nurse doing her rounds after lunch checked in on her. The nurse thought she had fallen asleep. But on closer inspection...’ his voice tailed off.

‘...She was dead.’ Phyllis finished off his sentence.

‘May we see her?’ Serena asked.

The doctor led them into Alicia’s ward. Alicia was lying in her hospital bed. She looked so peaceful and relaxed. And younger, free from all her worldly cares. In her hands she clutched a small photo album. The album was open at pages containing images of Serena and Phyllis.

‘I’ll leave you both to spend some time with her. If you have any questions, please let me know. I’ll not be far away.’ The doctor headed down the ward to speak with the charge nurse. Floods of tears cascaded down Serena's face. She could not stem the flow. 'Poor Alicia… to be so alone at the end. No one with her. To comfort her and to hold her hand.'

'I know, dear. It's so terribly sad.' Phyllis said, stroking Serena's face. 'Let them out, my darling. This was what she wanted. To just slip away. And, although she hid it well, to no longer to be in pain.'

'I know, but I can't believe she's gone. I'll miss her. Even if she did kill Amy.'

'Knowing Alicia, I'm sure she regretted doing so. However, she was adamant Amy was going to kill you and wanted to stop her. Whatever the cost, she felt. That's what she told me.'

'I understand that. But still…' Serena stood up and contemplated the view from the window. The battleship grey sky matched her mood. 'So, what happens now?'

'We arrange her funeral.'

Alicia's funeral was held in the Borders Crematorium at the end of March.

Arriving there with Phyllis, Serena was struck by the prettiness of the countryside. Spring had arrived. Lambs cavorted in the fields bleating after their mothers. Daffodils and crocuses bloomed in the flower beds surrounding the crematorium. *How could it be so lovely on such a sad day*, she thought?

Phyllis read her mind, 'I know, Serena – I know. How can it be so beautiful on a day like this?' She tucked Serena's left arm through the crook of her elbow and together they entered the crematorium.

Sitting solely in the front pew with Phyllis, Serena was comforted to see Mary with Henry and Ginny with an unusually sombre looking Rory in a row of pews further behind. She would go and talk with them later. People arrived in dribs and drabs. There would be no difficulty in locating a seat. Very few people were attending Alicia's funeral. Alicia's adopted parents were conspicuous by their absence. Either they could not or had elected not to attend Alicia's funeral. Serena was sad, thinking of this. After all, Alicia had been their child from babyhood. And barring recent events, must have been truly proud of her and her accomplishments. Tears sprang to Phyllis's eyes when she noticed the coffin with the gorgeous white lilies placed on it. They would be sent to the local hospital. Phyllis couldn't bear the elegant flowers to be devoured by the flames.

The minister started to talk about Alicia. No mention was made of Amy. Of how thrilled Alicia was to locate Phyllis and meet her half-sister, Serena. To live in the Scottish Borders, close to her birth mother. He described Alicia's talent as a painter of animals and her love for them. Pointing out that although she had only resided in the area for a fleeting time her paintings graced the walls of many prominent county houses. The service passed quickly, much to Serena's relief. She managed to hold it together until the last hymn was played, 'Abide with me.' Only by fixating on the beamed ceiling of the crematorium chapel did she manage to prevent the tears which had welled up in her eyes from pouring down her face. Leaving the chapel to the strains of 'My heart will go on' by Celine Dion – Alicia's favourite song – they were then out, into the brilliant sunshine. Serena, alongside Phyllis, thanked her friends and the other people who had attended the funeral.

Chapter Twenty-six
The Bank, Edinburgh

Following Alicia's funeral Serena immersed herself in work. The atmosphere in the office, however, remained strained. Only Mary really spoke to her, although Graham now managed a brief hello when passing in the corridor. Serena felt like she had the plague, people averted their eyes if they encountered her and heaven forbid if they were forced to speak to her. Their conversations were very brief and stilted.

'I'm thinking of applying for a new job. A fresh start,' Serena announced to Mary one lunchtime.

Deserting their habitual lunchtime canteen visit for a local Indian restaurant, Mary wolfed down her beef rogan josh. Serena picked at the chicken tikka masala in front of her. She wasn't hungry. Mary regretfully contemplated the now clean plate in front of her and put down her fork. She then looked up and stared at Serena, without speaking for a few minutes. 'Yes. Maybe it's for the best,' she said.

'Not you too!'

'Why, who else?'

'My mother thinks I should go and work somewhere else. New beginnings,' she mused. 'Perhaps she's right,' Serena checked the time on her watch, she had a meeting after lunch.

'Well, she has a point. You're a brilliant developer and there's always jobs for people like you. Especially a techie who isn't a diva and talks in English, so to speak, to others who don't understand technical terms. And is very patient with others too.'

'I'm glad to hear I'm not a diva or a prima donna!' Serena smiled.

Mary hadn't seen Serena smile for months. The last time was at the Ball. That Ball had much to answer for. She deliberated venturing into dangerous territory. After all, she was Serena's best friend at work. 'Speaking of the Ball,' she started, not knowing how Serena would react to her mentioning the fateful evening again.

Serena's eyes narrowed. Her jaw tensed. She glared at Mary. Her eyes, icing over, became those of a stranger. 'Well? What about it?' She slammed her empty water glass down on the table.

'Well...' Mary began, 'Have you heard from Robin?

A single staccato laugh emitted from Serena's lips. Her eyes sparked hostile green fire.

'What do *you* think?' Her voice oozed sarcasm. 'I've never spoken to him, nor heard from him since the night of the Ball. *He* thinks I killed Amy. Once when I met him in a corridor at work, I tried to speak to him. He made it clear he wanted nothing further to do with me. This was before he left the company.' Serena folded her arms and scowled at Mary. 'So that's how it is. End of story. I don't want to talk about it anymore. To *anyone*. Ever again. Finis.'

Mary judged it was a sensible idea to change the subject. She dabbed her mouth with the linen napkin. She thought for a moment.

'Did you know Amy's Mum sent her dog to the

Edinburgh Dog and Cat home? No? Well, none of her family wanted him. Her mother hates animals. I wasn't sure whether to mention this or not. I would have adopted him, but unfortunately Henry's allergic to dogs. I know how much you love animals. All animals.'

'Poor Amy. That's such a shame,' Serena said. 'Poor dog, too, losing Amy *and* his home. What is he like?'

'He's a large white poodle. Mr Boye. Amy's pride and joy. He used to win prizes at dog shows. When Amy showed him. A great temperament too, or so I've been told,' Mary explained.

'Yes I remember the photos she had pinned up behind her workstation. How do you know all this?'

Mary didn't know where to look and stared at the empty plate in front of her. 'Graham told me.'

'So, he still speaks to you then, does he?' Serena raised an eyebrow.

'I think he's too ashamed to speak to you after the Ball. I think he blames himself for Amy turning on you. Do you know they had a terrible argument? No? You didn't?' Mary glanced at Serena's mutinous face, 'I'm sorry – I thought you did.'

'Not your fault. Or Graham's,' Serena said, 'Shame about the dog, though.' She looked thoughtful and started to eat her lunch.

Chapter Twenty-seven
Kelso, The Scottish Borders

The day of the Border Union show dawned clear and bright. The second largest agricultural show in the country. Held in a large park on the outskirts of Kelso, this prestigious event took place over two days, towards the end of July. People travelled from all over Scotland and farther afield, to attend, exhibit their animals, visit the trade stands, enjoy the ambiance and hopefully pleasant weather. Serena had planned to go on the Saturday with Phyllis and meet Mary there. She had arranged to stay the night with Serena after the show.

A major change had occurred in Serena's life. She no longer worked at the bank in Edinburgh but, instead, remotely for a London investment bank. This meant she had to travel to London for a couple of days each month. Her home was now in the Scottish Borders, in Kelso, in Alicia's house which had been bequeathed to Serena.

Serena was devastated by Alicia's death. She continued to mourn her, although she could never forgive Alicia for killing Amy. She wished they had never gone to *that* Ball. Then Amy would still be alive and, herself, an item with Robin. Possibly.

Life flowed at a slower pace for Serena, she enjoyed working from home, her laptop strategically placed in front of a window, so she could enjoy the stunning garden where the herbaceous borders were now in full bloom. Although she still had the continual nightmares featuring June and Belinda, she felt more able to cope with them and recognise them for what they were. Just bad dreams she told herself.

Arriving early at the show, Serena and Phyllis went their separate ways; Serena to watch the retrained racehorse class and Phyllis to the craft marquee to display the homemade raspberry jam she had entered in the Preserves and Produce section.

Serena dawdled past the cows, sheep and goats being shown, and the numerous trade stands. She soon arrived at the collecting ring for the retrained racehorse class. She had always loved thoroughbred horses and was worried about what happened to them when their racing days were over. She was delighted the show included this class which encouraged people to take on ex-racehorses and compete with them.

At the far end of the collecting ring, Ginny was warming up her exquisite liver chestnut thoroughbred mare, Samandy. The mare moved delicately, almost floating, pointing her hooves as she trotted across the grass. Ginny halted next to Rory who started to polish Samandy's gleaming coat, looking for non-existent specs of dust. The steward called them forward, ready to start the class. Serena just had time to give Samandy a quick pat and wish Ginny good luck before she entered the show ring.

Sitting on a bench at the ringside, Serena counted sixteen other horses in the showring. She eyed up Samandy's competition. Most of the horses were geldings and predominately bay in colour. A number resembled good old-fashioned steeplechasers, like

Rubstic. A Borders-trained horse, fondly remembered, he had won the Grand National in the late nineteen seventies. There were a couple of other mares too, although none as classy nor beautiful as Samandy, in Serena's opinion.

The two judges stood in the centre of the ring conferring. The bandy, bowed legs of the judge who was riding the horses contrasted with the lady judge's whose legs were as slim and elegant as any thoroughbred's.

Following the initial walk, trot and canter by the competitors en masse, the judges selected the order in which the horses were to be lined up. Serena was ecstatic to see Samandy was pulled in third. Each horse and rider had to perform an individual show which included a short gallop at the end. Samandy behaved well, responding to Ginny's kind and tactful riding. Then it was the turn of the judge to ride Samandy. Her ears flickered back and forward as the ride judge approached. He had been a famous jockey in his time, now being much sought in demand to judge show classes like these. Scrambling onto Samandy's back, the judge sat with his legs pushed forward, as if he were out hunting. Ginny holding onto Samandy's rein, whispered 'be good' to her and, after one final pat on the silken neck, the mare moved off. Samandy ignored two spaniels held on leads, growling and fighting each other at the ringside. Their owner's attention preoccupied on the ex-racehorses, devouring their large ice cream cones, oblivious to the snarling dogs.

Out of nowhere, angry shouting followed by loud cursing could be heard. A small herd of young Belted Galloway cows had broken free from where they were tethered, at the opposite end of the park. They were heading towards the horse area. Obviously deciding they were missing out on seeing what else was happening at the show, they cavorted and galloped towards the entrance to show ring where the retrained racehorse class was taking place. Serena could barely watch. The horses in the ring were going crazy. They reared, bucked and bolted with their riders. A couple of horses, that were old hands at this, having been there and done that, stood placidly beside their now dismounted riders. They were the exceptions. Serena held tightly onto the dog lead in her right hand.

All eyes round the ring focused firstly on the escapee cows. Their entry into the ring was barred by a group of intrepid young farmers. A sturdy, red-headed lad managed to grab the lead rope of one of the heifer's halters and persuaded her that she really didn't want to join the horses in the ring and then managed to capture another delinquent. The remaining fugitives decided they had had quite enough excitement for today and were ready to re-join their better-behaved companions back in the show's livestock area. The crowd gave a small appreciative clap as the renegade black cows with white 'belts' encircling their tummies were led away. They could now focus on the ex-racehorses again, hopefully with no further unwanted interruptions.

For, amid all the furore, Samandy had been an angel. Walking serenely in a circle beside Ginny. The judge was a skilful rider, well used to calming nervous racehorses on the way to the start of a race. Patting Samandy's glossy neck, he put her through her paces, finishing with a short gallop. He pulled up with a flourish beside Ginny, dismounted and handed her the reins.

'What a super mare she is. Nothing obviously phases her if she doesn't bat an eyelid at those naughty cows!' He smiled broadly, obviously enjoying himself.

'Thank you! She was so sensible just now,' Ginny said.

'I just wish they were all like that!' the judge said, giving Samandy a final pat, he moved down the line, to ride the next horse. The runaway cows still obviously rattled some of the horses, so he had his hands full, both mentally and physically.

Eventually, the riders remounted the horses and were asked to walk around the ring. Serena crossed her fingers, while waiting for the judges' decision. Samandy was pulled in first place.

'What a well-behaved horse you have and she went so beautifully,' the lady judge said to Ginny pinning the rosette on Samandy's bridle. 'She deserved to win especially after those cows tried to enter the ring!'

The ex-jockey judge was equally complimentary. 'Look, if you ever want to sell that mare let my office know. She is a cracker,' he added. Patting Samandy.

Ginny thanked the judges. After all the other placed riders had been handed their rosettes, they led a victory gallop around the ring.

Serena waited in the collecting ring. Rory joined her. Not so dashing and debonair today. Dressed in an old Barbour jacket and muddy jeans sticking out the tops of his Hunter wellies. He smoothed down the corners of his black moustache and ran his hands through his dishevelled hair. 'Thank goodness that's over. I need a drink. After that. A large drink!' He grimaced. 'Can you *believe* these cows!?'

'Me too! Yes, those cows were frightful, I'm just relieved they were prevented from entering the ring. There would have been utter carnage! But wasn't Samandy brilliant?'

Ginny rode over on Samandy. 'Yes, she was wonderful.' She dismounted from Samandy, retrieved a packet of polos from her show jacket pocket and began to feed Samandy polos. The mare took them daintily one by one from Ginny's palm.

'Anyway,' she handed the reins to Serena, 'she's yours now.'

Serena's old mare, Rose, had died in April. Serena was heartbroken. She missed Rose and her fiery nature. Since then, Serena had never had the time nor the inclination to look for another horse. But she had always coveted Ginny's horse, Samandy. She was undoubtedly the most beautiful horse Serena had ever seen. Rose, although endearing in her ways and appearance, was a workmanlike Belgian Warmblood. In human terms, though, Samandy was a supermodel and Rose the pretty girl next door. The mare was accident prone, jumping into fields, breaking fence rails, resulting in long layoffs. Only in the past year had Ginny and Samandy finally managed to achieve their successful joint act together, justifying Ginny's faith in the mare.

'What do you mean? Really!?' Serena couldn't believe her luck. She hugged Samandy who then nuzzled her face. 'Are you sure you want to sell her to me?'

'Well, yes, if you still want her, that is?'

'Of course, I do. I just can't believe she'll be mine. After all these years. After all that's happened.' Serena was over the moon – maybe her luck was about to change?

'Serena, sorry but we really need to go. I must sort out the other horses at home. Phone me on Monday. Enjoy the rest of the show,' with that Ginny handed Serena the first-place rosette and stalked off to her horsebox. Rory retrieved Samandy from Serena, and he was then towed in Ginny's direction. Samandy knew she was going home. The mare was overexcited at the thought of returning to a field full of lush grass and being reunited with her friend, Woolly the black Suffolk ewe.

Serena loitered towards the main ring. Pocketing the rosette, she still couldn't believe Samandy would soon be hers. Turning round she noticed Mary strolling towards her. *She must have recently arrived*, Serena thought.

The showground was heaving, but Mary would

have been easy to spot. She was wearing spearmint cropped jeans, the top button above the zip straining to stay shut around her generous tummy and a shocking pink V-necked jumper which clashed with her copper hair. Mary broke into a grin when she saw Serena.

Serena grinned back at Mary. 'Mary – it's so lovely to see you. I've missed not seeing you since March.' They hugged.

Although Mary was delighted to see Serena, her attention was taken elsewhere. 'What on earth? Where did you get that dog? He's massive!' she exclaimed. 'It's not...'

'Yes, this is Mr Boye, Amy's dog. When I decided to move to Kelso, I thought I'd see if he was still available to be rehomed,' she explained as she adjusted the lead on the white poodle's blue collar.

'Well, now that I have a garden I felt so sorry for him. After finding out that he got on well with cats I was determined to provide a home for him.' Serena gave Mr Boye's head an affectionate pat.

'What a kind thing to do,' Mary said.

'Well, you told me about him, I couldn't bear the thought of him languishing in the strays home. No one wanted him. I felt I owed it to Amy.'

'You didn't owe Amy anything. But I'm sure she would be gratified if she knew,' Mary beamed.

'I hope so,' Serena said, but she wasn't entirely convinced.

They sauntered past the poultry show tent. Ducks, hens and geese quacking could be heard from within.

'Mary – remind me to pop into see the poultry later. Mum's friend is showing her young Cayuga ducks.'

'What are they like?' Mary asked.

'Oh, they're handsome ducks with black plumage which has an iridescent green lustre. I'd like to own some. One day.'

'When you have your estate. You mean!' Mary laughed and linked arms with Serena. 'Anyway, it's great to see you. Now where's the ice-cream stall you always rave about at this show. Some firm in Northumberland makes it, you said. Come on, let's go and buy a huge cone each!'

Leaving the food hall with cones containing large scoops of ice-cream, Serena and Mary sat down on a bench looking onto the main ring and concentrated on savouring the delicious ice-cream.

Mary was the first to speak. 'So, how's things? I miss you not working at the bank. I used to enjoy our lunches and night outs out together.'

'I miss you too. And of course, all those Beachcomber Babies!'

'Yes, thought you would miss them. What about the new job. Do you like working there?'

'It's fine,' Serena said, feeding Mr Boye the last remnants of her cone. 'Work is going well; I'm enjoying working for the investment bank. I usually travel down once a month to meet my manager and stay for a couple of days. Though, it's not the same, not seeing friends like you. The fun night outs. Even

Daisy and her ways. But I felt I had to leave. You know why. Move on. The work is quite different though from what I did before, but I enjoy it.'

'And a new start too,' Mary commented.

'Yes, but what happened to Amy is never far from my mind. I'm haunted by what happened to her. I can't forgive Alicia for what she did. That's why I took Mr Boye to do a good deed for Amy.'

'She never did any good deeds for you when she was alive,' Mary said.

'I know that, but she's still dead before her time.'

There was no response to that, as Mary knew. They sat together for a few minutes or so watching the hunter championship which being held in the main ring. Serena favoured the lightweight hunter, the horse reminded of Jubilee, her first horse. The lightweight hunter was chosen as the reserve champion.

Not having seen Serena for three months, Mary studied her appearance. Serena's figure was as lithe as before, the endless legs encased in slim-fitting, white jeans tucked into knee-high, black suede boots, complete with jade tassels. Mary noticed how closely she resembled Alicia. The delicate bone structure a bit too near the surface now and the dark under eye shadows which had not existed previously.

Putting the dark shadows down to Serena's new demanding job, Mary asked, 'Any interesting men there? In the office, I mean?'

'I don't really know. I've only met my team for meetings. No one goes for drinks after work there, not like at the bank.' She played with the neck of her navy cashmere jumper. 'Anyway, I'm off men just now.'

'Yoohoo! Serena! Mary! Wait for me!' A loud voice provided a timely interruption for Serena. She didn't really want to continue that conversation. Turning round on the bench, she saw Phyllis advancing towards where they were sitting, a cheesy grin on her face.

'I won!' Phyllis shouted.

'Your jam won?' Serena asked. Phyllis had never ever won any prizes for her jam. 'That's amazing!'

Phyllis was clutching a first prize envelope. She waved the tiny envelope, the coins jingling inside, in front of Serena. 'I won the competition for my raspberry jam. These are my winnings!' She smiled again. 'I can't believe it, I beat Mrs Biddlescomb!' the last four words were said very quietly, as a woman in a heavy brown tweed suit and sensible brown lacing shoes stalked past.

'Was that her?' Serena asked.

'Yes, and she's in shock by being beaten by the likes of me!' Phyllis smirked. 'It's probably something that's never happened to her before!'

'That's great.' Serena said, still observing Mrs. Biddlescomb. 'I'm so pleased for you,' she added.

'Congratulations!' Mary said, 'That sounds like a reason for a celebration!' With that Mary took them both off to the bar in the large marquee.

Deciding it was warm enough to sit outside at a picnic table and bench, they raised their glasses of Pimms.

'Here's to your good health and happiness,' from Phyllis. 'Anyway, how are you doing Mary? It's great to see you again. In happier circumstances.'

'I'm good, thanks. It's lovely to be here. I've missed seeing Serena. The office is not the same without her,' Mary replied.

Sipping their drinks, Phyllis spotted a friend from the SWRI and hared off to join her. 'I'll see you girls later,' she said.

Mr Boye stood up abruptly, pricked his ears and started to bark. Serena looked round, she couldn't see who or what had caught his attention. He tugged on his lead and Serena had difficulty restraining him. 'Steady boy. Sit down. Sit!' she said to the exuberant dog.

'Mr Boye? It's lovely to see you!' a familiar sounding voice said. A man ran over and ruffled Mr Boye's ears. It was Graham. Serena stared at him.

'What are you doing here? Why are *you* here? No doubt you've seen Mr Boye on many occasions,' she said glaring at him. He was no longer one of her favourite people. And no longer featured in her life.

Graham stopped patting Mr Boye and turned to face Serena. He ignored Serena's comment about Mr Boye. 'Well, Mary mentioned she was going to the Border Union show and, since I hadn't been before, thought I'd come along too,' he said, lingering to see what was happening in the main ring. 'Nice to see you too, by the way,' he added.

Serena glared at Mary. Then looked daggers at Graham. 'So, you came by yourself, did you?' she asked.

'Erm no – not quite.' He looked over his shoulder to where the bar was.

Serena followed his gaze. A familiar tall lanky dark-haired man was strolling towards them, carrying a plastic glass of beer in each hand.

'Did you know about this,' she asked Mary. 'You should have told me!'

Mary shook her head. 'Most definitely not.' She wouldn't have engineered a meeting like this. Never. Ever. Kind of sneaky, it struck her. 'No. Not *my* style,' she said.

Serena turned to Graham. 'So – is this *your* idea of a joke?' she said.

Graham flushed and his face turned a tomato red. 'No, but it's my way of apologising for what happened at the Ball. To make up for it. I'm sorry I never really spoke to you after that evening. I was so ashamed of myself. I antagonised Amy so maybe that was why she went for you.'

'Explain, then. What do you mean by that?' Serena said.

'Well, earlier that evening I asked her out and she turned me down. I then told her Robin would never look at her in a million years and he only had eyes for you. She stalked off in a towering rage.'

'I see. I think.'

'I'm sorry. Look, I know I can never make up for my past behaviour, but I thought I could make things right between you and Robin. I told him all about what happened that night. It might explain why Amy was gunning for you.'

'That's an unfortunate turn of phrase to use.' Serena glared at Graham. 'Don't you think?' She looked him up and down. 'And not one *you* should be using.'

'I know. I'm sorry. I just didn't think.' Graham looked at Serena, his eyes not meeting hers.

'That's the problem. You *never* think. Do you?' Serena retorted. She had nothing more to say.

No one said anything and contemplated their drinks.

That terrible night. Serena would have given anything to rewind time. She peeped at Robin who wasn't far away. Robin glanced back at Serena. Lowering her eyes, she continued stroking Mr Boye's head.

Robin drained his beer. 'Graham – your round next,' he said. After handing Graham his empty glass, Robin sauntered over to Serena and Mary. 'Hi, guys! How are you? Serena? Mary?'

Neither Serena nor Mary responded to his greeting. Minutes passed. They remained silent.

Robin shifted his weight from one foot to the other and decided to try another approach. 'Now who's this?' Robin motioned with his hand towards Mr Boye.

'Mr Boye. He was Amy's dog, nobody wanted to look after him, so soon after Amy died, he was sent to a pet rehoming centre in Edinburgh and put up for adoption. That's where I got him from,' Serena said. She sneaked a glance at Robin. 'I just wanted to give him a nice home.'

Robin's brown eyes softened. He smiled when Serena explained about Mr Boye. Serena hadn't seen him smile like that since before midnight at the Meridian Club Ball. 'And how kind of you to give him a home,' he said pushing his fringe back off his forehead.

'When I heard about him, I felt so sorry for him and after what happened to Amy…' Serena said, the sentence tailing off.

Graham raised his eyebrows at Mary and they wandered off together, towards the trade stands.

'I know,' Robin said, 'I just wish that horrible night had never happened. Graham told me afterwards what had taken place between him and Amy earlier on in the evening.'

'You mean before Amy's death?' Serena said.

'Yes,' Robin said. 'You know I never believed you killed Amy. I knew you couldn't have…'

'Or wouldn't have, you mean?' Serena interrupted.

'Yes. And for what it's worth, I'm sorry.' Robin said. 'I should have spoken to you before.' He reached out to touch her hand, then on seeing the expression on Serena's face, changed his mind.

'Yes. Yes, you should have. Then.' Serena gazed at Robin. The words 'not now' remained unspoken. Things would never be the same between them. The night of the Ball had changed everything. They couldn't go back; they had crossed the Rubicon. She forced herself to speak. 'It is good to see you again,

Robin,' permitting herself one last look at the chiselled cheekbones and the wide brown eyes partially obscured by the habitual floppy fringe.

They stood and stared at each other. Wordlessly. Serena fidgeted with Mr Boye's lead. Robin crossed his arms.

Graham and Mary rejoined them.

'It was nice to see you today, Graham,' Serena said. 'Enjoy the rest of the show.'

'We will, thanks. Take care, Serena. It's been lovely to see you,' Graham half-smiled.

Robin said nothing but smiled a tight-lipped smile. After that dreadful business with Amy, he had vowed to have nothing further to do with Serena. But when Graham suggested attending the Border Union shown and knowing Serena would be there... Seeing Serena again had re-ignited the spark. For him, at least.

'Look, I think it's time we headed off to meet my mum. She'll want to go home shortly,' Serena said to Mary. Her shoulders drooping, she turned round, trudging off in the opposite direction, Mary plodding behind. Serena didn't notice Mary making apologetic hand gestures to Robin and Graham.

Chapter Twenty-eight
Kelso, the Scottish Borders

'Serena!'

'Wake up!'

'Serena – *Please* wake up!'

Mary shook Serena's shoulders back and forwards. Serena's eyes were open. She was far away, in another world. Mary tried again. Serena was in a trance. Her eyes unseeing. Mary rushed over to the small hand basin of the sink and filled a glass with water. Swiftly returning to Serena's side she flung the contents of the glass, over Serena's face. Serena spluttered. Blinking several times, she focussed with difficulty on Mary.

'What the hell?' she said. 'Are you trying to drown me?' Serena wiped her face with the sleeve of her dressing gown.

'Thank goodness – you're ok,' Mary breathed a long sigh of relief. 'I was so worried about you.'

Shadow, the grey cat, her tail bushy like a Christmas tree, padded over on the bed to Serena. Serena leant over and patted Shadow's velvet head. Shadow turned her head and hissed at Serena, the cat then retreated to the far end of the bed and started to wash her paws.

Mary observed Serena's face. Her eyes concentrated on Serena's. Mary was reassured to see Serena now looked better, her eyes clear and alert, meeting Mary's. 'Do you want to tell me what happened?' She asked Serena. 'What was that all about?'

'What was I doing?'

'You were screaming at the top of your voice. I thought you were being murdered.'

'I nearly was,' Serena murmured under her breath.

Mary glanced over at the alarm clock on the bedside table. It was three-thirty on Sunday morning. After a delicious, barbequed meal outside, setting the world to right, accompanied by lots of wine it didn't seem like five minutes had passed since they had gone to bed.

'Look, why don't I make us some camomile tea and you can tell me what that was all about?'

'That would be lovely. Thanks.'

Serena lay back on the bed. Her head was thumping, some chilly water would help. She dragged herself out of bed and lurched over to the small bedroom sink. Turning on the tap, grains of sand poured into the sink. She gave a small yelp and jumped back into bed,

Mary returned to the bedroom. Seeing Serena shivering violently. She asked, 'What is it? What's, what's happened – now?'

'There's sand in the sink.' Serena mumbled.

'*What*! *Why* would there be sand in the sink?' Mary got up from the stool in front of the dressing table and went over to the sink. There was nothing to be seen. She ran the taps. Only water discharged. Sitting down again, she looked anxiously at Serena. 'So, what's going on? You don't appear to have slept well for weeks?'

'I haven't,' Serena admitted.

'I put it down to your new job, but it isn't that is it?'

'No.'

'Why don't you tell me what's going on, you'll feel better for doing so?'

'Possibly. But I doubt it'll make any difference.'

'Well, it's worth a try. You can't go on like this? Can you?' Mary regarded Serena's ashen face. 'And it's not the first time, either, this has happened. Is it?'

'No, you're right. I can't. And no, it's not the first time,' Serena sighed. 'OK, I'll tell you,' Serena sat up in bed and took a sip of her camomile tea. 'It's not a pleasant story. And you'll not think me a very nice person for the part I played part in it.'

Mary sniffed. 'I don't think so. Anyway, let me be the judge of that.'

Serena related the events at the Devon beach, which had occurred, a decade or so ago. She then explained about Belinda, that she never knew how Belinda had died, until Amy told her.

'Amy held me responsible for her cousins' deaths. I can't say I blame her. Their lives *were* cut short. And now Amy's.' Serena slurped her tea and continued. 'It was such a tragedy. That poor little girl and her guilt-stricken sister. Belinda – she must never have had a moment's peace. But I still think that she should have taken better care of June. That day.'

'Yes, she should have,' Mary echoed.

'That's what I thought. At the time. Now I'm not

so sure,' Serena said.

'Well, I still think she should have. She was her sister *and* you told Belinda you were swimming back to the shore.'

'I know. But I can still see June in her little pink and white spotted swimsuit turning cartwheels on the sand,' Serena said.

Mary shook her head. 'You need to stop this. Get a grip of yourself. Just tell me what happened last night.' She pulled her dressing gown tighter around her waist and looked encouragingly at Serena. 'Come on – keep going.'

'Alright!' Serena clicked her fingers and Shadow proceeded down the bed to settle alongside Serena. Mr Boye had crept into the bedroom and stood trembling beside Serena's bed.

'It all started shortly after Amy joined the bank. The nightmares, I mean. I think. Or maybe they are ghosts and I'm being haunted by them?'

'So, it sounds like Amy starting to work there – back in your life was what triggered them?'

'Yes, that's right. She was the catalyst. I had managed to deal with what had happened before, in my head. But that all came to a stop from the first day I met Amy again in the office,' Serena took a mouthful of tea and patted Mr Boye's head. He slunk out of the bedroom, his tail clenched between his hindlegs.

'Anyway,' she continued, 'one night I was aware that Belinda and June were at the foot of the bed in my bedroom in Edinburgh. They were pointing accusatory fingers at me. I told myself it was a bad dream. Nothing more.' Serena grimaced. 'You know – I even dreamt about them in the police cell...'

'As if that wasn't bad enough being locked up in a police cell,' Mary interjected.

'I hoped the dreams and nightly visitations would cease when I moved to the Borders. One of my reasons for doing so.'

'But they didn't, did they?

'No. They're getting worse. Even more frightening is the figures are now drawing closer and closer towards the top of my bed.'

They sat in silence and stared at each other.

'And last night?' Mary prompted.

'The ghastliest yet. Amy now accompanies Belinda and June. In my bedroom, they're standing beside where my head lies on my pillow, their fingers only a fraction from my head. They just stop short of touching my face. What made it even worse was the new appearances of the figures... or apparitions. Before they looked almost normal. A bit pale in the face. Almost alive and vibrant. But now...?' Serena's voice tailed off, 'They are different. Quite shocking in appearance...' Serena shuddered and put her hands over her eyes.

'Serena, please tell me,' Mary shivered and reaching over patted Serena's right hand.

'Last night, I'm positive it wasn't a dream. In fact – I'm sure they are ghosts and they are terrifying or more likely terrorising me!'

'They *were* here. In the room. June in her adorable bathing costume, but her blonde pigtails now entwined with seaweed and seawater splashed down her face. Amy looked pretty much as she did the night of the Ball except the bodice of her strapless dress was lopsided. Her hair was sticking up at the front, a large bruise was present on her forehead.'

Serena stopped talking.

'And Belinda?' Mary prompted.

'Belinda was the worst. Her face bleeding. Droplets of blood gushing down over her once enchanting features. Her body encased in a ripped tartan dress was broken and bruised due to what happened with the train. She could barely stand beside the bed. Using one of her bloodied hands she propped herself against the bed, the other hand gesticulated at me. Just like her companions. She is the most upsetting of the trio to look at.' Serena shivered.

'That's absolutely awful.' Mary shivered.

'It is. Isn't it?'

'But what are you going to do? What *can* you do?'

'I don't know. But I need to do something. The… these manifestations – are really getting to me. I've tried sleeping pills, prescription ones I got from my doctor, they made no difference. The figures are edging closer and closer… What will they do next? But what can I do?'

Mary had no answer. 'Well, at the end of the day it's still just a dream.' She added, 'it *has* to be!' A no-nonsense person, she would sooner have dismissed the idea of ghosts as something made up to scare children. But now she wasn't convinced. The Serena of old she knew wasn't given to wild fancies and those dreams certainly appeared to be having a calamitous effect on her.

Serena broke in on Mary's musings. 'I'm not entirely sure. Sometimes I think I've woken up and they're in the room beside me. I try to tell myself they're only ghosts and can't hurt me. But I'm worried one day I'll wake up with bruises around my neck or something far worse.' She decided to downplay the ghost angle. It was obvious Mary didn't believe in the supernatural. Neither had Serena. Before. 'The dreams are driving me nuts and I need to deal with this soon.'

'Maybe having told me about it will make them go away?'

'I hope so, but I doubt it,' Serena leapt out of bed and opened the curtains; dawn was starting to break. *Thank heavens,* she thought.

'Serena – you must find a way to make the dreams stop. You'll drive yourself mad, if you don't do something.'

'I know – you're right. I'm just not sure what the remedy is, though.' Serena shook her head.

Mary left shortly after breakfast. She gave Serena a hug. 'Now don't leave it too long until we meet again and in the meantime, don't do anything rash. Call me if you need me. Anytime. You know where I am.'

'I wish you could stay.' Serena waved her off.

'I know. Me too. But we'll meet up again soon. I promise.'

*****

The day flew by. Serena arranged to see Ginny about buying Samandy the following weekend. *Something to look forward to*, she thought. She kept herself busy, cleaning the house and taking Mr Boye for a long walk in Bowmont forest. The day having flown past, conversely the evening crawled on and on. It was an unseasonably cold August day, so Serena lit the wood burning stove in the living room. The flames cast eerie shadows onto the walls. To take her mind of the impending night, she leafed through recent photographs, sticking those she liked best into a photo album. Later she poured herself a large gin and tonic, before settling down to watch a favourite detective series on TV. Then it was time for bed.

After a deep lavender oil scented bath, Serena retired for the evening. It had been a pleasant enough day and she expected to drift off to sleep. Unfortunately sleep eluded her. She tossed and turned from side to side, watching the illuminated clock hands reach one am. Eventually an uneasy sleep arrived.

A door banging woke her up. It was as if someone or something had opened her bedroom door and crept in. The room was pitch-black. Serena reached out her hand to turn the clock round to face her. Earlier on, she had deliberately moved it so she couldn't see what the time was. Four am. Around the usual time. Her hearing, sharpened from the disturbed nights she was experiencing, discerned the sound of feet padding on the carpet. Blinking her eyes, she could see nothing in the darkness. Straining her eyes – a whisper of white light appeared to emanate from underneath the bedroom door. She looked again. The room was empty and still. Thank goodness. Resting her head back on the pillow, telling herself it was just another bad dream, Serena closed her eyes.

A pitter patter of feet. Silence. Then again. Now, the sound of *something* being dragged over the bedroom carpet. Her eyes snapped open. She *was* awake. She reached over and switched on her bedside lamp. The three spectres of the previous night were in the room and advancing towards her from the bottom of the bed. There was something deliberate and calculated in their movements. Closer and closer they came. Last of all was Belinda, pulling herself along. Nearer and nearer. Serena wanted to put her head under the duvet, but she was mesmerised by the figures. She couldn't tear her eyes away. They stopped beside her pillow. The trio towered above her. Heads peering downwards. Their fingers made stabbing movements, less than an inch from her head. Serena forced herself to gaze at them. The phantoms, similar in appearance to the previous night, grinned evilly at her. Serena shook with fear when she stared up into their faces, each with gaping black sockets on either side of the nose. No eyes.

'Wh-what d-do you w-want?'

'*You*,' Amy hissed.

Amy reached forward and proceeded to place icy fingers around Serena's neck. With a malevolent smile on her lips, she continued to tighten her grip.

Amy's fingers were remarkably strong and Serena began to find it an effort to breathe... Gathering what strength she had, Serena dug her nails into Amy's hands. Amy let go. Without a sound, thrusting her hands towards the spectres, Serena attempted to shove them away. Her hands passed through what would have remained of Belinda's body.

'Th-that is enough!' Serena yelled at the top of her voice. '*Go. Away. Now*!' The figures raised their heads and turned towards each other. Seemingly astounded, at hearing Serena's raised voice, they vanished.

Serena half-fell/half-jumped out of bed. She wanted to get out of the room. Now. She slammed the bedroom door shut and headed for the kitchen. Everything was reassuringly normal, the red Aga grumbling away in the corner, Shadow and Mr Boye sound asleep in their baskets. The first fingers of dawn, peeped out from under the red-and-white spotted blind. Making a cup of tea in the kitchen, she couldn't stop her fingers from shaking. The liquid spilled out of her mug as she tried to drink it. *This is the end. I can't go on like this. I must do something. I-I need to exorcize my demons. Today. Now,* she thought. Entering the living room, she lay down on the comfortable old sofa and fell into a troubled sleep.

Sunlight blazed into the small living-room. Shadow licked Serena's face. She stirred and gently pushed Shadow away. *Cripes – what time is it?* Glancing at the mantelpiece clock, *Nine am. I should be working*. Reaching for her mobile phone she dialled her manager's number.

Looking out over a grey and dreary London morning sky, Mike Gregson straightened his navy and maroon striped tie before answering his phone. 'Good morning, Serena. How are you, this rainy Monday morning?' he said.

'Good morning, Mike,' Serena replied. 'Actually, I'm not great so I was wondering if I could please take this week off. I'm not terribly busy at present. The project I'm working on is still in the analysis stage. The design phase is not due to start for two weeks or so?'

Mike liked Serena, the newest member of his team and considered her development work excellent. Although she had only worked at the investment bank for a few months, he sensed this behaviour was out of character.

Serena twiddled the biro pen in her right hand. She hoped Mike would say 'yes'. The apparitions had to be stopped.

'I know it's terribly short notice. It's just that I have something I need to deal with. Urgently. Please?' she added.

Mike mentally hummed and hawed to himself. The project team could probably manage without her, for this week only. The current project had an aggressive deadline looming. 'OK, Serena, take this week off, if you must. But I expect you back next week. Monday morning.'

'Thank you, Mike. I really appreciate this.' *You don't know how much,* Serena thought. She was so grateful he had agreed to the time off.

'Don't say I'm not good to you. Speak to you on seventh of August.' With that, Mike hung up.

Serena immediately phoned Phyllis. She had arrangements to make.

Chapter Twenty-nine
The Scottish Borders

After speaking to Mike Gregson, Serena had scrambled her possessions together. Jeans, t-shirts and shorts were thrown into her small suitcase. Arriving at Phyllis's house shortly before twelve, she handed her bewildered pets over to Phyllis.

'Where are you going? What are you doing? You *must* tell me?' There was no response from Serena. 'You must let me know when you've arrived. So I know you're safe.' Phyllis was distressed and needed hear more about Serena's plans. Her younger daughter taking off somewhere out of the blue was completely out of character. Everything about Serena was controlled and organised. Usually.

'I'll be back by the weekend. I expect,' Serena said. She gave Shadow a quick hug and caressed Mr Boye's floppy ears. 'Thanks for looking after the animals. Be good, guys,' she added.

'That's no problem. I'll love having them. You haven't told me where you're going yet. I'm really worried about you.' Phyllis had noticed the uncommon dark shadows below Serena's previously sparkling eyes. Today her eyes were an insipid green. Bringing Shadow and Mr Boye into the house, they were greeted by Pimms and Tosca, whom Phyllis had taken in after Alicia's death. Shadow put out a paw to touch Pimms' head. Pimms spat at Shadow and hid behind the coat stand in the hall. Marmalade, the long-time sole resident cat took one look at the intruders and retreated upstairs.

'Not a great start,' Phyllis commented. Holding Serena's hands she said,' Now, darling, please. *Please* tell me where you'll be staying?'

Serena unclasped her hands from Phyllis's. Walking back to the car she slid into the driver's seat.

'Devon,' she said.

Phyllis sighed. What she had been dreading to hear. 'Look – phone me when you get there. I just want to know you've arrived safely and that you're OK.'

'Will do. Now I really need to go.' Serena said. She turned the keys in the ignition and the car's engine purred into life.

After one last wave, Phyllis retreated into her house. The animals crowded around her legs. 'I'm guessing it's nearly lunchtime for you two,' she said, addressing Shadow and Mr Boye and pouring dried pet food into the cats' and dogs' bowls.

Phyllis was anxious about Serena. Surely this still couldn't be about that awful business more than ten years ago, when the little girl drowned. Serena seemed obsessed by what had transpired, never more so than now. Not being party to the story of the apparitions, Phyllis was mercifully unaware of the effect they were having on her daughter's life. Nevertheless, sitting down to a hasty lunch, she was unable to settle to eat it. Never had her favourite prawn mayonnaise roll looked less appetising. Dumping the remains of the roll in the pedal bin, she took Tosca and Mr Boye out for a walk. The August day which promised to be warm had turned chilly. Slumped on a bench, watching the dogs chasing each other around the park, Phyllis pondered about what to do. Then she thought of Mary.

Chapter Thirty
Edinburgh

Throwing her work satchel on the hall carpet, Mary pushed open the sitting-room door and collapsed on the leather sofa. It was almost seven-thirty pm. What a day it had been! Up to her eyes in meetings, reviewing the detailed requirements for the bank's latest product and no time to break for lunch. The bank 'production line' never stopped and she felt like a hamster permanently running on its wheel. Henry entered the room bearing a large vodka and tonic. Mary grabbed it with both hands and drank greedily.

'Thanks, Henry. Just what I needed! You're a star!'

'Hey, steady on!' Henry said. 'It's only Monday night.' He sat down on his armchair and resumed reading his newspaper.

Mary smiled as she drained the dregs from the crystal tumbler.

'That bad, was it?' Henry put down *The Times*.

'Yes. Abysmal,' she contemplated asking for a top-up. 'There's now the additional problem of Serena.'

'Serena? What do you mean?' Henry inwardly cursed. He wasn't overly fond of Serena. He was relieved when she had moved onto another job. Mary and Serena had been as thick as thieves. He thought she had been a bad influence on Mary, dragging her off after work for drinks on a Friday. Introducing her to Mary's now favourite cocktail. What was its name?

Something stupid no doubt. A Beachcomber Baby. In his mind, but never directly to Mary, he alluded to Serena as one of Mary's drunken friends.

Mary on the other hand was very fond of Serena. She missed not seeing Serena every day and their canteen lunches. They had worked well together for several years. True they argued at times, but each valued the other's professional opinion, knowing they only wanted to develop the best products that they could for the bank. Serena had been a tower of strength when Mary's father had unexpectedly dropped dead after returning from a winter's day walk. Mary felt protective towards the younger woman, sensing an air of vulnerability about her. She was now aware of what demons existed in Serena's head and had tried not to subscribe to the ghostly visitations. But following on from Phyllis's near hysterical phone call, it was obvious to Mary that Serena was determined to attempt to exorcise her demons forever.

'Well, I think she might be in danger.'

'What sort of danger?' Henry asked. He was very dismissive of Serena and didn't get what Mary saw in her. Serena had always gone out of her way to be pleasant to Henry. Because of Mary. Although they had had a super evening at the Ball. Until that awful business with Amy and Alicia...

Mary placed the empty glass on the oak coffee table. 'I don't know exactly. I just need to do something,' she said, though exactly what she wasn't quite sure.

Henry rolled his eyes and sighed as Mary left the room.

Scrolling through the list of contacts on her mobile phone, Mary kept searching for inspiration. Only one name stood out. The one she was loathe to contact. Robin. Surely if he liked or loved Serena, once, he would help her. She dialled Robin's number. He answered after two rings.

'Hi, Robin, it's Mary. From the bank. How are you getting on?'

'I'm fine, Mary. Now what can I do for you? I'm a bit busy just now.' Putting his glass of Rioja down on the occasional table, Robin picked up the remote control, idly flicking between channels on the television.

This wasn't the response for which she had hoped. Mary considered trying a bit of small talk.

'It was jolly nice seeing you at the Border Union show. Did you enjoy it? Is your job going well?' she added.

'The show? Oh, *that* show. Not particularly, it wasn't really my kind of thing. The job is fine, thank you for asking.' Robin wondered why Mary was phoning. She wasn't exactly a close friend. Or a friend at all. Now. Although probably still a staunch supporter of Serena. Placing the remote control on the tweed sofa, he drummed his fingers on the arm of the sofa. He could think of better ways to spend his evening and that didn't include indulging in idle chit-chat with Mary.

Silence.

Mary was unusually stuck for words. How to broach the subject of Serena?

Robin broke the rapidly becoming awkward quietness. 'Look, it's getting on timewise. I have things to do. Is there actually any reason you phoned me?'

'It's about Serena.'

All was quiet again at the other end of the phone. Mary waited.

'Serena.' Robin's eyes lit up at hearing her name. Time had not diminished his feelings for her. Despite telling himself to forget her he couldn't, however much he persevered. 'What's happened to her?'

'I think she might be in some sort of trouble, possibly danger.'

Mary related Phyllis's conversation to Robin.

'If you still care for her, Robin. I know you once did...'

Robin cut in. 'Do you know what the place is called where she might be heading?'

'Queenston. In Devon.'

'Let me think what I can do. Don't worry about Serena,' he said.

'I *am* worried. She's my best friend,' Mary retorted.

'Everything will be fine. You'll see,' and with that he hung up.

Luckily Robin was on holiday that week. He had arranged several golfing outings, including one in the Scottish Borders. That was the reason he had agreed to go to the Border Union Show with Graham. To discover what the golf courses were like in the area. And on the off chance that he might meet Serena at the show. Graham had mentioned that Mary had let slip she was meeting Serena there.

Glancing at his watch, it was eight pm. Robin considered an early night was in order to drive the long journey to Devon the next morning.

*****

The blue Subaru Impreza hurtled down the narrow hedge bordered Devon roads. Serena revelled in the power and speed of the car, much as she would do a thoroughbred horse. Checking the time on the car's clock Serena ignored the idyllic surroundings as they flew past. Her room was available from two pm.

Chapter Thirty-one
Devon

'This is gorgeous. Thank you,' Serena commented to the stout landlady, who owned the bed and breakfast, where she was staying. The pretty bedroom was decorated with Laura Ashley poppies wallpaper and coordinated soft furnishings.

Mrs Chase smiled. She smoothed down her frilly apron over her tight-fitting plaid skirt. 'You're very welcome, dear. Now is there's anything else I can get you for you?'

'No, I'm fine. Thank you.'

'Then I'll be off then. Must finish the tidying.' Mrs Chase closed Serena's door quietly behind her as she left.

A lucky cancellation had arisen. This meant Serena was able to stay for a few days in a bed and breakfast situated in the village. She had arrived early in the afternoon. Flinging her small suitcase in the corner of the room, she stood in front of the window. There was a marvellous view, looking out over the village. In the distance the beach could be glimpsed.

Serena made herself a cup of tea, choosing from the generous selection of beverages and biscuits on the hospitality tray and sat down on the edge of the bed. Thinking. Drinking her Earl Grey tea, she was unsure what to do now she was here. And why she was here? Good question. What *did* she hope to achieve? To confront her demons? Would it change anything? Only one way to find out. A stroll down to the beach.

Where it happened. Changing into shorts and a t-shirt she left her room.

The communal willow green living room was cluttered with every conceivable form of Beswick animals in glass display cases which surrounded the room. Mrs Chase was bustling around cleaning ornaments and checking for dust. She put down her feather duster and looked up as Serena came into the room.

'I'm just going to the beach,' Serena said.

Mrs Chase carefully shuffled round the Royal Doulton figures standing on the demi lune table. 'You watch yourself,' she said.

Serena stared at Mrs Chase. 'What do you mean?'

'Now you be careful on that beach. There was a child who drowned there not more than ten years ago. That poor little mite, she was such a pretty little thing.' Mrs Chase sniffed and dabbed her eyes with a hanky. Smoothing her apron down she continued with her dusting.

'I will be. I've never really been all that keen on the sea.'

Gently closing the front door, she wandered down the street in the direction of the beach. After a five minute walk or so, the beach lay roughly a few hundred yards away.

Queenston beach enticed. The gleaming white walls and peppermint green framed windows of Burgh Island hotel could be seen in the distance. The Sea Tractor, transporting guests to their island destination, was meandering its way along the golden sand.

Serena descended the short slope to the beach entrance. Wide enough for a single car to be driven onto the sand, it was filled with holiday makers making their way back to the village. Looking around it was as if she had never been away. Everything appeared the same as before. It was as if time had stood still. Except she was older and wiser. Realistically only older. The sun had retreated behind a cloud, leaving a dull sky and there was now a cool breeze getting up. Children played with their buckets and spades, building sandcastles. Others paddled in the shallow water. Teenagers lobbed a ball back and forward to each other over a high net. One solo wind surfer was braving the waves. Unobserved by Serena, Robin lounged on a beach towel behind a windbreak.

Robin had literally left at dawn that morning. Allowing himself only short breaks he had driven the long journey to Devon at breakneck speed in his Audi A6. Unable to find a bed and breakfast with vacancies in the village, he had booked a room in Kingsbridge, a quaint market town. However, Robin wasn't here for sightseeing. After checking in at the guesthouse, he had driven immediately to the beach carpark.

Serena settled down on the beach towel she had brought and surveyed the beach. The lone windsurfer was still in the sea, just visible from where she was seated. No other people were in the water. Although the summer had been hot, the sea was still chilly. Unpacking an apple and a paperback she concentrated on catching up on the next chapter of the Daphne du Maurier novel she was reading. An hour or so passed. The windsurfer retreated from the sea, sprinting towards his towel. Pulling her cardigan tighter around her, Serena stood up. It was getting decidedly blowy. Strolling down to the water's edge, Serena dipped her toes in. Freezing! She drifted along the beach. Gazing out to sea she spotted the rock which Belinda, Josh, June and herself had attempted to swim to. Deceptively close – yet again it didn't appear far away. That had been their mistake. Squinting her eyes, she stared at the rock. Nothing and no one were present. Focusing again on the rock she was sure there was something there. A person? If so, they were holding on with difficulty to the edge of the rock. It couldn't be. Could it? Looking around the beach no one else seemed to have noticed the figure. Her eyes must be deceiving her. Giving her head a shake, she focused on the rock again. There was someone. *I can't let this happen again,* she thought.

Flinging her cardigan onto the sand, without a second thought, she raced into the sea. The icy water made her gasp, but she ignored it. Striding on further into deeper and deeper water until she could walk no more. Starting to swim, front crawl, as fast as she could, keeping the rock in her sights. The figure with its long blond hair billowing in the wind, still appeared to be clinging onto the side of the rock. Minutes passed. She was almost there. The figure gestured with one hand the other clutching onto the rock.

'I'm nearly there!' Serena shouted. 'Hang on.'

The figure smirked. In the gloom, its features were blurred, but there was no mistaking the toothy grin spread across its face.

An unexpected wave caught Serena unaware, forcing her away from the rock. Serena shook her head. She didn't need this. Now that she was close. Concentrating on swimming she finally reached the rock. There was nobody there. Serena swam round to the other side. The figure had gone.

Serena hadn't swum much for years; not since the last time she visited Devon. Suddenly she felt worn out by her exertions. She gave herself a shake. She had to find that person. Another tragedy must not be allowed to happen. Putting her head underwater, she attempted to see if there was a body in the water. Sinking deeper into the gloomy depths. Nothing. Gasping, scrabbling at the front of the rock, she endeavoured to hold on, but it was very slippery. Her hand kept sliding off. Allowing herself one last look, Serena thought, or imagined, the figure was now farther away. A hundred yards or so beyond the rock. Arms flailing above its head. One arm waved to her. 'Come on' the figure seemed to be saying. This galvanised her limbs into action. She started to swim again...

Without warning, pain shot through her left leg. Cramp. The pain was excruciating. Serena could not swim any further. She found it impossible to tread water. With difficulty she managed to float on her back. Large waves lapped around her, becoming stronger and more frequent. The beach looked farther away. 'I'm sorry,' she whispered to the distant figure.

'Serena.'

'Serena!'

Serena glanced over her shoulder; she was sure someone was shouting her name. But she couldn't quite make out what they were saying.

It was Robin. Chatting to a group of wind surfers, he hadn't noticed Serena was no longer on the beach. Spotting Serena swimming far out in the distance, he flung himself into the water, oblivious of the cold. Being a strong swimmer, he reached the rock in half the time Serena did. There was no figure there. Only Serena. Drifting close by.

He could clearly see her. On the other side of the rock. Serena was lying on her back. Motionless. Suddenly, she disappeared under the water.

Serena shivered and shook herself. She kept trying to tread water. In vain. She felt as if someone or something was dragging her underwater. Into the beckoning darkness. Images from her life sped through her mind. *I can't let this happen to me*, she thought. *Mum... my animals*. Then, everything went black.

Robin reached where Serena had been drifting. Swimming underwater, at first, he couldn't see anything in the murky water. The water cleared and he was just able to make out her body, spiralling downwards. Diving down, he managed to snatch her, before the black abyss claimed her. He forced his way to the surface. Cupping her chin with his left hand he swam as quickly as he could back to the shore.

She wasn't breathing. Placing Serena on the damp sand he endeavoured to give her CPR. He pressed her chest repeatedly. Serena did not rouse.

'Come on, Serena. Please, Serena. Please don't die. I love you,' Robin said. A solitary tear fell onto her cheek. He continued pummelling.

'Here stop that! Let me.'

A middle-aged man had just appeared on the beach, being dragged along by his enthusiastic labrador. Splashing about in the shallow water, the dog was straining on his lead. Pulling the dog out of the sea, the man dashed towards Robin and Serena. Pushing Robin off Serena, he began CPR. Robin watched the man who obviously knew what he was doing. Unlike Robin.

The two lifeguards who had sprinted towards Serena and Robin, then hung back when they saw the man *correctly* applying CPR.

*****

Serena was in an ill-lit hall. Her eyes adjusting to the blackness she could glimpse flaming beacons, in the distance. She was unsure where to go. Tiptoeing along the hallway, she noticed there were doors on either side. She tried the handle of the nearest door. It swung open.

An idyllic sight greeted her. Serena found herself in a large meadow, surrounded by rolling hills on either side. Swallows soared overhead in the azure sky. A herd of horses grazed contentedly, side by side, tearing at the lush emerald blades. Foals galloped round the field chasing each other up and down the gentle slopes. Those tired of that game, lay flat out beside their mothers, the foals' stumpy tails swatting away the occasional fly. Horse heaven.

Stopping to stroke one of the foals, Serena noticed a girl was leading two horses along a stony path towards her. *Rather inappropriately dressed to be handling horses*, Serena thought. She rubbed her eyes and looked again. Alicia? She, she must be imagining things...

'Serena! What on earth are you doing here?'

The girl *was* Alicia. Looking years younger. Dressed in a full-length white tunic, embroidered with shimmering thread. A gold band encircled her smooth forehead. Her auburn hair shone, her skin was luminous and the glistening green eyes regarded Serena tenderly. Alicia and the horses came to a halt beside Serena.

'Alicia! I thought I would never see you again!' Serena was delighted to see Alicia obviously in good health. 'You look fabulous!'

Alicia smiled. And then pursed her lips.

The bright bay mare, with the white star on her forehead, reached out and nuzzled Serena's hand with her nose. The chestnut mare whickered gently to Serena.

'It can't be. Can it? Jubilee? Rose?'

Both horses' ears flicked back and forwards as she said their names. 'My girls! They look so well.' Serena attempted to hug them both at the same time.

'And happy,' Alicia added.

'But what about *you*. Are you happy too?' Serena

said.

Alicia ignored Serena's question. 'Why are you here? What, are *you* doing here, Serena? You *shouldn't* be here.' She shook her head. 'Not yet.'

'I don't know what happened. One minute I was swimming and now I'm here. With you.' Serena gazed at Alicia. 'I'm so pleased to see you! I miss you! How are you? Are you happy? You never said. Please tell me.'

Serena's question was unanswered.

'Time to let the horses go, Serena,' Alicia opened the gate into an adjoining field. After one last gaze at her old horses Serena removed their headcollars. Rose and Jubilee galloped off to join their friends.

'Thank goodness they're OK,' Serena said, 'I always wondered. And now I know.'

Alicia grabbed Serena's hand and led her through the door Serena had come from, back into the gloomy hall. They wandered along until they reached a large, studded oak door. Unlocking the door with a large barrel key, the door opened, through which a blinding light shone. Alicia attempted to persuade Serena through to the other side. 'And time for you to go. You must go, go back to...'

'I don't want to go away and leave you,' Serena interrupted. 'I'm not going until you tell me how you are. Are you happy?' she asked yet again. She needed to know. She gripped Alicia's hand.

'Yes. Very,' was the crisp response. Alicia unclasped Serena's fingers from her hand. 'Now, it's not your time, yet. Not for years. Please leave. Go and live your life and be happy. Please?' She gently pushed Serena through the doorway. With one final smile at Serena, Alicia closed the door.

*****

'We're getting there...,' the man gasped. Robin tightly clutched onto the dog's lead.

Water. Sea water? Why was her mouth full of sea water? Serena couldn't stop herself spewing great mouthfuls of sea water over her rescuer. Again. And again. 'I, I'm so sorry. Really sor...'

'It's quite all right. Now get it all out,' he said, smoothing Serena's soaking hair off her forehead.

Serena started to splutter. Her breathing was laboured. She struggled to sit up. Her eyes widened. 'Robin. Robin – what on earth. Why are you here?' She began to retch again. The remaining sea water in her mouth, making her gag.

'Easy girl, you've had a lucky escape. If it wasn't for that man...' Propping Serena up, so she remained upright, the man nodded in Robin's direction.

Robin jogged to the windbreak and returned with a large beach towel, which he wrapped around Serena. Sitting on the wet sand, she was shivering violently.

She began to speak. 'I, I can't really recall what happened. But I'm sure I saw someone clinging to the rock out there,' she pointed to the rock, now farther away in the distance. 'I, I had to help them, they – they looked like they were in danger...'

Robin cut in. 'You had swum out to that rock and *you* were in difficulties. There was no one else there.'

Robin scanned the horizon. 'It was fortunate that this man was out for a walk with his dog.' He gesticulated in Serena's rescuer's direction.

'I'm... I'm sure, in fact I'm *positive*, there was someone there.' Serena said.

The men turned and scrutinised the faraway rock. After several minutes they shook their heads.

Serena shrugged. 'Anyway, the most important thing. Thank you for saving my life,' she said, extending a shaky hand. 'I'm Serena.'

'I'm Simon,' He shook Serena's. He proffered a right hand to Robin.

Robin took it. 'I'm Robin and I am so glad that you were here today. On the beach just now. Thank you.'

'I'd just completed my shift at the hospital – I'm a surgeon. After work I always like to take my dog for a walk before we go home for our tea,' Simon continued. 'When I noticed what was happening to you.' He glanced at Serena. 'And what you were *trying* to do.' This was to Robin who blushed.

'Simon, I just... I can't thank you enough. You saved my life!' Serena trembled. She patted the fluffy white dog who laid his head against her knee. 'Is this where you regularly walk your dog? He's gorgeous. What's his name?'

'Moby.' Moby heard his name, stood up and shook himself beside Simon. Spraying droplets of seawater on Simon's Barbour wax jacket. A bit more water won't make much difference,' Simon patted Moby's head.

'I'll always be grateful to you, Simon – you don't know how much this means to me. Will *always* mean to me. Thank you,' Robin said.

Simon brushed off Robin's comments. 'No problem. I'm only glad I was here and able to help. I think I have a good idea how much,' following Robin's gaze until it rested on Serena.

'Now this young lady needs a change of clothing and a hot drink, Robin, and so do you.'

Serena smiled, 'I'll make my way back to the bed and breakfast where I'm staying.'

'Not on your life!' Simon grinned. He was relieved to see the colour returning to Serena's face. 'I'll drive you there myself. Robin – what about you?'

'My car is in the car park. I'll drive back to where I'm staying and grab some things. Thank you again, Simon. For saving my most precious girl.' Robin helped Serena to her feet. 'And 'I'll be round shortly to see how you are doing.' He nodded to Serena.

'Robin, thank you for being here too,' Serena said.

Robin smiled. 'I'm just so pleased I was there. It doesn't bear thinking about what would have happened if Simon and I hadn't been at the beach. See you soon, Serena.'

After ascertaining where Serena was lodging, Robin headed off for dry clothes.

Simon drove Serena the short journey back to the bed and breakfast.

Mrs Chase opened the door. She took one look at Serena's bedraggled appearance. 'What on earth happened?' she said to Simon.

'Serena was swimming when she got into difficulties. Her boyfriend swam out and brought her back to the shore. I gave her CPR.'

'Mrs Chase, this is Simon – my rescuer. He saved my life. Not Robin!' Serena said.

'Sounds like you and this Robin were *both* responsible for saving you,' Mrs Chase said. She opened the door wider and bustled Serena in. 'Now Mr...? Would you like to come in for a cup of tea or something stronger?' she said to Simon.

'My name's Simon Grieve and I only live a couple of miles away. Anyway, Moby and I need to get home.' He glanced at the dog waiting patiently in the car. 'It's been a long day...'

'And not every day you save a life!' Mrs Chase smiled.

Serena came back outside. 'Simon, I can't thank you enough. Can I have your contact details? If you're ever in Scotland...?'

Simon wrote down his and Serena's phone number. 'Let me know how you go. Yes, it's not something I do on a regular basis – rescuing someone from the sea. Thank goodness!' He beamed. 'And send me an invitation to your wedding. That young man is clearly besotted with you!'

'Simon!' Serena laughed. 'Of course, I will! Thank you again. I'll keep in touch.' She waved goodbye as Simon climbed into his car. He waved back and drove off slowly.

Mrs Chase fussed around Serena. 'Now, dear, you go upstairs and I'll run a warm bath for you. Come down when you're changed.'

This was the last thing Serena wanted to do. And see. More water. She felt that she never wanted to see an expanse of water ever again. *If Robin and she ever decided to marry, their honeymoon would be somewhere without a beach. And no water. A place like Death Valley would be perfect,* she thought. Images of Bedouin Tents and galloping Arabian horses flew through her mind.

Gingerly stepping into the warm, bubble filled bath, Serena burst into tears. She didn't know exactly who she was crying for. Alicia, Belinda, June, even Amy. All those who had been taken too early, their lives cut tragically short. Not wanting to linger in the water, she quickly washed and dried herself. After dressing in a green cashmere polo neck jumper and black jeans, she was, thankfully, warm at last.

In the communal living room Mrs Chase was waiting for her, a concerned expression on her face.

'Now dear, come in and sit beside the fire and get that hot tea down you.' Mrs Chase studied Serena. She noticed the deathly pallor which had returned to her face, despite the hot bath. A fire was roaring in the grate, she wasn't taking any chances with her guest. 'I've put some brandy in it to give you a lift.' Mrs Chase's distant relative was the baker on the Titanic who survived due to his bottle of brandy, or so she liked to say.

Serena sipped her tea. The hot liquid burned in her tummy, generating an inner fire. She hated brandy and had never drunk it since the night of the

Christmas Ball. Too many bad memories would return.

When Mrs Chase turned round to offer her a plate of thickly buttered fruit scones, Serena grimaced. But she forced herself to take one. The scones were delicious and Serena began to feel more like herself. Mrs Chase apologised for not doing traditional Devon scones with clotted cream topped with strawberry jam. Serena lay back in the armchair, watching the flames dancing in the fire.

'Now that young man of yours will be popping round later to see how you are,' Mrs Chase said. 'I can make you a nice bit of supper, if you like?'

'Thank you, Mrs Chase. That's very kind of you but I think we'll pop out to the local pub.'

'I'd recommend the Mermaid Inn. It's very nice.'

'Yes, I think that's where we'll be going.'

There was a knock at the front door. Mrs Chase answered it.

After a cursory greeting to Mrs Chase, Robin strode into the living room. Immediately going over to Serena, he planted a kiss on her forehead. 'How are you feeling now, Serena?'

'I'm fine, thanks, Robin. Feeling much better now.' Serena smiled at Mrs Chase.

Mrs Chase looked admiringly at Robin. What a dishy man. *They make an attractive couple*, she thought.

Robin turned to Mrs Chase. 'I want to thank you for looking after Serena. She's very dear to me.' Mrs Chase blushed as Robin gave her the benefit of his

Hollywood megawatt smile. Subconsciously, she rearranged the collar on her flowery satin pussy bow blouse and checked her hair in the mirror above the fireplace. 'It was no trouble at all. Mr...? '

'Dudley. But please call me Robin,' he said.

Serena went upstairs to fetch her fleece jacket. When she came back into the room, Robin and Mrs Chase were chatting together on the sofa just like old friends. Robin stood up immediately and put his arm round Serena's shoulder.

'I'll see you both later, dears,' Mrs Chase said, as she shut the front door.

Sitting in the centuries old Mermaid Inn, Serena barely sipped her Chablis. Robin meanwhile rapidly drained his pint. The inn was warm and welcoming. Serena felt chilled to the core and shivered profusely, despite sitting at the table closest to the Victorian open fireplace. She put both arms around her sides, hugging herself and watched the flames dancing in the grate. Robin was the first to speak.

'God, what a horrendous day,' he said.

'I know. Bloody awful,' Serena agreed, 'I just want to forget all about it.'

'You *were* sure you saw someone out there in difficulties, weren't you?'

'Yes. I wanted to prevent another tragedy. Atone in some small way,' tears were welling up in Serena's eyes. 'I tried. I *really* tried'.

'You have nothing to atone for. It wasn't your fault,' Robin had been filled in on the story of Belinda and June by Mary.

‘I know, but if I could have just somehow prevented them from swimming to the rock that day…’ Serena shrugged her shoulders, her palms upended in mute appeal. ‘If only I had done so.’

Robin reached across the table and caressed Serena’s hands. Serena pulled her hands away. Neither spoke.

‘Look, I’m terribly sorry about what happened with Amy and how rotten I’ve been to you. Can you ever forgive me?’ Robin toyed with the crested signet ring on his pinkie finger.

For a second or so she felt elated. Then unsure. Did she want Robin back in her life? Really? She thought for five minutes or so before she replied. Serena leaned forward and took Robin’s hand over the table.

‘Yes.’ They smiled at each other, holding hands.

Robin was reluctant to break the moment, but he was starving. Giving Serena’s hands a final caress, Robin rose to his feet. ‘Now time for food. I don’t know about you but I’m starving! Shall I go and order? ‘The oak beamed ceilings were low and Robin had to duck so that he didn’t bump his head.

‘I’m not hungry, you choose,’ Serena said. Despite not feeling particularly hungry, Serena devoured the crab salad, washed down with a fruity white Zinfandel. Chatting about their respective new jobs was a welcome respite from revisiting the day’s events. Taking a last regretful sip of the rosé wine, Serena yawned. It was time for bed.

Robin escorted her back to the bed and breakfast.

Mrs Chase was waiting up for them.

'Did you have a pleasant meal, dears?' she asked.

'It was delicious, thank you. I'm very tired now and I just want to go to bed,' Serena replied. *That should stop any further questions about today,* she hoped.

'Of course, dear, you've had a terrible experience today.' Closing the front door quietly behind them, she added, 'Now I've put some blankets over the large armchair in your bedroom for your fiancé to sleep in there tonight. He wanted to stay and make sure you were OK throughout the night.'

'Fiancé indeed!' Serena glanced sideways at Robin. He smirked at her. However, Serena was too tired to protest and it would be a pleasant change to have some company. On the off chance her nocturnal visitors dropped by, in Devon. She thought they just might.

Five-thirty am. Serena's eyes jerked open. Out the corner of one eye, she could see Robin snoring contentedly in the wingback armchair. The blankets had slipped down, exposing his striped pyjamas.

They were here. At the far end of the bed. All three staring at her. Lying in bed, Serena had the urge to pull the duvet over her head but resisted doing so. She must stand up to them. This time.

'What do you want?' She whispered, not wanting to wake Robin.

There was no reply.

Her eyes adapted in the gloom and Serena noticed the figures looked different. Vastly improved in appearance.

June now re-appeared as the pretty, fun-loving little girl she once was. The pink and white spotted swimming costume, sandless and dry. Her burnished blonde pigtails tied neatly with pink ribbons, were for once free of seaweed and no seawater trickled down her face. A 'gappy', toothy smile lit up her cornflower-blue eyes.

Belinda wasn't wearing the tartan dress, reduced to tatters from the incident with the train. Her long-tanned, colt-like legs now descended from a pair of orange shorts, above which a pink vest clashed gloriously. The same outfit she had worn, that long ago summer's day. The dark circles under Belinda's eyes, resulting from the sleepless nights she'd endured after June's death had faded. No longer did rivers of blood stream down the contours of her face. She looked like the lithe, carefree and beautiful sixteen-year-old girl she once was.

Amy. Well Amy was her usual truculent self. Unlike June, Amy was tight-lipped, those icy blue eyes staring straight ahead. Not a flicker of emotion chased across her statue-like face. Her blonde hair was perfectly coiffed, no hairs out of place and no creases spoiled the line of her strapless evening dress. The diamond necklace sparkled round her neck. In one hand was a seashell, dusted with sand.

The figures drew closer.

They came to a halt, directly beside her head on the pillow. All glared down at Serena. She gazed upwards.

‘I’m sorry. I tried. I *really* tried to save that person today. I wanted to prevent another tragedy,’ Serena said. She stuck out both hands to prevent the trio advancing. ‘I didn’t want anyone else to drown.’

Amy placed her almost skeletal hand on Serena’s. It was ice cold. She grasped Serena’s fingers.

‘I’m sorry. I don’t know what else I could have done,’ Serena persisted, unable to withdraw her fingers from Amy’s vice-like hold.

‘We know,’ Belinda spoke in tandem with June. Their voices sounded like a rasp being drawn over a rough piece of wood. ‘We saw.’

Amy remained silent. Her lips drawn together.

Addressing Amy, Serena said, ‘I’m sorry for what happened in the past and today, but neither were my fault. I’ve done my best. Go now. Please leave me alone.’

There was a slight loosening of the vice-like grip on Serena’s hand.

‘I’ll take loving care of Mr Boye. If that’s what matters to you?’ She stared into Amy’s eyes.

Amy’s tense shoulders moved slightly. Her body started to sway; her eyes focused on Serena’s, like a cobra toying with a mongoose.

Serena’s hand was suddenly free. ‘Be at peace. Please go?’ she said to the trio. She gazed at the three spectres floating before her. Amy, Belinda and June were obviously contemplating what to do next. Serena made the sign of a cross.

Amy’s eyes flickered. Turning to Belinda and then June, she nodded.

‘It’s time,’ Amy said. The guttural tone of her voice contrasted with her eyes. Those eyes now resembled Cinderella’s in Walt Disney’s original animated film.

All three apparitions joined hands. A wisp of a smile flickered across Belinda’s face.

A ray of sunlight crept in the room, from under the thick curtains. Serena was momentarily blinded. She shut her eyes. When she opened them, the figures had vanished. Amy’s seashell remained. Sand-free. On the edge of the bed. She cradled the shell in her hands.

Hardly daring to believe they had departed, Serena shut her eyes and re-opened them. Several times. Nothing. No one was there.

A sense of peace descended through Serena’s mind. All being well, they had gone. Forever. She had tried to make up for what had happened. Regardless of whether it was her fault or not. She still felt miserable about them, especially Belinda and June. Her eyelids became heavy and Serena fell into a deep sleep.

*****

‘Wake up sleepy head! It’s past nine o’clock!’ Robin caressed Serena’s shoulder.

Serena stared, bleary eyed at Robin. ‘Goodness I’ve not slept that long for ages,’ she said, deciding for now not to mention her early visitors.

‘Mrs Chase has promised us a slap-up English breakfast at nine-thirty. Do you think you can up and ready for then?’

Food. The thought of eating anything made Serena's stomach wretch, she swallowed, an acid taste appeared in her mouth. 'Great,' she said, 'I'll be down for then.'

'Mrs Chase thought you needed feeding up and so do I,' Robin said. He had noticed that Serena looked thinner than the Serena of old.

Dressing quickly and smoothing the duvet back on the bed, she remembered the seashell Amy had been carrying. Serena picked up the shell and packed it carefully in her suitcase.

Sitting down to a warmed plate containing three sausages, three rashers of bacon, two poached eggs, one hash brown, black pudding, Lorne sausage slices... Serena picked at one of the poached eggs. Naturally, it was perfectly cooked. Taking a sip of her Earl Grey tea, she concluded she had better eat something. She had plans for today.

Mrs Chase bustled into the dining-room. She placed a fresh pot of tea and more toast on the table. 'Now, dears, did you both sleep well?' She asked.

'Yes, thank you,' Serena and Robin said simultaneously. They both laughed.

'It's good to see how much better you look today.' This was to Serena. 'Now is there anything else I can get you?'

'No thank you, Mrs Chase,' Serena said, 'but is there a flower shop in the village?'

'No, but there's one in the town, not five miles away.'

'Thank you, Mrs Chase.'

Mrs Chase hovered expectantly, waiting to know why Serena wanted to purchase flowers. And who they were for. She mentioned she was particularly fond of blue irises.

'Mrs Chase, you've been simply marvellous, producing this delicious breakfast. But we're fine, thank you.' Robin said.

Mrs Chase swelled with pride. 'Well then, I'll be off, dishes to wash. Let me know if you need anything else.'

Breakfast done, Serena and Robin drove to the nearby town.

Robin was puzzled. For whom did Serena want flowers? 'Why do you want to buy flowers? They won't last long in the car on the long journey back.'

'I know that. But they're not for me. I'll also get some for Mrs Chase. She has been exceptionally kind.'

'Then who?'

'You'll see,' Serena smiled. She was deliberating about what kind of flowers she was going to buy.

Flowers purchased, they returned to the beach. A sunnier day than the previous one, it promised to be a beautiful day.

'Are you sure about this?' Robin said.

'Very.' Serena carefully removed the large cardboard box from the car. She left behind the bouquet of irises for Mrs Chase and strolled onto the beach. Slipping off her shoes, she stepped barefoot onto the cool sand.

The tide had been in but was starting to go out. Wet sand was apparent where only minutes before there was water. The rock Serena had swum out to was clearly visible, surrounded by a pool of water.

Robin caught up with Serena and took her right hand. Together they headed towards the rock.

The water around the rock looked deceptively shallow. Placing the cardboard box on the sand, Serena took out the contents.

'I'm not letting you go in. That water could be deep.' Robin said.

'I think I'll be fine,' Serena laughed. She stepped into the pool. Knee-deep. Robin followed her.

Climbing up onto the rock, one foot at a time, Serena reached up and placed the wreath on the crest of the rock. The wreath composing of fiery red, shocking pink and sunny yellow gerberas garlanded with grasses and foliage sat perfectly. The card pinned to the wreath read:

'Always remembered. Belinda, Amy and June. Love Serena X.'

After Serena jumped down from the rock and then back on the sand, Serena and Robin clasped hands. Serena said a small prayer, hoping the trio were now at peace.

They stood in silence, then turned and retraced their steps.

Taking one last look at the rock, Serena thought she could see a figure waving to her. She shook her head. Glancing back again the figure was no longer visible. It was probably her imagination. Her mind was as clear as a blank laptop screen for the first time in years. A sense of peace and calm descended in her mind. She was no longer the girl who lacked faith in herself. She had confronted her demons and won.

Holding hands, they meandered along the beach, paddling in small pools of sea water, as they went.

'Do you think they'll leave you alone now?' Robin asked. He knew of Serena's recurring nightly visitors. Mary had told him. 'I hope so.'

'Yes, I know so,' Serena raised her chin.

Robin raised an eyebrow. 'Are you sure?'

'They've gone. They won't be back.' Serena smiled. 'Time for me to go home.'

Robin inspected Serena. Serena stared back. A new Serena. There was iron in her jaw and her eyes observed Robin steadily. There was no hint of the timid girl. Now.

Serena stopped and turned to face Robin.

'Just one thing?' Serena said. 'What was that you said to Mrs Chase about me being your fiancé. Since when?'

'Oh, that?' Robin grinned. 'Well, I kind of assumed you were. So, I better ask you to marry me. Properly. Now.'

'Only if you get down on one knee?'

Despite the wet sand, Robin dropped down onto one knee.

'Serena Kennedy, will you marry me?'

Serena yanked Robin to his feet.

'Yes! Yes, of course I will, Robin!' she laughed.

Robin took her in his arms, bent down and kissed her. Serena opened her eyes and gazed into Robin's.

The eyes of a killer.

Robin had murdered Amy.

A dalliance took place, one drunken work evening, following an unsuccessful attempt to woo Serena. Amy had reminded Robin about this at the Christmas Ball. She threatened to tell all to Serena unless he became her lover. Robin followed Amy upstairs at the Club. He had waited, unnoticed by Amy and Serena, until Serena managed to escape from Amy. Seeing his chance and that they were alone, he flung Amy down the stairs. She landed in a heap at the foot of the stairs, her neck broken.

He had an inkling Alicia knew. Or was suspicious. Owning up selflessly to Amy's murder. After all, she knew she was dying.

He would make Serena happy. He was damn sure of that and was convinced Serena would never believe or think *he* was guilty of Amy's murder.

'Let's go home,' he said.

With one final look at the beach, Serena took his hand, and they strolled back to the car.